> *"He held the harp, bone-white as dragon's teeth*
> *And strung with moonlight's glow. He raised it*
> * high,*
> *And played, and when at last, the music ceased*
> *Like flowers killed by frost, the cities died."*

"What's that supposed to mean?" Flindaran demanded.

"That's part of an old song called 'King Loren's Lay.' It tells how King Loren destroyed Istrava and two other cities when they attacked him."

Flindaran stared at the harp. "And you think—"

"I think I know what this is," Emereck said with deadly quietness. "It's impossible, but it's the only thing that fits. This is the harp that ballad describes. The Harp of Imach Thyssel."

THE HARP OF IMACH THYSSEL

PATRICIA C. WREDE

ACE FANTASY BOOKS
NEW YORK

THE HARP OF IMACH THYSSEL

An Ace Fantasy Book / published by arrangement with
the author

PRINTING HISTORY
Ace Original / April 1985
Second printing / August 1986

ISBN: 0-441-31759-6

Ace Fantasy Books are published by The Berkley Publishing Group,
200 Madison Avenue, New York, New York 10016.
PRINTED IN THE UNITED STATES OF AMERICA

*F*or all those who have contributed so much to Lyran history, particularly Vabronen, builder of Castle Windsong, Neriwind, Karinobra, Macarato, Taldor, Virana, Nevarra, Calidion, Quain, Timlin ri Aster, Viella, Luan, Delmar, Icebolt, Philomel, Jeness, Iraman, Verrick Kyel-Semrud, Vallafana, Zylar, Colin, Halkana, Krendor, Maricor, Renalda, Marillion, Agis, Kaskani, Coral Starfinger, Araken, and anyone else whose proper name I may have forgotten.

One

*D*ark, still water reflected darker trees and a shadowed sky. As he rode along the lake, Emereck studied the scene, wondering whether he could capture it in words. It would make a good opening for a tragic song, and he'd been thinking of trying to do a new arrangement of "Corryn's Ride." He hummed the first line of music and paused to fit words around it. *Dark water, still water, darker yet the sky* . . .

"Emereck!" Flindaran's voice jolted him out of his reverie. "Is that an inn, or am I seeing things?"

Emereck glanced at his friend, puzzled. He looked at the lake again, and for the first time became aware of the town farther down the shore. It was a small village, hardly more than a cluster of cottages, but even at this distance, Emereck could see the bulk of an inn at its center. "For once you seem to have gotten something right. It's an inn. I take it you mean to stop?"

"Of course! I think we've earned a few small comforts after all this riding. A jug of Brythian wine, a pretty girl, a little entertainment . . ."

Emereck laughed in spite of himself. "Beer and bed is all you're likely to find here. And if there *is* any entertainment, we'll probably be providing it ourselves."

Flindaran looked at him suspiciously. "You don't expect me to sing for them, do you?"

"How else would we get a meal and a room?"

"We could *pay* for it."

"With what?"

"I've got more than enough to pay for both of us, if you weren't so sticky about—"

"We've been through that argument before, and you never win. Besides, this time it's not what I meant."

"It's not? That's a first."

Emereck ignored him. "If you're going to pretend to be a minstrel, you'll have to act like one. And no minstrel would pay for dinner if he could sing for it instead."

"Then I'll be a smith, or a soldier, or something instead."

"You'd give yourself away inside of three sentences. At least you know a little about music."

"After two years at the Ciaron Guildhall, I ought to," Flindaran muttered.

"Don't worry, you'll only have to do a few songs. Just enough so people don't wonder."

"They'll wonder if they hear me sing."

"You're exaggerating; your voice isn't that bad. But you don't have to fake it unless you want to. We could just tell them the truth."

Flindaran eyed him with disfavor. "You take all the fun out of things," he complained. "Besides, you'd still make me sing."

"Probably," Emereck said cheerfully. "So it really doesn't matter, does it?"

"All right, all right!" Flindaran heaved an exaggerated sigh. "The things I do for my friends."

"Oh? Whose idea was this? For that matter, who suggested leaving Goldar's caravan in the first place?"

"Don't remind me! I'll hear enough about it from my father when we get to Minathlan."

"Then why were you so pigheaded about taking this shortcut?"

"Because I'd rather be uncomfortable than bored. And the only thing more boring than spending four more weeks with a caravan of Traders is being a Duke's son and spending four more weeks with a caravan of Traders. I'm sick of their bowing and my-lording. Besides, the girls were all either too old or too young."

"I thought that might have something to do with it."

Flindaran grinned. "So I'm going to be a minstrel for a while. Come on, let's see what this inn has to offer."

The two men nudged their horses to a faster walk. A little farther on, the main road slanted away from the village to skirt the end of the lake. A smaller road, little more than a path, branched off toward the town, and in less than an hour they had reached their destination. The town was just as small as it had looked from a distance, but the people seemed used to travelers; only the children paid any attention to the two riders as they passed through the town and stopped before the door of the inn.

As they dismounted beneath the faded sign, a black-haired woman came out to meet them. She was small and neat and quiet-looking; a far call from the usual innkeeper, Emereck thought. Her eyes swept over the horses and their riders in cool evaluation, then she nodded. "Good day to you, sirs," she said in Kyrian. "And what do you wish from this house?"

"Whatever you would willingly spare a pair of minstrels in return for song and story," Emereck said in the same language.

"Song and story are very well, but there are few guests to be entertained tonight and the folk of this town have a choosy taste in such things."

"Including yourself?" Flindaran asked.

Emereck frowned, but the woman did not appear to be offended. "Perhaps, though I think my likes are somewhat different from those of the people of Tinbri," she replied calmly.

"You don't consider yourself one of them?"

"There are those who've lived half their lives in Tinbri and don't consider themselves townsfolk. But no, this is not my home. I'm keeping this inn for a time as a . . . favor to a friend."

"If songs are unwelcome, is there some other way we might earn your hospitality?" Emereck said. He heard Flindaran shift uncomfortably, and shot him a warning look. Two wandering minstrels would never offer to pay for a room in hard coin, and it was too late now to change their story.

The woman did not notice. "If you and your brother are willing to work, I think I can arrange something."

Emereck did not correct her mistake, though he grinned inwardly. He and Flindaran had frequently been taken for brothers during their two years in Ciaron, for they were both tall, brown-haired, and trimly built. Though they were not even distantly related, their resemblance had been of use to them before. Emereck glanced at Flindaran and said, "We're willing to do whatever's reasonable."

The woman laughed suddenly. Emereck blinked. There was music in that laugh, and a startled amusement, and the shadow of a joy as pure as sunlight, and . . . and his imagination was running wild again. Emereck shook his head as the woman said, "And we may differ somewhat on the definition of reasonable? Well, I will try not to be too stern. My stableboy has been ill three days, and the stable needs cleaning. Or there is wood to split, or you may help in the kitchen if you prefer. Is that to your liking, or shall I keep naming chores until you meet one that suits you?"

"No need!" Emereck protested, laughing. He glanced at Flindaran and made a quick, questioning gesture toward the horses. Flindaran nodded slightly, and Emereck looked back at the innkeeper. "By your leave, we'll begin with the stables."

"And see your own horses tended as well, I suppose. No, I do not mind; it does you credit that you think of your beasts before yourselves."

"If you'd rather choose the work yourself—"

"As long as the stable ends cleaner than it began, your motives are none of my concern; I'm simply glad it will be done at last. When you're finished, come to the kitchen and I'll show you your room. And if any question you in the meantime, say I sent you. I'm called Ryl."

Emereck bowed and gave her their names in return. Ryl smiled and directed them to an enclosed courtyard at the back of the inn. The stable was set on the far side, opposite the only gate into the courtyard. A large, sweaty man was forking hay into a small wagon just outside the stable door. He looked at them suspiciously, but when they mentioned Ryl's name he grunted and went back to his work. Flindaran looked at Emereck and raised his eyebrows. Emereck shrugged, and they went on into the stable.

Inside, they found five empty stalls and two occupied ones. The empty stalls were clearly in need of cleaning, but the occupied stalls had recently been swept out. Judging by the condition of the gear hanging beside her stall, the sturdy brown mare was a recent arrival. The roan gelding in the other showed signs of longer residence.

A variety of shovels and rakes were hanging on the wall beside the door; they each selected one and began on the stalls nearest the door, where they planned to put their own horses. Flindaran was in an excellent mood, since it appeared he would not have to sing for his supper after all.

"This is going to be even more fun than I expected," he said, pulling a clump of moldy straw out of one of the stalls with a long-handled rake.

"You call this fun?" Emereck looked skeptically at his friend.

"Not this, half-wit! The trip, the inn, the whole evening."

Emereck heard a familiar note in Flindaran's voice, and shook his head in amusement. "And Ryl?"

"What? No! I—Oh, blast you, Emereck, you know me too well. Yes, and Ryl."

"I'd be careful there, if I were you," Emereck said thoughtfully. "She certainly isn't what I'd expect to find in a village like this."

"Weren't you listening? She's not from this village."

"She also speaks as if she's well-born."

"She's probably from Kith Alunel; everyone there sounds like a noble or a minstrel or something."

"It's possible. But—"

"Oh, pack it up!" Flindaran poked his head around the end of the stall Emereck was working on and scowled at him. "You know, what you need is a girl of your own to worry about, instead of picking on mine."

"Don't start that again! All right, I'll quit annoying you. But I still wish I knew why Ryl didn't want us to sing."

"Is *that* what's bothering you? You ought to be glad I won't be ruining your reputation. Watch where you're stepping!"

Emereck glanced down and sidestepped. "It's not my reputation that's worrying me at the moment, it's Ryl. Innkeepers are usually happy to have a minstrel stay the night, but she wasn't even interested."

"Maybe she's just being careful about how she runs her friend's inn."

"Maybe." Emereck did not believe it, but he could think of no argument that would convince Flindaran. Particularly when Flindaran was clearly determined not to be convinced; Emereck had caught the note of stubbornness in his voice. He shook his head and said lightly, "And maybe she doesn't like minstrels. Where would that leave your plans for tonight?"

"Ryl may think she dislikes minstrels," Flindaran said with dignity, "but I intend to convince her otherwise."

"Oh? How?"

"Good looks and irresistible charm, of course."

"Is that what you tried on that farmer's daughter in Harmalla? The one who blacked your eye?"

"I'm sure Ryl has far more discriminating taste. You realize, of course, what a favor I'll be doing the Minstrel's Guild?"

"I'll make sure to let the Master Singer in Ciaron know as soon as we get back."

"Thank you. No doubt the Guild will find a way to return the kindness."

"Oh, if that's all you're worried about, I'll write you a ballad," Emereck said, bowing.

"You already owe me four ballads and a drinking song, and I haven't seen any of them yet," Flindaran said, unimpressed. "How long do I have to wait?"

"Quality takes time. But if you're in a hurry, I suppose I could dash off a third-rate epic poem or a few scurrilous couplets."

"What I'm in a hurry for right now is dinner," Flindaran said. "So pick your feet up! I'm ahead of you already, and I don't intend to do *all* the work."

The sun was setting when they finally finished in the stable and hauled their packs to the kitchen where Ryl awaited them. She studied them briefly with the same cool appraisal she had given them when they arrived, then led them to a room on the upper floor. The room was large, with a window overlooking the lake, and to Emereck's surprise, a tub of steaming water was waiting for them to wash off the dust and stable smells. By the time they descended the stairs once more, Emereck was willing to admit even to Flindaran that their hostess did not seem to dislike minstrels.

When they entered the kitchen, Ryl was stirring a large pot of something dark and spicy-smelling. She gave them each a bowl of it and sent them back to the taproom to eat, pointedly ignoring Flindaran's attempts to strike up a conversation.

The taproom smelled of beer, onions, and smoke. Several of the rough-hewn stables were already occupied. A tall blonde girl moved among them, serving beer and stew with bored efficiency. Most of the customers were clearly locals, but a wiry, white-haired man in a faded green leather uniform caught Emereck's attention. He nudged Flindaran and pointed him out.

"So?" Flindaran said after glancing toward the corner table where the man was sitting.

"So what's a Cilhar doing in a place like this?"

"Spending the night, the same as we are."

"I didn't think Cilhar traveled much on the east side

of the Mountains of Morravik." Emereck studied the man speculatively. "I wonder if he knows any of the Witrian song cycle."

"The what?"

"The Witrian song cycle. It's a series of Cilhar songs based on the Two Century War. I heard part of it from a Cilhar woman who stopped at the Guildhall last summer, and I've been looking for a chance to learn the rest ever since." Emereck set his bowl on an empty table and paused uncertainly.

"You're not thinking of asking him about it, are you?" Flindaran demanded.

"Why not? I may not get a chance like this again."

"Most people don't have your passion for obscure old songs. He's probably never heard of it."

Emereck started to reply, then paused. "What's worrying you? All I wanted to do was ask a few questions."

"I don't think it's a good idea to bother a Cilhar," Flindaran said with an uneasy shrug. "They like privacy, and it's not exactly healthy to argue with one of them."

"I see." Emereck felt a sudden perverse desire to walk over and strike up a conversation with the Cilhar for no other reason than to annoy Flindaran. He suppressed the impulse; irritating Flindaran did not seem a sufficient reason for ignoring his advice. He glanced speculatively at the Cilhar as he seated himself at the table. Perhaps he could persuade Ryl to introduce him to the man before they left. That ought to ease Flindaran's objections. Emereck shoved the matter to the back of his mind and began eating.

The stew was excellent, and they finished it quickly. Emereck accepted a refill from the blonde girl, but Flindaran, after a moment of indecision, shook his head. As the girl left, Emereck looked at him curiously. "Something wrong with your appetite?"

"Not at all," Flindaran replied, grinning. He picked up the empty bowl and balanced it on his finger, then flipped it into the air and caught it in his other hand.

"But you don't expect me to miss an opportunity like this, do you?"

"Opportunity?"

"I'm going to get my refill in the kitchen. Didn't you hear Ryl say we could?"

"Yes, but I got the distinct impression that she was interested mainly in getting you out of the kitchen at the time. And the stew's the same in both places."

"It's not the stew I'm after, idiot. I want to talk to Ryl."

Emereck stared at him, then shook his head. "Why don't you talk to that one instead?" he said, nodding at the blonde serving girl. "She's at least as pretty as Ryl is, and probably a lot more approachable."

"Ryl's a challenge." Flindaran paused and looked from Emereck to the blonde girl. "Why don't you—"

"No."

Flindaran looked at him and shrugged. "All right, then. See you later."

Emereck shook his head as Flindaran grinned and started to rise. He glanced toward the kitchen door, saying, "Well, I wish you—" He checked in mid-sentence as Ryl came through the door, wiping her hands on her apron. "—had better timing, I think," he finished, nodding in the innkeeper's direction.

"Oh, demons!" Flindaran dropped back into his seat, looking disgusted. "Now I'll have to think of something else. And on top of that I have to sit here and watch you eat while I do it."

"I didn't think it was food you were interested in."

"You have a low mind."

Emereck grinned and went on eating. A moment later he heard Flindaran mutter, "Demons take it!"

Emereck looked up in time to see Ryl seat herself across the table from the Cilhar he had noticed earlier. "Try to be a little patient; she'll have to get up eventually."

"So? You don't think I'd cross a Cilhar, do you?"

For a moment, Emereck could not believe Flindaran was serious. "He's old enough to be her father! Maybe even her grandfather."

"What does that have to do with anything? Besides, he might *be* her father, and then where would I be?"

"You've managed before."

"Not when a Cilhar was involved." Flindaran stared pensively at his empty bowl. "You know, I think I'd better ask for some more of that stew after all. No reason to starve myself."

Emereck looked at him suspiciously. Flindaran grinned, then turned and started trying to signal to the blonde serving girl. With a resigned sigh, Emereck went back to eating.

TWO

*T*wo beers and another helping of stew later, Flindaran and the serving girl were clearly well on their way to a mutual understanding. About the middle of the evening, Emereck left and went upstairs. The flirtation would keep Flindaran occupied for several hours at least, and Emereck wanted to practice.

He unpacked his harp and tuned it, then began with half an hour of the exercises Flindaran hated listening to the most. He worked for a while on the complex runs in the middle of "The Lay of Long Tormoran." When he was satisfied with his progress, he stopped and stretched.

He paced the room, then paused at the window, unable to decide what to do next. A glint of moonlight on the lake caught his eye, and he remembered the song he had started on the ride into Tinbri. With renewed enthusiasm, he went back to the harp and began picking out chords, pausing frequently to try different variations of words or music.

Flindaran did not return until nearly midnight. When he arrived he was clearly well pleased with his evening. As the door closed behind him, Emereck looked up from the small harp. "Flindaran! Listen to this and tell me what you think."

"Dark water, still water, darker yet the sky;
  Shadowed was the path beyond and cold the wind
    on high.
  Black forest, clouded road, where still the blood-
    stains lie;
  Dark the day and dark the way when Corryn went
    to die."

"I like the tune," Flindaran said.

"I think there's something wrong with the third line."

Flindaran shrugged. "It sounded fine to me. But don't you ever write any cheerful songs?"

"I should know better than to ask you for criticism." Emereck set the harp down. "What are you doing back already, anyway?"

"There are still two customers left downstairs, and Sira won't be available until they're gone. So I left, to provide them a good example."

Emereck shook his head, half in envy, half in admiration. "I don't know how you do it."

"Talent, hard work, clean living . . ."

"Luck, more likely. Much more likely. Though, knowing you, I'd be willing to believe you'd stacked the odds in your favor somehow."

"Certainly not," Flindaran protested. "I come by it honestly, whatever it is."

"How can you come by something like that honestly?"

Flindaran shrugged. "It runs in the family. Father has seven or eight half bloods at home, and Gendron has been flipping skirts for years."

"You mean your whole family is as bad as you are?"

"Oh, no. Gendron's the heir; he has to keep up family traditions. Oraven isn't nearly as bad, and the girls are too young."

"I can see it's going to be an interesting visit," Emereck said dryly.

"You're too stiff in the backbone. Now, if you'd just—"

A loud shout from just below their window interrupted Flindaran in mid-sentence. Emereck glanced toward the window, but Flindaran shook his head. "Drunks," he explained, "only get noisier if you shout back."

"Who's shouting? And if you're going to talk about drinking, I think you've—"

This time the interruption was a scream, ending in a choked, gurgling sound. Flindaran and Emereck lunged for the window.

Two armored men stood in the courtyard below. One held a drawn sword that glistened wetly; a body sprawled in front of him, half in, half out of the pool of light that spilled down from the windows of the inn. As the swordsman bent to wipe his blade clean, Flindaran stiffened and sucked in his breath. "Syaski!"

"What? They can't be!"

"No one else wears that kind of armor; I got a good look when he leaned over."

"Maybe they're just a couple of stragglers," Emereck said, but even as he spoke, four men rode out of the darkness to join the first two.

"So much for that theory. That means there are at least eight of them; they've probably left two more in back of the inn."

"I don't believe it," Emereck muttered as the six men in sight spread out around the front of the inn. "Syaskor is nearly a week's ride north! And they wouldn't risk provoking Kith Alunel like this."

"Tell it to them," Flindaran said grimly. "But keep a dagger handy while you do. They don't look much like figments of your imagination to me."

"What're they after in a town this small?"

As if in answer the Emereck's question, one of the men outside shouted. "Ho, Narryn! Come down and play!"

"Come fight, Cilhar scum," added another in a heavily accented voice. "Or we burn you out."

"Now you know." Flindaran stepped back from the window and glanced around the room, then began scooping their belongings into their packs. Emereck stayed where he was, frowning down at the soldiers and listening intently to their continued taunts. Something was wrong about this; he was sure those weren't Syaski accents, though he couldn't quite place them. Then the light outside changed, and he tensed. "Better hurry up," he said over his shoulder. "They've set the building on fire."

"Bloodthirsty half-wits." Flindaran buckled his sword-belt in place, then shoved the packs and the harp case at Emereck. "Here, take these. I'll go first."

Flindaran pushed the door open. The hallway was dark and already filling with smoke. Muttering curses, he stepped out of the room. Emereck followed as closely as he dared. He could hear shouts and screams from the lower floor, and the sounds of fighting outside. He tried to ignore them, and concentrated instead on the steady, muffled cursing ahead of him. If he lost Flindaran now, they might never— The cursing stopped. Emereck hurried forward and almost immediately ran into his friend from behind.

"Ouch! Demons take it, can't you watch where you're going?" came a furious whisper.

"In the dark? Anyway, why'd you stop?"

Flindaran hesitated. "I think we've missed the stairs."

"Keep going. There ought to be a service stairway at the end of the hall, and we still have a little time before the fire gets here."

Together they blundered on. When they reached the end of the hall there was a moment of confusion; then Flindaran found the right door and they half fell into the narrow stairwell. Emereck shoved the door closed, shutting out most of the smoke. They groped their way to the foot of the stairs. The door at the bottom was closed, but sounds of fighting came clearly through the cracks around the edges. Cautiously, Flindaran eased it open far enough for them to see what was happening on the other side.

They were standing at the rear of the kitchen near the back door of the inn. Ryl and the white-haired Cilhar stood on the other side of the room. Three Syaski faced them, their backs to Flindaran and Emereck. Wisps of smoke curled up from the edges of the far wall. The door leading to the main taproom was already ablaze. Ryl was fending off one of the Syaski with a long chopping knife, while the Cilhar's sword danced back and forth between the blades of the other two. A fourth Syask lay motionless on the floor beside the Cilhar.

Emereck had only an instant to absorb the scene; then Flindaran flung the door open with a crash and leaped forward. Emereck followed, wishing momentarily that he had some weapon. He saw Flindaran pounce on one of the Syaski. Another was a fraction too slow in recovering from his surprise, and the Cilhar ran him through. The third Syask stepped back and glanced quickly around.

Automatically, Emereck shifted his weight and swung one of the packs in a slow arc. It hit the man's head with a satisfying thud just as he opened his mouth to give the alarm. He collapsed with only a huff of air. Feeling a little surprised, and rather pleased with himself, Emereck hefted the pack and looked for another opponent.

There were none. Flindaran was just dispatching the last of the Syaski. The Cilhar wiped his sword on the cloak of one of the fallen Syaski, then glanced at the burning wall behind him. He looked at Ryl. "I don't suppose—"

"It would take too much concentration," Ryl said.

"Then we'd best get out of here. Quickly."

Emereck did not wait for the suggestion to be made twice. He took a firmer grip on the two packs and the harp case, and kicked the outer door open. A moment later he was standing in the courtyard behind the inn, waiting for his eyes to readjust to the darkness and hoping fervently that none of the Syaski would spot him in the interim. He heard the others behind him and turned.

Flindaran and the Cilhar came out of the doorway first, their swords held ready. The Cilhar seemed to have no trouble adjusting to the relative darkness of the courtyard. He scanned the shadows thoroughly, then sheathed his sword with an absentminded flourish. An instant later, Ryl appeared, dragging the body of the

Syask Emereck had knocked down. Emereck looked at her in surprise as she dropped the man in the shadows a short distance from the doorway.

Ryl saw him and frowned. "You'd rather I left him to burn to death? He'll not wake until we're gone."

Emereck's lips tightened, but he did not feel like explaining that his expression had been caused by Ryl's strength, rather than her actions. Dragging an armored Syask for even a short distance would be a heavy task for a large man, much less a small woman, but the innkeeper wasn't even breathing hard. Then the last half of her statement registered, and he said, "No, he should be coming to any minute now. I didn't hit him *that* hard."

Ryl looked at him. "I did. Now, shall we get the horses?"

As Emereck turned toward the stable, he heard Flindaran ask, "Where's Sira?"

"Heading for the woods with the rest of Tinbri," Ryl said. "She fled while we were holding the Syaski. You need not worry about her; she's safer now than we are."

The four headed for the stable. Their luck held; none of the Syaski appeared before they were safely out of sight. Inside the stable, they saddled their horses as quickly as they could. Even so, Emereck took time to make sure his harp case was securely fastened to his saddle. As they led the horses to the door, the Cilhar said, "I have not thanked you for your assistance. Will you give me your names?"

"Emereck Sterren of the Minstrel's Guild," Emereck replied, and glanced at Flindaran.

"Flindaran Sterren," Flindaran lied, bowing. "Both from the Guildhall in Ciaron."

The Cilhar raised an eyebrow. "I am impressed by your training. It is unusual to find a minstrel who is also such an excellent swordsman. Your skill does you credit."

Flindaran flushed with pleasure. "I am honored by such praise, especially from a Cilhar."

"I owe you a life," the Cilhar replied. "And if chance

ever takes you to the Mountains of Morravik, claim hospitality there in the name of Kensal Narryn."

"First we have to get away," Ryl said. "And if there are more Syaski coming . . ."

Flindaran leaned forward and peered out a crack in the stable door. "Looks quiet; they must still be around front."

Kensal Narryn shot a sharp look at Ryl. "When we're clear of the yard, turn to the left and head southeast around the lake toward the woods," he said as they left the stable. "If there are more of them, they'll be coming down the road on the west side of town, and we'll gain a little time."

Flindaran nodded and swung himself onto his horse. "Anything that keeps us out of the way is fine by—Uh oh."

Four Syaski stood by the corner of the inn, silhouetted against the flames. Emereck mounted hastily, hoping that they still had a chance of escaping if they moved quickly enough. When he looked again, the Syaski had not moved, but a row of mounted men had joined them, completely blocking the only exit from the courtyard.

"So there was a sentry," Kensal said calmly. He and Ryl had not yet mounted, and he had to look up to study the horsemen.

"Of course," said the man on the end of the line. "Now, throw down your weapons, grandpa, and we'll let you live."

"Will you indeed?" Kensal's voice expressed mild curiosity. His lips curved in a faint smile. Emereck thought he had never seen anyone look so dangerous.

"Even a Cilhar can't win against ten men at once. And there are your friends to—"

The Syask's speech was interrupted by a shout from the other side of the inn. As he turned in his saddle, another Syask appeared, running toward his mounted companions. He called a warning as he came, and Emereck stiffened as he recognized the language. "Lithmern!" he blurted in shock. "That's why the accent was wrong. These aren't Syaski, they're Lithmern!"

Flindaran turned and stared at Emereck as if he had gone mad. Kensal looked at Ryl, his face an expressionless mask. The innkeeper herself stood motionless beside him, staring with tense concentration at the riders.

The leader of the false Syaski glared at Emereck, then transferred his attention to the runner. "Well?" He spoke in Lithran; apparently he had decided there was no further need for pretense.

"The sentry's back," the runner panted. He took a deep breath and poured out a stream of Lithran. Emereck caught the words "Syaski" and "road," but most of the speech was too rapid for his meager knowledge of the language.

The leader gestured impatiently and the runner fell silent. The leader sheathed his sword and reached under his cloak. He drew out a small pouch, opened it, and sprinkled a pinch of black powder out of it into his hand. Carefully, he closed the pouch and replaced it, then hesitated and glanced at Kensal. "I'm afraid we're out of time. My apologies; I was looking forward to the fight."

With his last words, he stretched his hand out to one side and began to chant. The words were harsh and repetitive, and they bore no resemblance to any language Emereck knew. He could tell from the way the soldier spoke that the words had no meaning for him either; he was speaking from memory alone. Emereck glanced uncertainly at his companions. He saw Kensal half draw his sword, but Ryl put her hand on his arm and stopped him. She said something in a low voice, and then Emereck's attention was jerked back to the chanting Lithmern.

A thread of blackness moved in the man's upturned palm, like a wisp of smoke or a thin black snake. It curled and coiled around the Lithmern's hand, moving almost too rapidly to follow. Emereck's horse moved uneasily, and the riders nearest the spell-caster shifted nervously in their saddles. The smoke began to grow, and the leader flinched slightly, though his voice did not falter in the chant. The blackness thickened, and the man's arm sagged with the weight of it. Suddenly the blackness dropped to the ground and flowed toward Emereck and his companions like a carpet of clouds unrolling rapidly.

Emereck's horse reared, and he almost lost his seat. The blackness rippled slightly and came on. The horse came down fetlock-deep in darkness, and stuck fast. Emereck could feel the animal's muscles straining, but not a foot stirred. Flindaran's horse was caught, too, and the smoky carpet had almost reached Kensal and Ryl. Kensal was eyeing it measuringly, as if trying to decide whether his chances were better if he remained standing or tried to mount his skittish horse. Ryl's eyes were closed; she seemed to have withdrawn completely.

The blackness touched the hooves of Kensal's mare, and the animal rolled its eyes in fear. Suddenly, Ryl's voice cut across the chanting, crying out in a language that pulled at Emereck though he knew he had never heard it before. "*Miramar! Niterbarat cebarrel ja rykar rinarnth!*"

The chant faltered, and the advance of the blackness slowed. Nothing more seemed to happen. Kensal and Ryl stepped back a pace, then another, until their backs almost touched the stable wall. Then Emereck saw something move out beyond the fence that enclosed the courtyard; a fog on the surface of the lake. It thickened into a dense wall of gray wool and swept toward them. In another instant, it reached the fence that surrounded the courtyard and covered it.

The Lithmern leader faltered again at the sight of the unnatural wall of mist, then redoubled his efforts, chanting more loudly than ever. It had no effect. The mist rolled on over the courtyard. Emereck saw Ryl smile as she vanished into it; then Kensal and Flindaran were swallowed up as well. Emereck had time to hope that he would be as pleased as Ryl by this unexpected development, and then the fog engulfed him.

The mist was warm and damp and smelled, impossibly, of halaiba flowers. Emereck could make out a few dim shapes where the Lithmern stood; then the mist thickened and they were gone, leaving only an orange glow on his right to mark where the burning inn stood. He could hear the leader's voice calling instructions to his men in Lithran, and the answering shouts of the soldiers. Wondering what good a concealing mist would do them if they couldn't move, he looked down. The black smoke was slowly dissolving where the mist touched it. As the last of it disappeared, Emereck's horse reared again, screaming, and bolted.

All he could do was hang on and hope that the horse was still heading toward the courtyard gates. He passed Flindaran in a rush and was among the Lithmern. One of the soldiers started to draw a weapon; another tried to grab his horse's reins. Then he was through them, and out of the courtyard.

Behind him he heard shouting and the clang of steel on steel. He hauled on the reins, but the horse ignored him. Gradually, the sounds faded into the distance. He hoped fleetingly that the horse would not stumble; at this speed they'd probably both break their necks if it went down.

Suddenly the horse shied violently, nearly unseating him. As he struggled for balance, Emereck glimpsed the startled face of an armored rider. He saw the man's sword coming down, and tried to twist away, but he was not quick enough. The shock of the blow grated along his ribs. Pain lanced through his side. His horse gave a shrill, frightened whinny and bolted into the mist once more.

Grimly, Emereck clung to the saddle. He had never been more than an adequate horseman; staying with his terrified mount taxed his ability and the pain of the wound only made matters worse. He had no idea what direction they were going, for the mist hid everything. The ride quickly became a nightmare of figures looming unexpectedly out of the gray darkness and then vanishing again. Some were men; some were trees; some, Emereck was sure, were only his imagination.

He did not know how long it was before his horse slowed at last. He was vaguely aware that the animal had settled into an exhausted plodding, but by then it took most of his concentration just to stay in the saddle. He had lost a good deal of blood, and he was having difficulty thinking clearly. He knew he should stop and rest, but he was afraid that if he did, he would be found by the Syaski or the Lithmern or whoever they really were. Besides, he doubted that he would have the energy to start again once he stopped.

As he went on, the mist changed, so slowly that at first he did not even notice it. The air grew cold, and the smell of flowers faded. The mist thinned fractionally, barely enough for Emereck to tell that he was moving through trees. It seemed to be darker as well, though that was probably only his imagination.

A long time later, he realized that the horse was no longer moving. If I'm not riding I should dismount, he thought fuzzily. He tried to swing his leg up, but his muscles did not seem to be working properly and he overbalanced. He felt himself falling, and then the ground hit him and he lost consciousness.

Shalarn sat in the darkened room, staring at the dying embers in the brazier. Her black hair hung loose around her face, and her hands were clenched in tense concentration. The room was silent except for the sound of her breathing and the occasional faint crackle of the fire.

Slowly a picture formed in the air before her, framed in swirling smoke. Men in armor stood before a large building, shouting words she could not hear. The scene shifted. Firelight flashed on steel, and a man fell. Her eyes narrowed angrily; she had ordered them to avoid fighting! With effort she controlled herself before she lost the vision, and saw that the scene had changed again. A line of mounted men blocked a courtyard gate, and dark smoke flowed out from them.

Shalarn leaned forward eagerly. They had found him, then! She tried to shift the viewpoint, and caught a glimpse of two young men on horseback just in front of the line of soldiers. Behind them was a shadowy blur. She struggled to focus the spell, and suddenly a curtain of mist hid the scene. Shalarn gasped. Even through the seeing-spell, she could feel the echo of sorcery.

The mist swirled, then parted to show one of the young

men from the courtyard. His side was wet with blood, and he was alone. As she watched, he swayed and fell from his horse.

On impulse, she murmured another spell. The picture shivered, and the other man appeared. The room faded from her awareness as she concentrated on him, drawing him in the direction she had chosen. It was much easier than she had expected. She brought him to a point almost on top of the wounded man, then let go of her spells. As the picture vanished, she wondered absently whether the two men even knew each other. Well, she had done what she could, and those blundering soldiers would have much to explain when they returned.

With a sigh, she released the last threads of the seeing-spell. She would learn no more tonight. She stretched her cramped muscles and sat back, wondering whether she should try again the following night. The seeing-spell was unreliable at best, and it required considerable power. Then, too, there was always the chance that Lanyk would discover what she was doing. Her men would return in seven or eight days; perhaps she should wait until then for an explanation.

Shalarn frowned. The raid had failed; that at least was clear. And there was sorcery involved, strong sorcery. The Cilhar had wizard friends, then. Perhaps that was the key to his importance. Or was he himself the wizard?

Her frown deepened. There was still too much she did not know. The thought of a foretelling crossed her mind, but she dismissed it at once. She knew from bitter experience how misleading oracles and auguries could be. Again she considered making a second attempt at the seeing-spell. But a sorcerer might detect it, and that could bring everything to ruin once more.

Shalarn straightened in sudden decision. She would wait the seven days for her explanation. In the meantime, she would build her strength for whatever confrontation might come. Her face relaxed into a smile, and she rose and left the room. Behind her, a wisp of smoke curled up from the brazier and vanished as the last of the fire winked out.

Three

*E*mereck awoke to the smell of smoke and the hissing sound of fat dripping into a fire. For a moment, he was sure that this was their previous camp and the entire episode of the inn had been a dream; then he tried to move and the pain in his side told him otherwise.

He opened his eyes and looked down. His chest had been crudely wrapped in the torn remnants of his tunic. He blinked, then rolled cautiously onto his good side and raised himself up on one elbow to look around.

Judging from the sunlight, it was late morning. He was lying under a tree in the middle of a forest or a grove of trees. He saw no sign of the mist, the lake, or the village. His horse was tethered nearby, along with another mount he recognized as Flindaran's. Flindaran himself was sitting on the opposite side of a small fire, scowling at a rabbit he had suspended over the flames. Emereck stared at him in disbelief.

At the rustle of Emereck's movement, Flindaran looked up, and his expression lightened. "Emereck! You haven't—I mean, you're . . ."

"Flindaran, what are you doing here?" Emereck demanded.

Flindaran's answering grin held profound relief. "Taking care of you, you ungrateful croaker. You're lucky I found you."

"I'm not sure 'lucky' is the right word." Emereck pushed himself up to a sitting position, wincing as he did. "What happened to Ryl and Kensal? And how *did* you find me in all that mist?"

"I don't know. We had to fight our way out of the courtyard. I lost Ryl and Kensal just outside, so I turned left and headed for the woods, the way Kensal suggested. I thought I saw Ryl ahead of me a couple of times after I got into the trees, and I tried to follow her. I lost her again just before the mist started to clear, and then my horse practically tripped over you. It was more luck than anything."

The explanation sounded a little odd to Emereck, but it was no more unlikely than some of the things Flindaran had done in the past. Emereck shook his head. "I can't get rid of you no matter how hard I try."

"Just for that, you get the burned section when the rabbit's done."

"You mean there's going to be a part that isn't burned? Your cooking must be improving."

Flindaran made a face at him and reached quickly to turn the rabbit. "Now tell me what happened to you. You went galloping through those Syaski like one of the heroic idiots in those tragic ballads you're so fond of; I was afraid you were going to get killed."

"They weren't—wait a minute, you don't think I took off like that *on purpose*, do you?"

Flindaran stared.

"My horse ran away with me."

A reluctant smile began tugging at the corners of Flindaran's mouth. "Well, you never have been much of a horseman. Go on."

Emereck described his encounter with the swordsman, but skipped lightly over most of the nightmarish ride that followed. When he finished, Flindaran shook his head. "I keep telling you and telling you, you ought to learn how to handle a sword. Maybe now you'll listen to me."

"I'll think about it."

Flindaran grimaced. "You're lucky all you got out of it was a scrape on the ribs! I'm not Philomel the Healer, you know."

"Just a scrape?" Emereck shifted, and winced again. "It feels a lot more serious than that to me."

"That kind of wound usually does." Flindaran paused, looking worried. "I tried to clean it off a little, but I'm not sure how good a job I did. And I wasn't sure which of your herbs were supposed to be good for bleeding, so I didn't use any."

"It's just as well, though I suppose you'd have managed not to kill me. But it sounds as if you did all the right things." Emereck stopped and studied his friend. "Don't worry so much. It would have been worse if things had happened the other way around."

"What do you mean?"

"What would your father say if the two of us rode up to his castle and *you* were the one with his chest wrapped up like this?"

"He'd probably say I deserved it. And he'd be right; those Syaski were lousy swordsmen."

"They weren't Syaski."

Flindaran shrugged. "Maybe the first bunch weren't, but I'll bet you a new harp the second batch were."

"The second . . . That's what he meant!" Emereck said, startled.

"What who meant?"

"The soldier who came charging around the inn right before the one on the horse started doing . . . whatever it was. I only caught a few words of what he said, but it fits. He must have been warning the Lithmern that there were real Syaski coming down the road!"

"You're sure they were Lithmern?"

"Positive. Their accents were right, even if their armor wasn't."

"Maybe they're just hiring their swords to Syaskor for a while. That would explain the armor."

"Lithmern working for Syaskor?"

"Sure. Half the Lithmern army has turned mercenary

in the past couple of years. There wasn't much else they could do after Alkyra wiped out their invasion."

"It's a pity Lithra and Syaskor aren't neighbors," Emereck commented. "They deserve each other. But if the Lithmern we saw were working for Syaskor, why were they worried about more Syaski showing up?"

"I don't know." Flindaran frowned. "I don't like the smell of the whole thing. Lithmern in Syaski armor, real Syaski who can't fight—none of it makes any sense!"

"Don't forget the magic."

"Magic?"

"What do you *think* Ryl and that Lithmern were doing, reciting Varnan poetry?"

"Oh, that. That's not what I was talking about; magic never makes any sense."

"At least not to swordsmen."

Flindaran ignored him. "I wish I knew why they thought Kensal was important enough to send a raiding party for him."

"We could go back and look for him; maybe he knows."

"Are you out of your mind? We barely got away as it was."

"It was just a suggestion."

"Your curiosity is going to get you killed one of these days. Besides—are you sure you should ride?"

"I don't have much choice. We can hardly camp here for a month while my side heals."

"We have a couple of weeks to spare before we'll be missed at Minathlan; Father's expecting us to come in with the caravan. At the rate Goldar was going, it'll be at least three and a half weeks before they get there. We should be able to do it in a week, once your side is healed."

"You'd go out of your mind from sitting here doing nothing, and I'd do the same from watching you. Riding may wear me out, but I doubt it'll do me any real harm."

Flindaran looked at him sharply, then grinned. "All

right, then. We'll head for Minathlan. But first we eat."
He leaned forward and reached for the rabbit.

It was mid-afternoon by the time they were ready to
leave. Flindaran helped Emereck mount, then swung
himself into his own saddle. "All right, pick a direction."

"I thought we had decided to go on to Minathlan."

Flindaran grinned. "Yes, but which direction is that?"

"You mean you don't know where we are?"

"I haven't the foggiest notion."

"Oh, we've mist our way?"

Flindaran groaned. "I surrender."

Emereck shook his head. "Why didn't you mention
this earlier?"

"What difference would it make? We'd still be lost."

"You and your shortcuts. I don't suppose you have
any idea how to get us out of this?"

"Well, we don't want to go back to Tinbri, and I think
that's west of us. Minathlan ought to be somewhere
north and east. So why don't we . . . why don't we . . ."
Flindaran frowned, staring into the trees. "That way,"
he said suddenly.

"What?" Emereck squinted up at the sun, then looked
at Flindaran in puzzlement. "But that's almost due east;
you just said we have to go northeast to get to Minathlan."

"It feels right."

Emereck stared. "What are you talking about?"

"It feels right," Flindaran said stubbornly. He hesitated, then continued with more confidence, "Besides,
it'll be easier to find out where we are if we go east."

"Oh, really."

"There's a road the caravans take that runs northeast
from Kith Alunel; we should come to it before too long.
Then all we have to do is follow it and we'll get to
Minathlan."

"That sounds as if it makes a little more sense."

"And when we get to the road, we'll be on a regular
route again."

"You just convinced me."

Flindaran nodded absently and they started off. Flindaran went first, and Emereck followed, gritting his teeth. Despite his reassurances to Flindaran, he was in no condition to enjoy the ride. Even at a deliberately slow walk, his side was painful. He tried to take his mind off it by watching the trees, but it only made matters worse. The trees all looked the same; watching them gave him a headache.

Flindaran moved surely through the forest, seldom checking their direction. After a time, Emereck began to feel uneasy. How could Flindaran be so certain of their way? Emereck looked up, trying to determine the position of the sun for himself, but the heavy canopy of leaves made it almost impossible. Finally he rode up to Flindaran and asked bluntly, "Are you sure you've never been in these woods before?"

"Of course I'm sure. What kind of question is that?"

"I just thought—" Emereck was suddenly at a loss for words to explain his nebulous suspicions. "Never mind. I'll just be glad when we're out of this forest."

"You will? Why?" Flindaran's voice was surprised and puzzled. "I like it. It's so green." Emereck did not reply, and Flindaran went on in a musing tone, "You know, my grandfather claimed our family originally came from somewhere around here, back when Minathlan was still desert."

"Really? I didn't think there were any records that went back that far."

"There aren't. It's just a family legend about some ancestor who left this area and settled in Minathlan." Flindaran looked up at the trees. "No doubt he had a good reason," he added sourly.

Emereck swallowed the reply he had intended and said nothing. Flindaran did not speak often of his home, but Emereck had heard descriptions from minstrels who had been there. Minathlan was a flat country with few trees, tending to a dusty yellow-brown in summer and a muddy gray-brown in winter. The land had been reclaimed from desert many centuries before by some anonymous wizard, and the Dukes of Minathlan had worked it well since then. But neither magic nor diligence could coax more than a mediocre harvest from most of the land, and though Minathlan was not poverty-stricken, it was far from prosperous. Emereck did not find it surprising that Flindaran preferred the forest.

They rode on in silence. Emereck's headache receded, but his side still pained him. He bore it as long as he could, but finally he was forced to call a halt. Though it was still early they made camp, and Emereck fell quickly into an exhausted sleep.

In the morning they went on. Though Flindaran was as sure of their way as ever, they rode for most of the morning without finding any sign of a village, a road, or even of the end of the forest. "Are you sure we haven't been going in circles?" Emereck asked at last. "I thought we should have found that road of yours by now, even at this pace."

"No," Flindaran said absently.

"No, we're not going in circles, or no, we shouldn't have found a road?"

"I meant—" Flindaran stopped and his head turned. "What was that?"

Emereck paused, listening. The forest was silent; not even a breath of wind rustled the leaves. "I don't hear anything."

Flindaran pulled his horse to a halt and gestured. "It was over that way."

Shaking his head, Emereck peered into the trees. A sudden gust of wind swept through them, bringing with it, faint but clear, a whisper of music.

"There!" Flindaran said. "Did you hear it?"

"I heard it."

"Who would be playing flutes in the middle of a forest?"

"I don't know. But those weren't flutes, or any other instrument I've ever heard. And if you don't mind, I'd like—"

"—to go find out what they are," Flindaran finished. "And you claim I have a one-track mind!"

"It didn't sound as if they were too far away," Emereck offered.

The two men looked at each other. Flindaran grinned. "Let's go, then." They swung their horses around and started off in the new direction.

Four

As they went on, the stirrings of wind became a steady breeze and the music grew gradually louder. It was a haunting tune that changed constantly just as it seemed about to slide into a familiar ballad or song. It made Emereck uneasy even as he admired the skill of whoever was improvising it. He thought of the legendary swamp-spirits of Basirth, whose flickering lights lured unwary travelers on until they became hopelessly lost. The music behaved similarly; whenever Emereck and Flindaran began to drift off the path, a breath of wind would bring them another snatch of melody.

Emereck shivered. He realized with a start that he had fallen well behind; Flindaran was just disappearing over the top of a low rise. Emereck called to him to wait and urged his horse forward, heedless of the pain it caused in his side.

At the top of the rise, the trees stopped. Emereck squinted against the sudden sunlight and took a deep breath, then coughed at the heavy, unexpected scent of flowers. Belatedly, he realized that the slope below was a solid mass of blue halaiba flowers. A wake of crushed and bent plants marked Flindaran's route down the hill, and the air was sweet with their scent.

The flowers ended at the base of a long, high wall almost in the center of the open area. Even from where Emereck stood, the milky stone of the wall showed signs of weathering. Treetops showed above the wall, and Emereck could see a flash of white further on that might be a tower. The scene had an air of unreality about it, like a mountain seen through bright haze on a summer day.

Flindaran stood beside the wall, studying it, while his horse placidly cropped flowers. He looked up and waved. "The music's coming from inside," he said as Emereck came up beside him. He looked back at the wall. "I think I can climb it."

"Well, I can't, and you're not going in there without me. Besides, I think we'll get a much warmer welcome if we're a little more conventional about getting inside. Don't be so impatient. There has to be a gate somewhere."

"You have no sense of adventure," Flindaran complained as he remounted.

"You just want to have all the fun."

Flindaran grinned and denied it, and they started around the wall. About a third of the way around they found a massive iron gate, which swung smoothly open at Flindaran's touch. As they rode inside, the music changed sharply. Emereck glanced around for the players, and froze in surprise.

They stood at the edge of a garden, somewhat overgrown but still lush and green. The trees were immense, and a steady breeze added to the impression of shady coolness. Scattered almost at random among the flowers and trees were a number of stone pillars and spirals and abstract forms. Emereck realized with shock that it was the wind blowing through the various shapes that made the music they had been hearing. He heard a low whistle beside him as Flindaran discovered the source of the music. "Emereck . . ." Flindaran said.

"I noticed."

"It gives a whole new meaning to the idea of wind instruments, doesn't it?"

"You could say that." Emereck was only half-listening

to Flindaran's words; he was intent on the music. "Wait for me a moment, will you? I want a closer look at them."

"Shouldn't you check with whoever lives here first?"

"Lives here?" Emereck said blankly.

Flindaran gestured. For the first time, Emereck noticed the building in the center of the garden, half-hidden by trees and vines. Though it was large enough for a castle, it was more open and airy-looking than any castle Emereck had ever seen. It was made of a smooth, almost translucent white stone. The door facing them appeared to be made of carved and tarnished silver. No steps led up to it. Instead, an area the size of Ryl's taproom had been covered with the same white stone as the building, forming a terrace just in front of the door. The place looked abandoned. One wing had collapsed, and another seemed on the verge of it.

"You really think someone might be living in that?" Emereck said.

Flindaran shrugged. "We might as well look." They dismounted and tethered their horses to the gate, then walked toward the building. The door was ajar. As they approached a small bird flew out of it, scolding angrily. They found no sign of a knocker or bell-rope, and no one answered their calls.

"Let's go in and look around," Flindaran suggested.

Emereck shook his head. "No, thanks. I don't want the roof coming down on my head," he replied, gesturing toward the ruined wing. "Besides, I want to get a look at those wind-music makers first. I've never heard of anything like them, and I'll wager no one else in the Guild has, either."

Without waiting for Flindaran to answer, he started for the nearest sculpture. He examined it carefully. He got no better idea of how it had been made, but his opinion of the designer rose even higher. The stones were old, ancient, yet the wear of time had not diminished the quality of the music they made. He finished and started toward the next sculpture, wondering whether the wind ever ceased. It might not matter; the sculptures seemed to be scattered all around the central building, so no matter which way the wind blew, some of them would . . .

Emereck stopped. Slowly, he scanned the garden, sorting out the complex melody in his mind. He paused, staring at the trees on either side of the castle, and realized that Flindaran had joined him. "Have you found something?" Flindaran asked.

"The wind," Emereck said. "Look at the way the wind is blowing."

Flindaran gave him a puzzled look. "It's blowing the same way it was when we got here, from . . ." He stopped, just as Emereck had done, staring. "Demons in a chamber pot, it's blowing in a circle!"

"I'm glad I'm not imagining that. Come on. I want to look around the other side of this place."

Slowly, they circled the castle. The grounds were much the same: attractive, slightly overgrown, and dotted with the music-making statues. Emereck stopped several times, as much to rest as to examine the sculptures. He had not realized how tired he was. As they returned to the gate, he stumbled and nearly fell.

Flindaran was beside him in an instant. "Emereck, you idiot, why didn't you say something? Here, sit down, let me get—"

"Stop fussing! I lost my balance, that's all."

"People don't turn white just because they lose their balance. You're being an idiot."

"You said that already."

"Great truths bear repeating." Flindaran helped Emereck to the nearest tree. "There! Sit still, and don't do anything stupid. I'm going to make camp."

"Already? But it's not even noon!"

"So? We don't know where we're going; it won't matter if it takes us a little longer to get there. And you don't look as if you're in any shape to do more riding today."

Emereck considered the justice of that comment. "You're right, I wouldn't mind resting. But are you sure making camp is a good idea?"

"Why not? I thought you'd want to do some exploring later."

"I'm interested in exploring, all right. I'm also worried. I don't think even one of the adepts from the Temple of the Third Moon could build something like this, and I'm not sure it's safe."

"It's safer than camping in the woods."

"I suppose so. But don't go looking around without me. You might turn into one of those statues or something," Emereck said, half-seriously.

"Don't be ridiculous. Besides, I'd be off-key and they'd change me back right away." Flindaran grinned at Emereck's expression. "Stop worrying. I won't let you miss anything." Emereck nodded reluctantly, and Flindaran left to unsaddle the horses.

Emereck was more tired than he had admitted, and the throbbing in his side was worse than it had been the previous day. He spent much of the afternoon falling in and out of a fitful doze, but by late afternoon he felt more like himself. After they had eaten he got out his harp. He tuned it and ran a quick scale, then settled down to some serious practicing.

For a long time, Flindaran sat and watched. Finally, during one of Emereck's pauses, he said, "Emereck, what would have happened if you'd broken your arm falling off that horse?"

"I'd have been rather badly in need of practice once the splints came off. Why?"

"I just wondered whether there was anything that would keep you from playing those infernal scales."

Emereck laughed. "Sorry. How's this?" He began improvising a harp accompaniment to the strange tune the wind played on the garden statues.

Flindaran leaned back and smiled dreamily. "Much better," he said. "I don't think I've ever heard you play so well. How do you do that?"

"Improvise? Practice, that's all. It—"

"No, no! I mean, how do you make it sound like two harps?"

"Two harps?" Emereck listened closely for a moment, then abruptly muted the harpstrings with his palms. As the sound died, he heard what he was listening for. Beneath the constant swirling of the wind-music was the small, silvery echo of another harp. He looked at Flindaran. "That wasn't me! Did you hear it?"

"I think so," Flindaran said cautiously. "Try it again."

This time the echo was more distinct. The sound pulled at Emereck like a cherished memory, and he could tell from Flindaran's expression that it drew him as well. As the echo died, Flindaran rose. "It's coming from inside," he said, taking a step forward. He hardly seemed aware of Emereck at all. "Do it again; maybe I can follow the sound."

"No." Emereck forced the word out, and his own longing to run into the castle in search of the harp diminished.

"Why not?" Flindaran spoke without turning, but Emereck could hear the tension in his voice.

"Perversity."

"*What?*" Flindaran turned sharply. "Emereck, that's the stupidest reason I've ever heard."

"At least you heard it."

"What are you talking about?"

"Do you still want to go charging in there after that harpist, or whoever it is?"

Flindaran frowned. "I'm still curious, but . . . no, I don't. At least, not the same way I wanted to a minute ago." He looked up, puzzled. "What—"

"I think we were both spell-struck."

"I see. And I thought this place felt so friendly."

There was a long silence. "Now what do we do?" Flindaran asked finally. "Whatever it is, we can't just ignore it."

"I know. Well, maybe we can find it without the music."

Flindaran hesitated, eyeing the castle dubiously. Then he shrugged. "You're right; let's go. But you'd better bring your harp, just in case."

Emereck nodded. Their preparations were completed quickly, and they started into the castle. The slanting rays of the early evening sunlight streamed through long windows on the west side of the building. Their footsteps echoed through the stone corridors. The air felt heavy, like a summer day streaked with the first few drops of a coming thunderstorm. The rooms they passed were all but empty; one held a massive stone table, another a pair of carved marble benches, and that was all.

"It looks as if someone's taken everything in the place," Flindaran said. He sounded disappointed.

"Or as if everything's been carefully put away so it will be ready when the owner comes back," Emereck said.

"What made you think of that?"

"I don't know. This place gives me shivers; I feel like someone's watching me behind my back." Emereck stopped and swung his harp into reach. Carefully, he plucked a single string.

The echo answered, more pronounced than it had been outside but somehow less insistent. The sound still tugged at Emereck, but not as strongly, and his mind remained clear. He turned in the direction from which the echo had come.

They had to retrace their steps a short distance before they found a side passage that led in the right direction. Twice more, Emereck stopped and called up the silver echo with his harp. Finally, they turned down a short, featureless hall, and Emereck stopped short.

The hallway ended in a pile of rubble; beyond was the collapsed wing Emereck had noticed earlier. "Just my luck; it would have to be somewhere under all that," Flindaran said disgustedly. He stepped forward and began lifting stones aside. Emereck stayed where he was, frowning. How could the other harp—if there was another harp—make any sound if it was buried under the rubble? Still frowning, Emereck reached down and plucked a string of his harp once more.

The note seemed to go on and on, mingling with the sound of the second harp, ringing around him with a pure clarity. The air brightened; he saw Flindaran begin to turn, slowly, like a fish trying to swim through honey. A door-shaped section of wall beside him shimmered and vanished. As if in a dream, Emereck set down his harp and walked through it.

The room was washed with gold. Even the air seemed to shimmer. In the center of the room stood a pedestal of white marble. On it, glimmering faintly with a cold, white light, stood a harp. A corner of Emereck's mind noted the absence of any scrollwork or inlay; this instrument needed no embellishment. He moved forward and reached for it.

Something shot through him as he touched the harp—a flash of power or pain or joy, so intense he could not identify it with certainty. He stumbled backward, clutching the harp, and tripped. He fell, and found himself sprawling on the floor of the hallway, facing a blank, featureless wall of white stone. He still held the harp.

"Emereck!" Flindaran's voice, full of worry and amazement, shocked him out of his daze.

"I'm all right," he said as he picked himself up off the floor. "Let's get out of here." He reached down for his own instrument, and realized suddenly that his side no longer pained him. He swung his left arm experimentally, then stretched it. He did not feel even a twinge. He scooped up his harp, and turned to leave.

Flindaran gave him an odd look, but he did not say anything. They left hurriedly. Once they were safely out of the castle, Emereck explained what had happened to him. While he talked, he examined his side carefully. The wound seemed to have healed completely; the only sign left was a band of white tissue, like an old scar. Moving his arm was no longer painful and he felt only a small twinge when he probed the scar with his fingers.

"What is that thing, anyway?" Flindaran said, eyeing the harp with respect and a little wariness.

"A harp. What does it look like?"

"That's not what I meant, and you know it."

Emereck shrugged. "How should I know what it is?"

"Maybe if you played it . . ."

"No. Not until I know a little more about it."

"Then *I'll* play it."

"No!"

"But how else—"

"Magic is dangerous if you don't know what you're doing. This is stronger magic than any I've heard of outside legends, unless you believe those stories about the way Alkyra fought off the Lithmern a couple of years ago. And with this, neither one of us knows what we're doing."

"Sitting there won't tell you anything. The least you could do is look at it."

Emereck nodded. Reluctantly, he picked up the harp. This time there was no shock when his fingers touched it. The strings seemed to glow faintly silver and red and silver-green in the fading twilight. They were made of an unfamiliar material that was neither metal nor gut, and Emereck saw with surprise that they were fixed in place without tuning pegs. The body of the harp seemed to be made of bone or ivory, and it had been carved all in one piece, though Emereck knew of no creature with large enough bones to supply a piece of that size.

A snatch of melody ran through the back of his mind, and his eyes widened. Slowly and with great care he set the harp down and stared at it, unseeing. With a corner of his mind, he heard Flindaran's questions, and he murmured the words of the song in reply.

> "He held the harp, bone-white as dragon's teeth
> And strung with moonlight's glow. He raised it
>   high,
> And played, and when at last the music ceased
> Like flowers killed by frost, the cities died."

"What's that supposed to mean?" Flindaran demanded.

"That's part of an old song called 'King Loren's Lay.' It tells how King Loren destroyed Istravar and two other cities when they attacked him."

Flindaran stared at the harp. "And you think—"

"I think I know what this is," Emereck said with deadly quietness. "It's impossible, but it's the only thing that fits. This is the harp that ballad describes. The Harp of Imach Thyssel."

Five

*F*lindaran looked from Emereck to the harp and back. "The Harp of Imach Thyssel? Isn't that the one Marryl the Avenger used to play the shadows out of Harwood?"

"No, that was Neriwind's Harp," Emereck said. Talking was a welcome distraction from the tangle of emotions the discovery of the harp had roused in him, and he went on, "Neriwind's Harp has been in the Hall of Tears for nearly three hundred years, so this can't be it. I wish it were," he added under his breath.

Flindaran caught the comment and frowned. "Why? Is there something wrong about this one?"

"Not exactly. It's just that I'd know what to expect from Neriwind's Harp. It was made during the Wars of Binding, and it's been used several times since then. I know enough of the songs and histories to have a good idea of what it does and what to do with it."

"And the Harp of Imach Thyssel?"

"It's even older than Neriwind's Harp. No one knows when it was made, but it was before the Wars of Binding. It is more powerful, too. The Master Minstrel who first told me of it said that only the Lost Gifts of Alkyra might be its equal in magic." Unconsciously, Emereck slipped into the formal phrasing of a trained storyteller. "Twice was it used with known purpose: Once to bring fair winds to the fleet of the Kulseth sailors when their war with Varna failed and they were forced to flee, and once when Calzen, Istravar, and Toltan made war together upon the city Imach Thyssel, and were destroyed.

"In Imach Thyssel the harp was called the Luck of the City, for they said that the presence of the Harp kept them peaceful and prosperous, and so it was for many years. Yet despite the magic of the Harp, the city was at last betrayed and destroyed. Then the Harp of Imach Thyssel was played for the third time, and for what purpose is not known. But that day storm winds toppled the spires of Imach Thyssel on the heads of the invaders; fire took the city's walls; the earth shook; and at the end the sea swallowed armies and city alike. And since that day, none has seen or heard of the Harp of Imach Thyssel, the Luck of the City."

Silence fell. At last Flindaran shook himself and looked around. "I wish you'd warn me when you're going to do that."

Emereck laughed self-consciously. "I'm sorry. It's just habit and training."

"Don't apologize; it was wonderful. But distracting. Are you sure that *this* is the Harp of Imach Thyssel?"

"No," Emereck said without conviction. Flindaran looked at him sharply. Emereck sighed. "Yes, I'm sure. I don't know why. There have been other magic harps made, and for all I know half-a-dozen of them could fit the description in that song. But I'm still sure."

"And if it is . . ." Flindaran leaned forward and stared at the Harp with growing excitement. "Emereck, if this *is* the Harp of Imach Thyssel, think of what you could do with it!"

"I'd rather not."

"What? Why not?"

"Lots of reasons." Emereck shifted uncomfortably. "If I think about it too much I'll be tempted to use it. And I wouldn't trust myself with that kind of power, even if I knew enough to be sure I wouldn't make any mistakes."

"You mean you don't want it?"

"I want it, but I don't want to want it, if you see what I mean. And there's the price to consider."

"Price?"

"Everyone who has ever tried to use the Harp of Imach Thyssel has paid a price, and usually a heavy one. The Kulseth fleet escaped from the Varnan wizards, but their Prince was crippled by the power he had used. King Loren didn't just destroy the armies that were attacking Imach Thyssel, he destroyed all three of their home cities as well, down to the last child within their walls. And his betrothed had been visiting in Istravar when the war broke out; he never really recovered from losing her. As for Imach Thyssel itself . . ."

"It could all just be coincidence."

"The Master Minstrels don't think so."

"Oh." Flindaran paused. "What are you going to do with it?"

"I don't know. I ought to leave it here," Emereck said, knowing even as he spoke that he could not bring himself to do it.

"You wouldn't!"

"No. But I'd like to. It would make things . . . simpler." The Harp made Emereck profoundly uneasy. He knew that finding it marked the beginning of changes he could not imagine or anticipate, and he wanted to run from it. But he could not explain that to Flindaran.

Flindaran remained silent for a long time, staring at the Harp. Darkness had fallen, and the glow of the harp-strings was easier to see. It was a cool, diffuse light that illuminated little beyond the Harp itself, like starlight, Emereck thought. Flindaran looked up and said tentatively, "If you don't want it, Emereck, I could take it."

Emereck tensed and peered into the gloom, trying to make out Flindaran's expression. "I'm afraid that wouldn't help," he said cautiously. He hesitated, then asked, "Did you want it for something specific?"

"Well . . ." Flindaran's shoulders hunched slightly, then he said in a rush, "If it really is the Harp of Imach Thyssel, and it can do all those things you said, I thought . . . well, that it might make things in Minathlan better."

"Guardians of Lyra, Flindaran, are you crazy? Or haven't you heard anything I just said?"

"I heard you," Flindaran said. He waited until Emereck looked and their eyes met, then added softly, "It might be worth the price."

Emereck could not answer. This was a side of Flindaran that he had never seen. At last he swallowed hard and said, "No one should use that Harp until one of the Guildmasters has had a chance to study it."

Flindaran was still watching with that disquieting expression. "Then your answer is no?"

"The answer is no."

Flindaran shrugged and sat back. "All right, it's your Harp." He grinned suddenly. "But it was worth asking. You should have seen your face!"

"It's not funny. It's bad enough that one of us will have to pay a price to that thing, without you getting involved, too."

"One of us . . . you mean because it healed your side?"

"Yes."

"But you weren't *trying* to use it. You didn't even play it."

"I don't know whether that matters. But I suppose I'll find out." Emereck tried to sound cheerful, but he did not succeed in keeping the strain out of his voice.

There was another long silence. Finally Flindaran said, "Well, what *are* you going to do with it?"

"There's only one thing I can do. Take it back to the Guildhall, and hope someone there knows enough about it to decide what should be done."

"You're not thinking of going straight there, are you?"

"Of course. The sooner I get there, the less time I'll have to spend worrying about it."

"I was right, you're not thinking. Look, Ciaron is over a month's journey from here, even if you go through the Mountains of Morravik instead of around them. You have hardly any supplies, and there are Syaski and Lithmern and demons-only-know-what-else wandering around somewhere in that direction. You'd never make it."

"You have another suggestion?"

"Yes. Come to Minathlan with me, the way we planned. It should only be about three or four days' ride. That'll give the Syaski and the Lithmern plenty of time to kill each other off or go away or something, and I can give you whatever you'll need for the trip."

"Well . . ." Emereck hesitated. He had been firmly resolved to head straight back to Ciaron, but the mention of the Syaski and the Lithmern gave him pause. If either of those countries got their hands on the Harp of Imach Thyssel . . . "All right. I'll admit I don't like the idea of dodging all those soldiers, so Minathlan it is. We'll have to think of some way of wrapping up the Harp, though; I'm not about to ride around with it dangling from the side of my saddle for all the world to see and wonder at."

"That's the first sensible thing you've said all night," Flindaran said. He poked the coals of their dinner fire into a cheerful blaze, and the ordinariness of the action made the whole unlikely situation seem more manageable. Emereck relaxed, and the converation turned to plans for the remainder of the journey. They talked until late that night, and by the time he went to sleep, Emereck's niggling sense of worry over Flindaran's request for the Harp had vanished.

The ride to Minathlan took nearly eight days, and it was one of the least pleasant in Emereck's memory. For the first three days it rained intermittently, and even when the drizzle stopped, the leaves above them dripped in cool, heavy splashes on their heads and horses. On the fifth day they came out of the forest onto a rolling green plain. Shortly after that the rain stopped and the sun appeared. The light and warmth were welcome at first, but under their influence the water began to evaporate, and soon the plain was a steambath.

To add to Emereck's discomfort, he was not sleeping well. It began as a simple restlessness and developed through bad dreams into full-fledged nightmares. Twice

Emereck woke sweating in the early hours of the morning, unable to recall any details of his dream beyond a deep sense of horror and grief. After that he began taking the second watch, and the dreams subsided.

As they drew nearer to Minathlan, the country grew flatter, dryer, and dustier. Flindaran seemed to stiffen as the land changed, as if he were bracing himself against something. Emereck's uneasiness returned, though Flindaran did not bring up the subject of the Harp again. He did not even mention its existence, but his request lay like a reproach in the back of Emereck's mind as they rode past the dry, brown fields. Emereck found Flindaran's restraint profoundly disturbing. It was unlike him, and Emereck began to wonder if he was being wise to bring the Harp to Minathlan.

The Cilhar sifted dead ashes through his fingers while the wind played an endlessly changing song on the statues that dotted the garden behind him. "There were two of them, I think," he told the dark-haired woman beside him.

"How long have they been gone?"

"About three days. We might have gotten here before them if we hadn't followed those Lithmern for so long."

Ryl shook her head. "We could have done nothing else. I owed somewhat to the people of Tinbri for bringing all that on their heads. Besides, the time wasn't wasted; we learned a fair amount."

"I wasn't criticizing."

"I know. I was talking more to myself than to you, I fear. One always has a tendency to justify one's mistakes, and this will make matters far more difficult for us."

"Difficult? Their trail's three days old, and the rain will have all but washed it away. It may not be quite impossible to follow, but it's sure to be close to it."

"There will be no need to strain your abilities; I think I know where they are going. Minathlan."

"Minathlan?" Kensal looked startled. "I hadn't even considered it a possibility. Why Minathlan?"

"Because at least one of them is of the family of the

Duke of Minathlan. There is no other way they could
have found this castle."

"I don't quite follow your logic."

"Castle Windsong is protected from discovery by
anyone but the family of its builder, and the Dukes of
Minathlan are the only remaining branch of that family.
An ordinary person traveling through these woods would
never realize that there was anything here, but one of the
Duke's blood-kin would be drawn to this place like steel
to a lodestone."

"I see." He looked at her curiously, but decided not to
comment on their own presence at the castle. Every rule,
after all, had exceptions. "And you're sure they have the
Harp?"

"Yes. I think the castle gave it to them."

"*Gave* it to them?"

"Sometimes Castle Windsong has . . . a mind of its
own." Ryl smiled slightly as if at some private joke.

"But why?"

Ryl's smile faded. "One of them, I think, must have
been a real minstrel. For such a one to come to this place
in company with one of the heirs of Minathlan . . . it was
very nearly inevitable that Windsong release the Harp. I
fear the blame is in part my own for rousing this place,
however slightly. I should not have called upon Miramar
so close to here."

"Called on Miramar?"

"In the courtyard of the inn. There is an ancient
friendship between the . . . spirit of Lake Miramar and
that of Castle Windsong. I should have thought that
waking one might disturb the other."

"You did what you had to, and it's too late now
anyway." Kensal straightened. "Shall we go?"

"Where?"

"To Minathlan, of course, to get you that Harp."

Ryl smiled and shook her head. "I don't think it will be
quite that simple, my friend. The Harp of Imach Thyssel
does not move easily from one owner to another. We may
have to . . . persuade them to cooperate. And there are
the Lithmern to consider as well; it seems that one of them

at least has some inkling of what we seek. Are you sure you wish to continue aiding me?"

"Everything fun is complicated. Besides, I owe Valerin a life. Mine. If it will take you and this Harp to repay him, I'll gladly help."

"Thank you." She bowed her head in acknowledgement. "I only hope we will be in time."

He looked up sharply. "There's a time-limit? You hadn't told me that."

"It wasn't relevant when all we had to do was pick up the Harp and take it north. But now . . . We should have three weeks, four at the most. And every day it will become more difficult."

"Then we're for Minathlan, and quickly." Kensal started for the horses.

"Not quite so fast. I've one thing left to do, unless it will disturb you to ride with one who has a stranger's face."

He turned, frowning. "A stranger's face won't disturb me, but is it really necessary?"

"I don't want one of them recognizing me when we arrive; I wish to study them before they grow suspicious."

"You're sure it's safe?"

"I'm safer here than anywhere but Silvermist itself, which is why I wish to make the change before we leave. It will not take long." As she finished speaking, she closed her eyes.

He saw her form begin to shimmer and grow; there was a ripple of motion, and suddenly a different woman stood before him. She looked younger, barely twenty, and her hair was a dark blonde. Where the dark-haired woman had been almost beautiful, this woman was almost plain. She was taller and more solidly built, and her movements were slightly awkward. She smiled. "Will it do, do you think?"

"If I hadn't seen you do it myself, I wouldn't have believed it. I don't suppose you could teach me that trick? Particularly the getting younger part . . ."

Her laugh held an undercurrent of sadness. "I'm afraid not."

"I thought you would say that. Have you anything else

to do here? Then we'd better get started." He helped her to mount and they left the castle without looking back.

In the highest tower of the castle of Lanyk, Prince of Syaskor, a tall figure in a hooded cloak stood staring out a south window. The information had been correct; something important was moving. First had come the arrival of that sorceress, Shalarn, and now there was the business with the Cilhar at the inn. Lanyk's men had bungled it, of course. They should have waited to attack until the disguised Lithmern had the man fast. But Lanyk's men had no more patience than their ruler, and they had lost him.

The Lithmern Captain had not done well, either. Of course, no one had expected the innkeeper to be a sorceress. The hooded one frowned. Who was she? The Dark Ones in the north had given no warning of her presence, but surely they must have known. Someone with the power to undo one of their spells could not have gone unnoticed.

At least Shalarn did not know that the leader of her men was working for someone else as well. The unseen lips curved. Did the Lithmern sorceress really think the Captain could have cast the spell of black mist alone? But Shalarn seemed to have no suspicions.

So the effort at the inn had not been totally wasted. The Captain of Shalarn's men was now firmly committed; he would be very useful. And Lanyk was at last convinced that magic would be used against him. He would be more amenable to reason now, more inclined to listen to advice. And the net of subtle power and influence, three years in the making, would close even tighter around the Prince of Syaskor.

The hooded one was very patient indeed.

Six

*E*mereck's first impression of Castle Minathlan was of a weathered mountain of gray stone. It was a
huge, almost shapeless pile, surrounded by a litter of
thatched huts and a maze of narrow streets. The people
seemed friendly, and Flindaran greeted many of them by
name as they rode up to the gates.

Inside the castle courtyard, Flindaran led Emereck to a
quiet corner and said, "Wait here while I find out who's
here and which rooms are free. I'll be back in a minute or
so."

"But not before I've finished unloading, I'll wager."

"Would I do that?"

Emereck nodded as he dismounted. Flindaran grinned
and left. Emereck began unloading the horses, taking
particular care with the bundle that contained the Harp
of Imach Thyssel. He suppressed a desire to unwrap it
right there in the courtyard, and reached instead for the
case that held his own harp.

"Welcome to Castle Minathlan, Minstrel."

The unexpected voice behind him made Emereck
jump, and he almost dropped the harp-case. He turned
and met the level gray gaze of a woman standing behind
him. She was young, and her chestnut hair was pulled

back from her face in a severe style. "Fair morning to you, Mistress," he said. He took in her dusty leather attire and the sheathed sword by her side, and added, "Or should I name you Warrior?"

"In Minathlan the proper term is Sword-Wielder, but few here worry much about titles." Her voice was light and noncommittal; it made a sharp contrast to her attire.

"Even so, I thank you for the correction." Emereck bowed.

"Then perhaps you'll take another suggestion. If you've something to keep secret, you'd do well to train yourself to be less easily startled." Her eyes flickered to the bundle at his feet, then returned to his face.

"I'll bear your words in mind," Emereck said. Inwardly he winced. Had he been that obvious?

The woman smiled slightly. "Don't worry that I'll give you away. I know how to keep my own counsel."

"I have no doubt of it. I think—"

"Kay!"

Emereck and the woman beside him turned to see Flindaran coming toward them across the courtyard. "I thought that was you!" Flindaran said when he reached them.

"Welcome home, Flindaran," the woman said. "You're a bit early, aren't you?"

"We hurried." Flindaran grinned, then his eyes dropped to her uniform and he shook his head. "Haven't you let Father promote you yet?"

"I've been promoted, in a manner of speaking. I'm a Free Rider now."

"I might have known you'd prefer something like that to a captain's job." Flindaran turned to Emereck. "In case she hasn't mentioned it, this is my half sister, Kiannar."

Emereck bowed and murmured politely. Flindaran ignored him and turned to Kiannar. "This is my friend Emereck Sterren from the Minstrel's Guild in Ciaron. He's even stubborner than you are, Kay."

"He's probably developed it from associating with you."

"The thing I like best about you is your tact. Who's home?"

Kiannar rattled off a list of names, most of them unfamiliar to Emereck. He listened intently, committing as many as possible to memory so that he could quiz Flindaran about them later. Kiannar finished her recital, and Flindaran frowned. "Oraven's not here?"

"He's out with the Riders on the western border." Kiannar's voice was all but expressionless.

"He's *what*? That idiot! He's going to get himself killed, I swear it. Why does he keep doing these things?"

"He has reasons."

Emereck looked quickly at Kiannar's face. Her expression had not changed. He looked back in time to see Flindaran press his lips together tightly. The thought flashed across his mind that there might be a deeper reason than he had supposed behind Flindaran's reluctance to speak much or often about his family, and then Flindaran said, "I know. How's the town generally?"

Kiannar shrugged. "No one's starving; it's been a fairly good year."

"Kiannar—" Flindaran began angrily, then stopped. "Never mind. Does Father still spend this part of the afternoon with the steward?"

"Yes, he does," Kiannar said, looking faintly surprised. "But I doubt that he's heard you're home yet."

Flindaran's jaw tightened. "I need to talk to him once I've shown Emereck to his rooms." His voice sounded strained. "Fare you well."

Emereck barely had time to make a polite farewell and pick up his harp-case and the Harp of Imach Thyssel before he was hurried off toward the castle. Kiannar merely smiled and nodded, but all the way across the courtyard Emereck was sure he could feel her eyes on his back. As soon as they were inside the castle and safely out of sight, Emereck turned to Flindaran. "What's possessed you?" he demanded. "We left the horses and most of our bags just standing there!"

"Oh, someone will take care of them. Probably Kay; she's good about that sort of thing."

"We could have done it ourselves if you hadn't been in such a hurry all of a sudden. What was that about, anyway?"

Flindaran looked back over his shoulder. "Kiannar is a grand person, and I'd trust her with my life. She also gets on my nerves every time we're together for more than about a tenth of a candlemark."

"Oh?"

"She's always right and it irritates me. Besides, I have a lot to do this afternoon."

Emereck raised an eyebrow inquiringly. Flindaran's answering grin was a little lopsided. "There are a couple of girls I want to renew my acquaintance with."

"I might have known."

Flindaran's grin broadened. "This way."

Emereck nodded. He did not ask any further questions, though he was no nearer understanding their encounter with Kiannar. It was plain that Flindaran did not want to discuss the matter. Emereck stored the incident in the back of his mind for further consideration and concentrated on remembering as much of their route as he could. The castle was even more jumbled on the inside than he had expected from its unorganized exterior, and he did not like the idea of being lost if he ever had to find his way around it alone.

Finally they reached the room Flindaran had chosen for him, and Emereck set down his bundle with a sigh of relief. He felt as though every servant and guard they passed had stared curiously at the awkward package. Though he knew he was only reacting to Kiannar's unnerving comments, he was glad that he, and the Harp of Imach Thyssel, were safely out of sight.

As he turned toward Flindaran, the size of the room registered and he frowned. "This is a little grand for a mere minstrel, isn't it?" he said. His gesture included the red-gold canopy over the bed, the tapestries covering the walls, and the gleaming wooden furniture that was scattered about the room.

"You're here as my friend, not as a minstrel." Flindaran sat down in one of the chairs and looked expectantly from

Emereck to the cloth-covered Harp. "Aren't you going to unwrap it?"

Emereck looked at him sharply, then reached for the bundle. Flindaran was right; he ought to make sure the Harp had not been damaged during the journey. As the wrappings fell away, Emereck blinked. The Harp of Imach Thyssel seemed much plainer than he remembered. It looked more like the battered instrument Emereck's first master had used to teach him to play than like a powerful maker of magic. He realized that Flindaran was watching intently, and he bent to his examination.

He did not find any new damage, but he scowled at the accumulation of centuries-old dents and scratches. None were serious, but still . . . He would have to have a proper carrying case made for it before he left Minathlan. Knowing that the Harp was protected by more than an old cloak or two would be worth the delay. Emereck looked up and his eyes met Flindaran's.

"Well?" Flindaran said.

"It's not hurt."

"Good. Then we can go see Father now and get it over with." Flindaran rose and started for the door.

"I'm still not sure I like this idea."

"I thought we'd settled this on the ride here. You can't bring a thing like that," Flindaran waved at the Harp, "into someone's house without telling them about it. Particularly someone like Father."

"Well—"

"Besides, he'd find out anyway, eventually."

"Not unless you told him."

"You haven't met him yet. He has his own ways of finding things out. Believe me, we're better off telling him right from the start."

"All right, but I still don't like it. And I'm not going anywhere until the Harp's out of sight."

"Why? No one even knows it's here yet!"

"Flindaran!"

Flindaran shrugged and glanced around the room. "Try sticking it in that chest in the corner; I think it'll fit. You can even lock it up if you want to. There ought to be a key around somewhere."

Feeling a little irritated by Flindaran's casual attitude, Emereck moved the Harp of Imach Thyssel into the chest. He covered it with some of the linen he found there, then rose and followed Flindaran out of the room. He tried to tell himself that no one except himself and Flindaran knew the Harp was there, but his attempts at self-reassurance only made him feel more uneasy than ever. Finally he forced the Harp from his mind and went back to memorizing corridors. He thought the twisting passages were beginning to make some kind of sense, when Flindaran stopped short at the juncture between two hallways.

"Lee!" Flindaran shouted, and took three strides down one of the passageways. Emereck reached the crossway and saw Flindaran a few steps away, hugging a tall blonde girl.

She was dressed in a blue gown too fine for a servant's but too plain for one of the nobility. She leaned back to look at Flindaran, and Emereck saw her face clearly for the first time. Serious brown eyes, straight nose, a mouth too wide for prettiness—and then she smiled, and she was beautiful. "It's good to have you home, Flindaran," she said, and her voice was warm and welcoming. Even though she was not speaking to him, Emereck felt at home.

Flindaran grinned. "You've gotten even prettier than you were when I left."

The girl smiled again, and an irrational stab of anger drove all thought of the Harp from Emereck's mind. Flindaran should know better than to pay empty compliments to a girl like this! She deserved better than a casual flirtation; couldn't he see that?

"Emereck, I want you to meet Liana," Flindaran said, turning. "Of all my sisters, she's my favorite."

Sister? Emereck bowed to hide his confusion and relief. "I am delighted."

"You mean that, don't you?" Liana said. Her voice was light and soft; it made Emereck think of distant flutes. Silver flutes, perfectly tuned. "I'm glad. And it will be nice to have music again. It's been a long time since a minstrel came to Minathlan."

"He'll probably only be here a few days," Flindaran cautioned her. "Don't start planning a feast or anything."

"But while I am here, I will be honored to entertain you as best I may," Emereck said. "I only hope my playing will not disappoint you, my lady."

Liana dimpled, and Emereck felt suddenly light-headed. "You are very polite, and I thank you very much," she said, "but you really shouldn't call me 'my lady.' I'm not entitled to it."

Flindaran frowned suddenly. "Who says so? You're my sister, aren't you?"

"Not entirely. Don't fuss about it, Flindaran, it's not that important."

"Well, you're my father's daughter. Isn't that enough?"

Liana sighed. "It's enough for me; I don't need more. And it makes some people unhappy when you insist on giving me courtesies I've no real right to."

Flindaran's frown deepened. "Liana, if someone's been stepping on the hem of your cloak, I can—"

"I told you it wasn't important to me," Liana said almost sharply. "I just don't like making people unhappy, especially about something as silly as a 'my lady' or two. What difference does it make?"

"I'm sorry. I thought . . . Well, all right, then. I won't say anything."

"Thank you." Liana smiled and curtsied. Then she stepped forward and tucked her hand under Flindaran's arm. "Now, tell me about your trip. You're almost two weeks earlier than we'd expected, you know. How did you manage it?"

Flindaran glanced at Emereck. "We took a shortcut."

There was a small pause, then Liana said, "Then it'll be another week at least before the caravan arrives? Talerith will be disappointed. She was looking forward to the fair, especially the dancing."

"Dancing? Talerith? She's still a child."

"Maybe she was when you left, but she's seventeen now. More than old enough for dancing."

"A great age indeed," Flindaran said solemnly. "Next thing you know she'll be getting married."

"I believe Lord Dindran has been approached about it at least twice already."

"What!" Flindaran stared at her, then shook his head. "I must be getting old. Talerith, married!"

Liana laughed. "Oh, not for a long time yet. Years, maybe. But she's certainly thinking about it." She paused and looked at him sidelong. "You should stop and see her. She'd like that."

"Maybe after Emereck and I talk to Father," Flindaran said carelessly. "We have some things to arrange before Emereck leaves."

"You haven't seen him yet? Then I've kept you long enough. But you'll come back later and tell me about Ciaron, won't you?" Her smile included them both.

"If Flindaran does not, I will be more than pleased to answer your questions," Emereck said.

"Of course we will," Flindaran said, throwing Emereck a surprised glance. "Later. Come on, Emereck."

They made their farewells and left. When Liana was out of earshot, Flindaran sighed and shook his head. "She really is my favorite sister, even if she's only half my sister. I wish I knew why I get along so well with her and so poorly with Kiannar."

"Why should you?" Emereck said, remembering the dark-haired warrior. "They're not much alike."

Flindaran looked at him. "They're twins. Didn't I tell you?"

"Oh. No. You didn't." Emereck fell silent. Flindaran did not seem inclined to continue the conversation, and they walked without speaking until they reached the study door.

Seven

*L*ord Dindran himself answered Flindaran's knock. If the Duke of Minathlan was surprised by the appearance of his youngest son two weeks earlier than expected, he gave no sign. He greeted Flindaran and acknowledged his introduction of Emereck with unruffled calm. Even Flindaran's request for a conference brought only a raised eyebrow and a nod of dismissal to the steward.

Emereck studied him as the steward left. The Duke of Minathlan was tall, lean, and gray-haired. His eyes were as dark and bright as a hawk's, and as unreadable. He was dressed with severe, almost ascetic simplicity. Emereck found it difficult to reconcile this man with the mental picture of the Duke that he had formed from Flindaran's conversation.

Lord Dindran seated himself and motioned for them to do likewise. He studied Flindaran briefly and said, "I see it has become the fashion in Ciaron to cover oneself with dust before presenting oneself in company. You will forgive me if I am old-fashioned enough to prefer the previous mode of behavior."

Flindaran flushed. "I beg your pardon, sir. We came straight here as soon as we arrived."

"So I observe. To what do I owe this . . . gratifying display of haste?"

"It's a long story."

"I am all attention," the Duke said politely.

Flindaran took a deep breath and plunged into the tale of their journey. Lord Dindran listened without comment, his expression unreadable. When Flindaran finished, the Duke inclined his head. "I am compelled to confess that for once you have surprised me, Flindaran."

"It was not my intention, sir."

"Nonetheless, you have succeeded admirably. I make you my apologies; you were indeed justified in coming directly here."

"Thank you."

The Duke nodded in acknowledgement, then looked at Emereck. "And I commend your discretion, Minstrel."

"I fear I do not understand you, my lord," Emereck replied.

"It appears from my son's narrative that the Harp of Imach Thyssel has not yet been played. Knowing him, I infer that yours was the restraining hand. Consequently, I applaud your prudence."

"My lord is too kind."

A gleam of amusement crossed Lord Dindran's face, so swiftly that Emereck wondered whether he had imagined it. Then the Duke leaned back and said, "Just so. Now tell me, what are your plans for this impressive instrument?"

"My intention is to bear it to the Guildhall in Ciaron without delay, my lord," Emereck said firmly. Somehow, Lord Dindran's presence made him more uneasily aware than ever that he had neither the experience nor the knowledge to deal with the Harp alone.

"I regret that such a journey is not now possible." The Duke sounded only mildly apologetic.

Emereck stiffened. Flindaran frowned and said, "Why not, sir? From my experience with you, I expect you have some reason."

"You are correct. Your little encounter with the Syaski is only one of many that have occurred recently. Though I appreciate your desire to turn this Harp over to the Masters of your Guild, I cannot look with pleasure on the possibility of Syaskor obtaining it."

"Sir, the men we met were Lithmern, not Syaski," Flindaran said.

"That is one of the things that makes your tale so fascinating."

"Then you think the Syaski are involved as well?" Flindaran leaned forward eagerly. "That they're getting ready for something?"

"There are indications of it."

"Sir, if—"

"I do not believe I have indicated a wish to begin a discussion of the Syaski before I have finished my discussion of this Harp of yours."

"Again I beg your pardon, sir," Flindaran said, clenching his teeth.

"Quite so." The Duke studied him. "If you are determined to discuss Syaskor with someone, I suggest you seek your brother Gendron. He returned from Syaskor barely two days ago. No doubt he will be willing to indulge your curiosity."

Flindaran bit his lip and nodded. Lord Dindran smiled sweetly at his son, then turned to Emereck as though nothing had happened. "You see why I must advise against your immediate departure."

Emereck hesitated. "I share your concern about Syaskor, my lord. But I do not like waiting here with no sure course before me. If the western way is barred, perhaps I may go north into Alkyra, or south to Kith Alunel."

"I am afraid the northern roads will be washed out at this time of year," Lord Dindran said apologetically. "And I doubt that Kith Alunel is a better choice than Syaskor at the moment."

"Why do you say that, my lord? The Guildhall there has a good reputation."

"Unfortunately, the Guildhall in Kith Alunel is temporarily empty. A week ago King Birn banned all minstrels from the city."

"*What?*" Emereck could not suppress the shocked exclamation. Beside him, Flindaran stared at his father in surprise.

The Duke smiled. "Some trifling disagreement regarding a satiric verse, I believe."

"A week ago, sir?" Flindaran eyed his father with respectful skepticism. "Kith Alunel is two weeks' ride from here, at least."

"How perceptive of you to realize that," the Duke said in a gentle tone that sent chills down Emereck's back. "I do not, however, choose to enlighten you as to the source of my information. You will have to take my word that minstrels have indeed been banned from the city."

"Of course, my lord," Emereck said hastily. "In fact, if you have further knowledge, I would be grateful to hear it. I have some concern for my colleagues in Kith Alunel."

"Forgive me; I am remiss. You need not worry for your friends. I believe most of them have taken refuge with Count Kyel-Semrud until His Majesty sees fit to restore them to favor. I doubt that it will take long. His Majesty will undoubtedly require music for his daughter's wedding two months from now. In the meantime, however, I cannot recommend Kith Alunel as a suitable destination."

"Thank you, my lord." Emereck paused, considering. "It seems I have no choice but to accept your hospitality for a time."

The Duke's eyebrows rose. "I hope you will find it acceptable."

"Forgive me, my lord," Emereck said hastily. "I did not mean to sound ungracious. But the matter of the Harp weighs heavily on my mind."

"Quite understandable," Lord Dindran said dryly. He paused and looked from Emereck to Flindaran and back. "Be sure I will notify you as soon as your way is clear. In the meantime, I trust I need not caution either of you to be wary how you speak of this matter."

"Of course, my lord."

"Yes, sir."

"Good. You may go."

They rose, bowed, and left. Outside, Flindaran heaved a sigh of relief. "Whew! Thank goodness that's over."

Emereck half-nodded. He felt almost as wrung out as he had on the day he'd been tested for Minstrel's rank within the Guild.

"Cheer up. At least now you'll be able to stay a while," Flindaran said. He started off down the corridor.

Emereck followed automatically. After a few turns and an unfamiliar flight of stairs, it dawned on him that they were not heading for his rooms as he had supposed. "I hate to ask this, Flindaran, but do you know where we're going?"

"To see my sister Talerith, of course. Don't you remember, I told Lee we would after we saw Father?"

Emereck was not sure he wanted to face yet another member of Flindaran's unpredictable family just then, but he did not say so. "Are you sure we should?" he said instead. "After what your father said about dust and new fashions, I think I'd prefer to clean up a bit before I meet anyone else."

"Father's always like that," Flindaran said. "Don't worry; Talerith won't mind." He stopped and knocked at one of the doors. After a moment it opened, and Liana looked out. Emereck's misgivings vanished abruptly.

"Lee, what are you doing here?" Flindaran demanded.

"I'm Lady Talerith's waiting-woman today," Liana said, smiling. "But come in! I'm glad you remembered to stop."

She stepped away from the door, and they followed her into a comfortably furnished sitting room. As they entered a black-haired girl lounging on a couch near the window looked up, then jumped to her feet with a delighted shriek. "Flindaran! You're here! Oh, it's been such a long time. What's Ciaron like?"

"It's a city," Flindaran said, hugging her.

"I know that! I meant, what kind of a city is it? Gendron says they have dancing every night, and magic shows, and—"

"Gendron hasn't been in Ciaron for a long time."

"Was he only teasing me? He would!" The girl stepped

back, and Emereck got his first clear look at her. Even wearing a slight pout, her face was strikingly pretty. Her hair was arranged in an intricate series of curls, and her gown was a bit over-elaborate for Emereck's taste.

Flindaran, too, was studying her. "Lords, you've grown up pretty, Talerith!"

The pout vanished at once. "Yes, haven't I? Come sit down and tell me about your travels."

She started to draw Flindaran forward, but he pulled back and turned toward Emereck. "First I want you to meet—"

"Oh, you've brought a minstrel! Then we can have music at supper tonight." Talerith smiled up at Flindaran. "But I don't want music now; I want to talk to you."

"Emereck's a friend of mine," Flindaran said, frowning. "A visitor."

"Oh." She turned and looked at Emereck more closely. From her expression, Emereck judged she was not favorably impressed. Then she smiled brightly. "Well, if he's a friend of yours, then I—I'm sure he's very welcome."

Emereck bowed. He saw Talerith steal a furtive look at Flindaran, then she stepped forward and held out her hand. "I'm pleased—that is, welcome to Minathlan, Minstrel."

"I give you thanks for your welcome, my lady," Emereck said as he took her hand and bent to kiss her fingers.

The hand was withdrawn as soon as he let it go. "Sit down, please, and tell me about Ciaron," Talerith said.

As she turned to take her own chair, Emereck saw her surreptitiously brush her fingers against her skirt. Suddenly he felt tired, too tired to face a conversation of artificial courtesy. "I beg you will excuse me, my lady," he said.

Talerith's face brightened, then clouded again as Flindaran turned. "What? You're not serious, Emereck!"

"I'm quite serious. I'm . . . a bit tired."

"I suppose you want to practice some more of those boring scales." Flindaran studied him, then shrugged.

"All right, then, let's go. I'll be back in a minute or two, Talerith."

"Flindaran, you can't!" Talerith threw Emereck an angry look. "You just got here!"

"What's the matter with you? Look, I have to go. Emereck hasn't been in Minathlan before; he'll never find his rooms again without some help."

"Liana can show him. I want you to stay here."

"Talerith—"

"I have no objection to the lady Liana's company, if she is willing to lend me her help," Emereck put in.

Flindaran glanced at him in surprise, and Emereck felt his face grow warm. A look of sudden enlightenment replaced Flindaran's slightly puzzled expression, and he grinned. "Is that all right with you, Lee? Go on, then, I'll be by later. He's three doors down the hall by the library."

Emereck bowed again and turned to go. Talerith shot him a look of profound dislike as he left, and he wondered what he had done to earn her disfavor. Then he was standing in the corridor outside with Liana. He felt as though he ought to say something, but he could not think of a single remark that would not sound vacuous. Finally he settled for a simple thank you, which he thought had the merit of being sincere, even if it was extremely unoriginal. He cleared his throat. "I am grateful for your courtesy, lady."

"Oh, you don't need to thank me! Flindaran was right; you really do need someone to show you your way. Minathlan is a dreadful maze if you don't know how to get around it."

"Having you as a guide makes a pleasure of a necessity."

Liana laughed delightedly. "I'd heard that all minstrels had tongues of silver; now I believe it!"

"The phrases come from training and habit," Emereck said, flushing. "But the meaning is sincere."

"I don't doubt it." Liana smiled, then glanced back over her shoulder with a thoughtful expression. "It's a pity you couldn't have . . ."

Her voice trailed off, but Emereck had a fair idea what she was referring to. "It seemed to me that Lady Talerith would have been ill-pleased by my presence no matter what I did."

"Talerith is Lord Dindran's youngest daughter, and she's been alternately indulged and ignored since her mother died. I'm afraid it hasn't been very good for her."

Emereck considered that a masterpiece of understatement. He did not quite feel able to say so; such direct criticism of his host's daughter would be unwise at best. He said instead, "That explains a little, but I confess I do not see why she dislikes me so much. Or have I entirely misread her?"

"I think she would dislike anyone she thought might take Flindaran from her. He's always been her favorite brother."

"There is more than that, I think."

Liana bit her lip. "Talerith is . . . very conscious of her noble birth. Too conscious, perhaps."

"I see." Though Emereck's experience with nobles was slight, he had encountered enough of them to realize that minstrels were not welcomed everywhere with respect and friendship. Talerith was apparently one of those who felt that musicians were desirable, so long as they did not attempt to mingle with nobility on anything approaching an equal footing. He was silent for the remainder of the walk to his room, and though his parting from Liana was friendly, his thoughts were elsewhere.

The Duke of Minathlan sat in his study, thinking. After a time, he rose and went to one of the bookcases that lined the room. He selected an ancient, battered volume bound in green leather and returned to his desk. For nearly an hour, he worked his way carefully through the book, turning each page gently so that the brittle paper would not crack.

Finally he closed the book. He sat looking at it, his expression as unreadable as it had been during his discussion with Emereck and Flindaran about the Harp of Imach Thyssel. Then he pulled a sheet of paper toward him and reached for the inkwell.

When the letter was finished, he set down the pen and bent toward the thin strip of carving that circled the edge of his desk. A moment later, there was a barely audible click. A small drawer sprang out of what had appeared to be solid wood. The Duke removed a gold seal and a half-burned stick of sealing wax. With these he sealed the letter. The hot wax glowed briefly as the seal touched it.

The Duke smiled faintly as he regarded the image stamped on the wax—a tree with three moons tangled in its branches. He returned the seal and the stick of wax to the secret drawer and closed it. Then he rang for a servant to arrange for the letter's delivery.

The three dancers leapt and spun with supreme grace. Shalarn watched with an outward appearance of attention; it would not do to offend her host even slightly. Inwardly, she resented the necessity of attending this dinner. She would have much preferred a cold supper in a quiet room, and the chance to ponder carefully some of her most pressing problems.

Chief among these was the report her men had brought at last. Far from providing the explanations she had sought, it simply posed more questions. The Cilhar's purpose remained unknown, and he seemed to have acquired a number of companions. There were the two young men who might be mere counters in this game, or might be active players. Then there was the woman, who was clearly no mere innkeeper. No sorceress of such ability would waste her time sweeping and scrubbing for long.

Unfortunately, Shalarn had no idea who the pseudo-innkeeper might really be. For three days, ever since her men had returned, she had used every resource at her disposal to discover the name of the dark-haired woman who had destroyed her spell at the inn. She had not succeeded. Shalarn frowned. Surely *someone* must know her! A sorceress of such power—

"The dancing does not please you, my lady?"

Prince Lanyk's voice was almost in her ear, and it took

all her control to keep from jerking away. "It pleases me greatly, sire."

"Yet you frowned."

"I was but concentrating, to be sure of following the subtleties of their skill."

"Ah. I, too, admire subtlety."

"It is a valuable trait in a ruler," Shalarn said demurely.

Lanyk smiled and moved on. Shalarn did not quite breathe a sigh of relief. She could see his wife watching them surreptitiously—what was her name? Oh, yes, Tammis. It was a measure of her importance that Shalarn had been nearly a month at Lanyk's court and could still be in doubt of her name. Shalarn dismissed her with a mental shrug, and turned her attention back to the prince.

Was he yet another player in this intricate game? She thought of the tenuous web of rumor and innuendo she had followed. It had taken her two years of patient work to untangle the strands and trace their hidden meanings; Lanyk did not have the patience for such a task. If he played, he was a newcomer to the game.

But his comments hinted at some knowledge. Could he be aware of her hidden activities, then? Her eyes narrowed. The Syaski raiders who had interrupted her men at the inn—she had assumed their presence was a coincidence. But if it were not? Lanyk was no true sorcerer, but he might dabble enough that her spells had attracted his attention. Or there might be a sorcerer in his employ—that was more likely.

She studied him from the corner of her eye. Yes, it was possible. She had been careless. She looked at him again, and smiled inwardly. Prince Lanyk might rule his wife with a firm hand, and Syaskor with an iron fist, but Shalarn sa'Rithven he did not rule at all. Nor would he. She could manage Lanyk.

A timid hand touched her shoulder. Shalarn turned. To her surprise, it was Tammis. Shalarn inclined her head. "Princess. May I aid your works?"

"Oh! No, I—I just wanted to talk."

"It's only an expression from my home, my lady," Shalarn said reassuringly. The little mouse didn't even have sense enough to check up on the customs of her visitors. "What would you say?"

"I—" Tammis was cut off by a burst of clapping as the dancers finished. "I hope you are enjoying your stay."

"Of course. You and the Prince have been most kind."

"My husband," Tammis said, with a barely perceptible emphasis, "is always . . . kind."

So the little princess was neither oblivious nor indifferent to Lanyk's wandering eye! "Sometimes, perhaps, too much so."

"What do you mean?"

"Why, only that it can be difficult for a guest to refuse an unwanted gift when it is offered with such great kindness."

"Ah." Tammis inclined her head. "I pray you, do not feel constrained to accept such a gift if the Prince should urge it on you."

"Be assured, Princess, I will not."

"I thank you, my lady Shalarn. You have greatly eased my mind." Tammis gave a small, tight smile and left.

Shalarn stood looking after her and pondering on their conversation. Had it been the straightforward probe of her intentions that it seemed, or had Tammis been playing a more subtle game? Shalarn dismissed the thought; whichever it was, it did not matter. She had no intention of becoming involved with Lanyk. She had more important things to do. She smiled to herself, and went to take a seat as the minstrels began to play.

Eight

*T*he day after their interview with the Duke, Emereck and Flindaran finally tracked Gendron down. Emereck found the heir to Minathlan something of a puzzle. Gendron bore a strong likeness to Flindaran, though he was nearly ten years the elder. The resemblance was heightened by his cheerful, careless attitude, but there were occasional disconcerting flashes of the Duke—a turn of phrase, a gesture, a raised eyebrow.

They found him in a small sitting room, and after introducing Emereck, Flindaran immediately asked Gendron about Syaskor.

"Oh, Lanyk's up to something all right," Gendron replied.

"Yes, but what?" Flindaran said in exasperation.

Gendron laughed. "If I knew what he was after, I might not have had to come home so quickly."

"You *wanted* to stay in Syaskor?"

"You would have, too, if you'd seen the woman Lanyk's got visiting him. I think he has plans for her himself, but if I'd had another two days—"

"It takes you that long? You're losing your touch, brother."

"You rush things. I have more finesse. This woman's

a Lithmern noble, and you don't—"

"What!" Emereck and Flindaran said together.

Gendron stared at them. "She's a Lithmern noble-woman. Or rather, she used to be. What's so odd about that?"

"Father hasn't told you about our trip home, then," Flindaran said. Gendron shook his head. Flindaran frowned and quickly outlined their encounter with the Lithmern at the inn. He went as far as his finding Emereck in the forest, and finished with, ". . . and we camped for a couple of days and then came home."

Gendron looked curiously at Emereck. "It seems that minstrels are hardier than I'd thought. You don't move like a man who's been recently wounded."

"Your brother exaggerates its seriousness," Emereck said, with a warning look at Flindaran.

"Doesn't surprise me." Gendron turned back to Flindaran. "Well, now I see why you were interested when I mentioned Shalarn."

"Who?"

"The Lithmern noblewoman, idiot! But I can't believe she had anything to do with that raid."

"You know of any other Lithmern in Syaskor?"

"No. But Shalarn's too . . . too . . ."

"Good-looking?"

". . . too innocent for that."

"Then where did the Lithmern soldiers we fought at the inn come from?" Emereck said.

"She did bring a few of her men with her," Gendron admitted reluctantly. "I saw them once in a while around the palace."

"And you still think she had nothing to do with it?" Flindaran said sarcastically.

"Lanyk probably used her men behind her back somehow." Gendron scowled. "I wish I'd known; I'd have been more insistent about inviting her here."

"You mean you asked this Lithmern woman to come to Minathlan?" Flindaran said. "Are you out of your mind?"

"Not that I've noticed."

"Have you told Father?"

"Of course not! I don't really expect her to come, especially with the situation on the border the way it is."

"I'm afraid I am unfamiliar with the circumstances," Emereck said. "I would be grateful if you would explain."

"It's a bit hard to do clearly," Gendron said. "Prince Lanyk has always been twitchy about his borders; that's why Minathlan has the Free Riders. Lately, though, he's been worse than usual."

"Oh?" Flindaran said. "Father didn't mention that."

"He wouldn't."

"What do you mean by 'worse than usual'?" Emereck asked.

"His men have been raiding border villages, he's had Trader caravans searched, things like that."

"The Traders aren't going to like that," Flindaran commented.

"If it comes to that, none of his neighbors like it. He hasn't bothered Minathlan much so far, but Kiannar told me Father's doubled the patrols."

"She didn't mention that to me!"

Gendron looked at him. "How long did you talk to her?"

Flindaran reddened slightly. "Well . . ."

"You know, you're lucky you came home when you did. Another week or two and you'd have had to swing all the way south of Kith Alunel to avoid trouble."

"What makes you think I'd want to avoid trouble?"

"I thought you had sense. I see I was wrong."

"Then you believe travel west is unsafe?" Emereck broke in.

Gendron nodded. "At least it is as long as Lanyk keeps playing these games of his."

"And you have no suspicion as to the reasons for Prince Lanyk's behavior? Since you have come so recently from Syaskor, I thought—"

"Nobody there knows anything. Or if they do, they aren't talking about it." Gendron grinned suddenly. "*I* think Lanyk's trying to start a war in order to get away from that Cilhar icicle he's married to."

"Lanyk married a Cilhar?" Flindaran said in surprise. "When did that happen?"

"A couple of years ago, right after you went off to Ciaron. Didn't you hear about it there?"

"Yes, but I didn't know the bride was a Cilhar! I thought Syaski hated Cilhar."

"They do. But that didn't stop Lanyk. Myself, I don't see why he bothered."

"Oh?"

"Tammis is the dullest woman I've ever laid eyes on. She's plain, she's boring, she never says anything, and she creeps around after Lanyk like a shadow. It'd drive me crazy in three days."

"She doesn't sound much like a Cilhar."

"She's some sort of renegade from the northern mountains. Lanyk tries to keep it quiet, but it's common gossip at court whenever he's not around."

"And you have the biggest ears this side of the Mountains of Morravik."

Gendron grinned again, unoffended. "That's why Father sent me to Syaskor in the first place. Anyway, I think all Lanyk's really looking for is an excuse to get away from his wife."

Something in Gendron's tone caught Emereck's attention. "Looking for?"

Gendron shrugged. "The story is that Lanyk's looking for something he wants very badly. Myself, I don't believe it."

"Why not?"

"Because supposedly he doesn't know what it is he's looking for. Even Lanyk isn't that fuzzy-headed."

Flindaran and Emereck exchanged glances. "You're right," Flindaran said. "It doesn't make sense. Where'd you pick up a tale like that, anyway?"

"Servants," Gendron said with a touch of smugness. "No one else ever talks to them, but they find out everything."

"Except why Lanyk's acting like he wants to start a war."

"He probably doesn't know himself. If you ask me, he's not much for brains."

They talked for a few more minutes, then Emereck took his leave. As he walked down the hall, he could hear the brothers exchanging uniformly low opinions of Prince Lanyk, Syaskor, and the Syaski. Emereck ignored them. The conversation had disturbed him deeply, and he wanted to set his thoughts in order.

It was clear from Gendron's comments that there was no hope of leaving for Ciaron in the near future. Emereck accepted it, though not without misgivings. He had an uneasy feeling that something was forming out beyond Minathlan, a web of intrigue waiting to snare him. He could glimpse its outline only dimly, but he was nonetheless certain it was there.

But the hints he had were so vague! The Lithmern noblewoman in Syaskor—was she really a dupe of the Prince, as Gendron thought? It didn't seem to fit. And was Prince Lanyk looking for the Harp of Imach Thyssel? It seemed likely, yet how had he learned of its existence? And how was it that he did not know what he sought? Then there were Ryl, Kensal Narryn, and Prince Lanyk's Cilhar wife. None of them appeared to fit anywhere in the woefully incomplete pattern Emereck was trying to develop, yet he was sure they should.

Emereck shook his head. He should have found out more about the conditions in Syaskor before he had left Ciaron. There must have been some minstrels in the Guildhall who had been there. But how could he have guessed then what he would need to know? Feeling frustrated and confused, Emereck began looking for the way back to his room.

Emereck spent the next few days learning his way around Castle Minathlan and trying to remember the names and positions of Flindaran's assorted relatives. In addition to Gendron, Talerith, Kiannar, and Liana, there was another full sister, several half brothers, and a number of more distant kin. Emereck could only be grateful that Oraven had not yet returned to add to his confusion.

His friendship with Liana progressed well, in spite of Flindaran's heavy-handed assistance. Unfortunately, Talerith's dislike had also become more evident. Flindaran seemed to be the only person in the entire castle who was not aware of her attitude. Emereck avoided her as much as he could, and remained scrupulously polite when he could not.

In his spare moments, he worried about the Harp. He mistrusted the suave Duke of Minathlan, whose only response to his respectful request for further information had been a raised eyebrow and a few politely vague phrases. The Harp of Imach Thyssel would be a temptation indeed to any nobleman, particularly one whose neighbors were as troublesome as the Syaski. He mistrusted Flindaran, who appeared to have forgotten the Harp entirely. Emereck did not believe that was possible. Most of all, he mistrusted himself.

It would be so easy to take the Harp for his own, and use it to make himself a hero, a Healer, a great minstrel. Though he did not believe he would be successful in any of those roles, he found it difficult to banish their seductive pictures from his mind. At times he found himself wishing almost desperately for someone, anyone to take the Harp away from him before he succumbed. As a result, he grew more and more anxious to leave Minathlan.

To add to his mental discomfort, his nightmares returned. On his second night in Minathlan, Emereck woke sweating from a dream full of twisted shapes and screams. He paced the floor until his breathing was more normal, then lay down again, but he was unable to sleep. The experience was repeated again, and again. By his fourth morning in Minathlan, Emereck was beginning to feel decidedly out of sorts.

He was also, apparently, beginning to look less than well. "What's wrong with you?" Flindaran demanded as they left the breakfast hall.

"Nothing."

"Then you've been rubbing soot under your eyes."

Emereck laughed in spite of himself. "I hadn't realized I looked as bad as that."

"Well, you do. So what is it?"

"I haven't been sleeping well, that's all."

Flindaran studied him, frowning. "Maybe you shouldn't try to play for the feast tonight. Talerith will be disappointed, but—"

"Wait a minute! I'm supposed to play for a feast tonight? When did this happen?"

"Didn't Talerith tell you?"

"No. She didn't."

"That featherbrain! Oh, well, it shouldn't matter much. It's more of a family party than a feast, really; nothing elaborate."

"I see." Emereck did indeed see. He had no doubt that Talerith had deliberately neglected to inform him. It was a spiteful gesture, more irritating than truly troublesome; no minstrel worthy of the title would be unable to manage a spur-of-the-moment performance. Unless she had something else planned as well . . .

"I think it'll do you good," Flindaran said persuasively. "It won't hurt you to show off a little.'

"What? Oh, of course. I'll be glad to play, Flindaran. I was just . . . thinking about which songs would be appropriate." There was a ballad about a proud King's daughter who was outwitted by a swineherd and forced to marry him. With very little adjustment, he could make it pointed enough that Talerith could not possibly miss the hint. And there was another song about a woman who scorned her true love because he came dressed in rags. Talerith would be furious. Emereck began to smile. Flindaran was right; it could well be a very satisfying evening. He looked up. Flindaran was watching him with narrowed eyes. "Something wrong?" Emereck said.

"I've seen that expression on your face before, and it always means trouble for somebody. What're you up to?"

Emereck tried to think of a way of distracting him.

"How would you like to do a duet with me tonight?"

"You're mad," Flindaran said with conviction.

"I am not. It would give *you* a chance to 'show off a little.'"

"All the songs I know are the kind that shouldn't be sung in front of ladies."

"You know 'The Wandering Knight.' And you've done it enough that we wouldn't need much practice."

"I'd sound like a crow."

"Nonsense. A raven, at the very worst."

"For the last time, I won't do it!"

"Good. If that's your last refusal, you'll have to say yes when I ask you again."

Flindaran began to laugh. "You must be the stubbornest man east of the Melyranne Sea!"

"I'm good at what I do," Emereck said blandly. "Now, about the duet . . . ?"

"All right, I'll think about it."

"You're sure you won't—"

"I said I'll *think* about it! But don't plan on it."

"I suppose I'll have to be satisfied with that. I'm going to go practice; let me know when you make up your mind." Thoroughly pleased with the success of his distraction, Emereck took his leave.

He returned to his rooms and began drawing up a list of songs for the evening, along with a few alternatives he could use if his audience seemed bored with his original selections. He labored over it for some time, then set it aside and turned to "adapting" a few of the songs to suit his purpose. When he finished, he picked up his harp and began running through them.

He made a few more changes to the first song, and began on the next. He fell quickly into the rhythm of it. He let his fingers move automatically while his mind listened critically to the music. He was playing well today, he thought, very well. It was a pity he hadn't brought a better instrument with him; the little traveling harp was well enough for inns and taverns, but a nobleman's hall deserved something grander . . . .

Abruptly, Emereck drew back from that line of

thought. He became aware that he was staring at the chest in the corner of the room; somehow he had turned his chair as he played without realizing it. He felt suddenly chilled. His hands were still moving over the harpstrings; he pulled them away and the music died in a broken jangle. In the silence that followed, Emereck heard the fading silver echo of another harp.

Unbelieving, he stared at the chest. The Harp of Imach Thyssel was inside, wrapped in cloth and covered with linen. The strings should be muffled too thoroughly to make a sound. Slowly, he rose and walked forward. He knelt by the chest and raised the lid. The linen looked undisturbed. He removed it and lifted out the bundled Harp.

The wrapping fell away. He shoved it aside and picked up the Harp. He turned it over in his hands, running his palms along the ivory surface, feeling the occasional roughness of the scratches that marred its smoothness. It was plain, heartlessly plain—*bone-white as dragon's teeth*. Carefully, he laid a hand flat against the strings. A bead of sweat ran down his back.

Someone knocked at the door. Emereck jumped. His hand jerked away from the Harp, and the strings rang faintly. He stared, appalled. He hadn't locked the door! "A moment!" he called, but the door was already swinging inward.

"Demon's teeth, Emereck, what are you doing?" Flindaran demanded.

"I was . . . checking the Harp," Emereck said lamely. Inwardly, he was shaken. Anyone could have walked in and found him with the Harp! How could he have been so careless?

"What for? Oh, never mind." Flindaran paused, then grinned sheepishly. "I just came to—well, to tell you that I'll sing after all. If you're still interested."

"Oh! Yes of course I'm interested. I'm not going to let you out of it that easily. Just a minute while I put this away." With hands that trembled slightly, Emereck returned the Harp and the linen to the chest and lowered the lid. He let out a long breath, half sigh and half sob, then turned to discuss the coming performance with his reluctant friend.

Ryl leaned on the windowsill, her dark blonde hair falling loose around her shoulders like a girl's. "It's here," she said softly.

Kensal glance past her, to where Castle Minathlan stood at the center of the town. "You're sure."

"Of course."

"Then what's next? Taking it back?"

"First I must learn a little about the Duke and his family, and discover what obstacles we may face besides the Harp itself. The Harp—"

"—does not move easily from one owner to another. You've said that before," Kensal said, grinning. "What other obstacles are you anticipating?"

"There are many possibilities. The Lithmern who set on us at the inn, for instance. They may be working for Lithra, or for Syaskor, or for the Shadow-born themselves."

"Or for someone else entirely."

"Yes. And there is the current Duke of Minathlan to consider. I know little of him personally, but his family tends to be . . . resourceful."

"I believe the Cilhar have a somewhat similar reputation."

Ryl smiled. "It is one reason I am glad of your help. But I think your part will come later."

"How much later? We only have two weeks left."

"I do not know. Soon, I hope."

"If you plan to stay long, we'll need more than this." Kensal waved at the tiny, sparely furnished room they had rented.

"That I leave to you."

"You have other plans for this afternoon?"

Ryl's smile widened. "Castle Minathlan prepares a feast tonight. They will need extra servants for it. I believe I shall offer myself."

"You make an unlikely kitchen maid."

"No more than I do an innkeeper. Come, I am anxious to begin."

Kensal nodded. They left the room together. Outside the inn they separated. Kensal started toward the main part of the town to look for news of lodging places, while Ryl began the long walk up to Castle Minathlan.

Nine

*T*he feasting hall of Castle Minathlan was large and less than half full. Rich tapestries covered the gray stone walls, but Emereck could not help noticing that most of them were in older styles of workmanship. The linen that draped the tables was snowy white, and the graceful wine decanters were polished silver.

The guests included a few notables from the town around the castle, but most of those present were, as Flindaran had promised, "family." To Emereck's surprise, the group looked little different from the gatherings of merchants he had seen in Ciaron. He had expected a richer atmosphere among the nobility.

Talerith had arranged the seating, and Emereck found himself placed at the low end of the side table. He did not find this as annoying as he might have, primarily because Liana had somehow been seated next to him. "This is an unexpected pleasure," he said as he rose to greet her.

"It is? Oh, dear, I thought everyone was told about the seating arrangements in advance. Talerith . . ." Liana glanced toward the head table and sighed.

Emereck suppressed an urge to volunteer his opinion of Talerith. There was no reason to chance spoiling

Liana's enjoyment of the feast. "It is hardly of great importance," he said instead.

Liana looked at Emereck and smiled. "At least it was a pleasant surprise."

"Never doubt it."

"Perhaps now I can finally hear about your journey from Ciaron," she said as she seated herself.

"It was not particularly interesting, I fear."

"Oh?"

"One caravan journey is very like another."

"Talerith has been having a game with me, I see. I'll have to speak to her."

"What do you mean?"

"Oh, she's been dropping mysterious hints about Flindaran's trip home for the past few days. There's no harm in it."

"I see." Emereck looked toward the head table. Flindaran sat next to Talerith; he was reaching forward to fill her glass. He said something to her, and she laughed and tossed her head. Emereck frowned. Surely, Flindaran had enough sense not to trust the secret of the Harp of Imach Thyssel to such a spoiled child! But Flindaran did have a tendency to boast about his exploits. He might have tried to impress her with the tale of their fight at the inn.

Liana's eyes followed Emereck's. "I don't think it's Flindaran," she said, misinterpreting Emereck's expression. "He likes Talerith too much to tease her that way."

"Entirely too much," Emereck muttered. He had never actually asked Flindaran *not* to speak of the Harp; he'd just assumed . . . And Flindaran had been spending much of his time with his youngest sister since their arrival in Minathlan. He looked toward the head table once more. Talerith seemed to be teasing Flindaran about something. How much did she know?

"What did you say?"

"I believe you are correct. Flindaran is unlikely to have been teasing Lady Talerith in that fashion."

"I wish—" Liana stopped. She threw him a quick sidelong glance, then began studying her plate with a pensive expression.

"I hope I've not displeased you," Emereck said, noting her expression.

"Not exactly."

Emereck's heart sank. "Forgive me, lady. I—"

"There isn't anything to forgive." Liana threw him another glance and returned to studying her plate with renewed intensity. "I just wish you didn't feel you had to be quite so formal all the time."

"I beg your pardon?"

"It's the way you speak. When you're with Flindaran you relax, but whenever you're with anyone you don't know well, you sound like the Officer of Protocol at King Birn's court."

"I do?"

"I'm not sure whether it's because you don't trust yourself or because you don't trust other people, but it doesn't really matter. Maybe it's a little of both."

Emereck hardly heard her. "I hadn't realized."

Liana looked up and smiled slightly. "I didn't think so. Now tell me about . . . about Ciaron. Is the marketplace really larger than the one in Kith Alunel?"

Emereck welcomed the change in subject. He made polite conversation with one half of his mind, while the other half worried about Flindaran, Talerith, and the Harp. He watched the head table surreptitiously all evening. Talerith appeared to be enjoying herself enormously. Flindaran flirted outrageously with every woman who came near him. His father's presence appeared to have very little effect on his behavior. Gendron seemed more subdued, but Emereck noticed the lingering glances the serving women gave him, and decided that Gendron was at least as successful as his brother. Only one of the women, a tall, rather plain blonde, payed no particular attention to either of the two men.

The Duke of Minathlan observed them all with a detached, slightly cynical air. Several times Emereck saw the Duke glance in his direction. He added Lord Dindran to his list of immediate worries. The Duke was not a man he would care to cross, and if he had plans of his own for the Harp . . .

Emereck shook himself. This was ridiculous! He was beginning to suspect everyone of wanting the Harp. He had no real reason to worry about Lord Dindran, and Flindaran seemed no more interested in the Harp than he was in listening to Emereck practice. Gendron did not even know of the Harp's existence, unless Flindaran or the Duke had told him. Emereck frowned and told himself sternly to forget the Harp, at least for the evening. He was not successful.

The meal ended at last, and Emereck got up to play. He began with a well-known ballad and followed with one of the newer songs that had come east to Ciaron from Rathane. Both were well received. He sang the first of his "adjusted" songs, and grinned inwardly at Talerith's scowl. To keep her off balance, he played a couple of lively dance tunes, then swept into an even more pointed ballad.

Talerith's face, flushed from dancing, darkened as Emereck sang. He glanced at the Duke and saw a gleam of amusement on his face. Flindaran seemed as unaware of the barbs in Emereck's song as he had been of Talerith's attitude.

Emereck ended the song. Talerith opened her mouth, then licked her lips and closed it tightly. Emereck was surprised at her restraint. He'd expected her to make a show of temper at least. Perhaps she had some other plan, but unless she wanted to make a scene, she would have to wait until he asked for requests. He looked at her again, and suddenly he was certain that was why she was waiting. Well, he could avoid it easily enough.

He bowed and raised a hand, and the hall quieted. "It is a custom among minstrels to ask now what songs their listeners would hear," Emereck said. He saw Talerith lean forward eagerly, and he smiled and continued smoothly, "But tonight I plan something different. Lord Flindaran will join me for the next song—'The Song of the Wandering Knight.' Flindaran!"

Flindaran rose amid much applause, and Talerith closed her mouth in an angry pout. Emereck smiled as

his friend joined him, and with a flourish he played the
opening notes of the song:

> "A knight came riding down the road,
> > Her armor mirror-bright,
> Her sword was silver in the sun,
> > Her horse was purest white.

> *"Oh, she was fair and strong and brave*
> > *And none could match her might;*
> *No warrior, wizard, king or knave*
> > *Could best the Wandering Knight.*

> "She came to Riven's castle gate
> > Where seven rivers run.
> She stayed one night, and when she left
> > She stole Duke Riven's son.

> "The knight went on to old Rathane
> > And stole a Baron's horse,
> Then sold it to the Earl of Torn
> > For twice what it was worth!

> "A barman bet she could not drink
> > A quart of Kingman's Rye.
> The knight, she nodded carelessly
> > And drained the barrel dry.

> "She drove the thieves from Rotrin Wood
> > Until not one remained,
> And when the town refused to pay
> > She drove them back again.

> "She fought the Witch of Morlang Isle
> > From dawn to dusk of day;
> Then they went drinking in the town
> > Before she went away.

> "Six men set on her late one night
> > To steal her purse away.

When she killed two the others fled;
They're running to this day.

*"For she was fair and strong and brave
And none could match her might;
No sword that swung in all the land
Could best the Wandering Knight."*

The last chords of the song were drowned in applause. Emereck bowed, smiling, though he knew that the enthusiasm had more to do with Flindaran's participation than with the quality of the performance. Not that they had done badly. On the contrary, Flindaran had done very well indeed. Emereck made a mental note to persuade Flindaran to try performing more often. He bowed again, and noticed the blond serving woman watching them intently. So she was not as indifferent to Flindaran's charms as she pretended!

Flindaran returned to his seat, and Emereck announced his next song. Suddenly, he saw a stir at one of the side doors. He paused. Kiannar came into the hall, her face set. There was a buzz of conversation, which died as she strode toward the Duke. She spoke to him for a moment in a low voice, then bowed and stepped aside.

The Duke rose. "My apologies to you all, but I fear I must leave. You will oblige me by continuing the festivities in my absence." He bowed to the astonished assembly and turned to accompany Kiannar.

A babble of voices rose around the tables, then was cut short by a piercing shriek. In the open doorway stood a fat, red-faced woman, tears running down her face. "It's the Riders! The Free Riders are back, and dear Lord Oraven's killed!"

"Quiet, you fool!" Kiannar said harshly.

The fat woman did not seem to hear. "They've killed him!" she cried. "Oh, he's dead, he's dead, he's dead!"

Kiannar stepped forward and gave the woman a resounding slap. The woman threw her hands over her face and burst into racking sobs. Kiannar took her arm and pushed her out of the hall, then turned back to the crowd. "Oraven's not dead," she said in a loud voice. "I saw him myself before I came here."

"What's happened, then?" someone shouted.

Lord Dindran looked coldly in the direction of the voice, and abruptly there was silence. "A group of Free Riders have returned from the border of Syaskor," the Duke said at last.

An uneasy murmuring rustled through the hall, then quieted. The Duke bowed mockingly. "Thank you for your attention. My son Oraven has also returned. He is apparently gravely wounded—but not, I believe, dead. No doubt I shall learn the truth of this myself if I am ever allowed to leave."

No one said a word. The Duke's gaze swept the crowd. "Very good. As your curiosity seems satisfied, I will now withdraw. My son Gendron will preside until I return." The Duke bowed again and left the hall. Kiannar followed, closing the door behind them. In the stunned silence, Emereck looked back at the head table. Flindaran was white. Gendron was scowling angrily. Talerith sat hunched over her plate. As Emereck's eyes reached her, she looked up.

"Play, minstrel!" she said shrilly. "Play something gay. Play something!"

Emereck stared at her. He saw the guests shift uncomfortably in their seats as Talerith said again, "Play!" Then he raised his hands. Still staring at Talerith's angry, frightened face, he plucked the opening notes of the song he'd been working on since the night in Ryl's inn.

> "Dark water, still water, darker yet the sky;
>   Shadowed was the path beyond and cold the wind on high.
> Black forest, old forest, murky, dead, and dry;
> Dark the day and dark the way when Corryn went to die.
>
> Barren fields behind him stretched, and dark and empty rooms

Where lay the young lord's wife and child all silent
in their tombs.
His thoughts were set on vengeance then, as he
rode through the gloom;
Sorrow keen for child and queen drove Corryn to
his doom.

Past the lake and through the trees, up to his
brother's door,
He made his way, and—"

"Stop!" Talerith's voice cut across the song. "Stop
it!" she cried again, and burst into tears.

Emereck lowered his hands, shaken. What had
possessed him? "Corryn's Ride" was a grim song at any
time, but now when one of Flindaran's brothers was
badly injured and perhaps dying . . . He was dimly
aware of the shocked expressions of the Duke's guests,
and of Liana hurrying toward Talerith, but his attention
was centered on the head table and Flindaran's tightly
controlled face.

Gendron rose. As he bowed to the guests, his
resemblance to the Duke seemed much stronger than it
had been earlier. "Under the circumstances, I think it is
best to end this evening early. I am sure my father will
inform you of whatever news the Riders have brought.
In the meantime, I ask your pardon for this uncomfortable finish to our feast. Fare you well."

Emereck sat motionless, still watching Flindaran, as
the people around him began to leave. Liana helped
Talerith out through a private door at the back of the
hall. Gendron looked at Emereck. "You will answer to
my father for this, minstrel."

"Yes, my lord," Emereck said without turning.

At the sound of Emereck's voice, Flindaran looked at
him at last. His face was expressionless. Their eyes met,
and Emereck swallowed. "Flindaran, I—"

Flindaran made a chopping gesture with one hand.
"Later," he said, and his voice was strained. "When
I've . . . Later." He turned and left the hall. Gendron

stood watching Emereck a moment longer, then followed his brother.

With a muffled oath, Emereck sprang to his feet and all but ran out of the hall. He barely noticed the blonde serving woman in the shadows watching him through narrowed eyes.

Ten

*E*mereck was not sure how long he wandered through the castle halls, but it seemed as if it had been hours. The passageways seemed more mazelike than ever. He was unable to keep out of the way of the servants, and even if he had been certain he knew how to find his room, he was not ready to return to it.

Finally he blundered into the empty courtyard at the rear of Castle Minathlan. He sighed in relief as the door closed behind him; no one was likely to disturb him here. He walked down the staircase and seated himself on the bottom step, leaning back against the wall. The stone was cool against his back, even through the cloth of his tunic. Numbly, he stared up at the stars. Kaldarin had not yet risen; Elewyth was a lopsided silver-green oval overhead. The moonlight gave a faint greenish sheen to the stone staircase.

He did not understand what was happening to him. He knew better than to play death songs in the presence of the dying, yet he had allowed his resentment of Talerith to goad him into playing "Corryn's Ride." It was a mistake, he told himself, only a mistake, but he felt as if he had betrayed all the teachings of his Guildhall.

And why had the Duke's children reacted so violently to the song? It had been in extremely poor taste, but that was not enough to explain Talerith's wild burst of weeping, or Gendron's sharp anger. And Flindaran— Emereck flinched away from the memory of Flindaran's face as it had looked just before he left the hall. How could he have guessed that they would be affected so strongly?

He heard a door open behind him, and he leaned backward into the shadows. He did not want to deal with the castle folk yet. He wanted to think before he had to—

"Emereck?" a soft voice said tentatively. "Minstrel Emereck?"

"Liana!" Emereck rose and came forward in surprise. "What are you doing here?"

"Looking for you."

"I see." Emereck turned away. "You know I didn't intend—That is, I am sorry about . . . what happened."

"Of course." Liana sounded mildly surprised. "But it wasn't your fault, you know. Hesta started it. Though I can understand why she was upset. She was Oraven's nurse, you know."

"No, I didn't." Emereck hesitated. "How is he?"

"Very bad. The healer has been with him since he arrived."

"I'm sorry." Emereck could have ground his teeth at the inadequacy of the reply. I should never have come here, he thought. He was making one mistake after another, because he didn't know enough about this place and the people who lived here. He looked at Liana. "I could use an explanation."

"Of what?"

"Why everyone behaved like madmen when I sang that song," Emereck said bitterly. "I shouldn't have done it, but—"

"Oh. Flindaran never told you about Oraven, did he?"

"No." Emereck had trusted Flindaran to tell him the things he needed to know about Minathlan, and

Flindaran had not. Emereck suppressed a flash of anger at Flindaran's thoughtlessness; after all, part of the fault was his own. He had never asked.

"I thought as much," Liana said calmly. "That's why I came."

Emereck looked at her, startled. Her face was in shadow, and he could not make out her expression. "I'd be grateful if you would explain," he said at last.

"Come and sit down, then, and I'll tell you."

They settled themselves on the low stone wall that ran along one side of the staircase. Emereck looked at Liana expectantly.

"Oraven is . . . special," Liana began. "Special to everyone in Minathlan, even Lord Dindran, though he doesn't show it often. He's about five years younger than Gendron, and he's never been as wild as the Duke's other sons. He's a—a very sweet, generous person, and everyone loves him. . . ."

Emereck shifted uncomfortably. Liana's information did not explain anything. The reaction of the guests had already told him that Oraven was highly thought of. Surely there was more than that?

"Oraven's the only one of the family who was ever close to all of the others. But he was especially close to Flindaran, before Flindaran left for Ciaron. He taught Flindaran how to use a sword, and . . . oh, all sorts of things. Even after Oraven married—"

"Married?" Emereck said, surprised. "I didn't think any of Flindaran's brothers were married."

"They aren't, now," Liana said softly.

"Oh. I see."

"No, you don't. Oraven had been married a little over a year when he decided he wanted to study sorcery. Well, I think he'd always wanted it, but he felt he owed something to Lord Dindran and his brothers first. So he didn't do anything about it until Flindaran was old enough to be sent to school in Ciaron.

"Anyway, he went to Kith Alunel to see if he could find a wizard who would teach him. His wife was pregnant, but it was still early and he expected to be home before the baby came. Only he was delayed in Kith Alunel, and the baby was early, and his wife died of it. The child only lived a few hours."

"I'm sorry."

Liana smiled at him. Even in the moonlight he could see that her expression was strained. "Oraven blamed himself, though there's nothing he could have done. I think he still blames himself. After Flindaran left, Oraven gave up the idea of learning magic and joined the Free Riders. I think he's always hoped he'd be killed, and now . . ."

"And now he may have gotten his wish," Emereck said slowly.

"And everyone knows, but no one really wants to admit it," Liana said, nodding. "So when you sang . . ."

Emereck nodded slowly. Unknowing, he had played "Corryn's Ride"—a song about a man whose wife and child were dead, and who wanted to die avenging them. No wonder Gendron and the others had been upset! "And Flindaran—"

"He had to leave for Ciaron just one week after Oraven came home. He wanted to stay and help somehow—not that there was much he could have done—but he had to go. He was very unhappy about it."

"Couldn't he have delayed it a year?"

Liana looked down. "Minathlan isn't rich. Lord Dindran had already paid for the first year of teaching. I think he would have let Flindaran stay, but . . ."

"Flindaran would find it hard to ask him, I think."

"Yes. So he left."

"I see. Thank you. I understand much better now."

Liana did not answer. They sat for a long time in silence, while Emereck considered. Finally he looked at Liana. "Why did you tell me all this?"

"I thought you ought to know," she said simply. "Especially if—if Oraven . . ."

"He's not dead yet, and you said the healer was with him."

"No, he hasn't died. But I think he will. He doesn't want to live."

Emereck stared. "Where's Flindaran?" he said at last in a voice he hardly recognized as his own.

"With Oraven and the healer and the rest of the family. At least he was when I left, and I don't think he'd have gone anywhere else. Not now." Liana rose to her feet. "And I'd better be getting back in case . . . anything happens."

"I'm coming with you," Emereck said.

"But—"

"I have to see Flindaran before 'anything happens.' I have to explain—"

Emereck broke off as the sound of a single harpnote echoed through the courtyard, soft and pure. Another followed, and another, vibrating in his very bones. He turned and stared at the castle in horrified disbelief. Flindaran wouldn't, he couldn't have—but the silver sound kept on. The music pulled at him far more strongly than it had before. For a moment he resisted, then with an incoherent shout, he ran into the castle.

Shalarn's eyes flew open. For a brief instant she lay staring into the darkness, then she threw the bedclothes aside and rose. She snatched her robe from the bedstand and shrugged it on as she hurried across to the door of the room where she performed her sorceries.

A wave and a muttered word dissolved the locking spells that protected her secrets from accidental discovery. Inside, she paused and concentrated. Yes, she still felt the tug of the magic that had awakened her. She had a little time yet. But how much?

She pushed the thought from her mind and whirled to the high chest beside the door. She yanked two drawers open and took the things she needed: four candles, a map, a bag of dried herbs, a small gold sphere at the end of a silver chain. In three steps she was beside the table. Her hands shook with the need for hurry as she spread the map flat and set the candles in their places—black to the north and south, white to the east and west. Carefully, she made a small pile of the crushed herbs at the point on the map where Lanyk's castle stood. Then she dangled the gold sphere above the herbs and began to chant.

A small figure slid silently through the forest south of Minathlan. Around him, rain fell in a slow, drenching drizzle. His bow and arrows made an oddly shaped bulge under the green cloak that protected them from the damp. His face was invisible inside his oiled leather hood.

His soft boots made no sound on the wet ground. Though there was no sign of a trail, he moved surely. Occasionally he paused to inspect a plant or to examine some nearly invisible mark on the forest mold.

Suddenly he stopped. He sniffed the night air tentatively, then stood motionless in an attitude of listening. Water collected in the hollows of his hood and dripped steadily from the hem of his cloak. He did not appear to notice.

The door opened and Kensal looked up. "Well?" he said as Ryl entered.

"In some ways it went very well."

"In some ways?"

"Both of those we sought are there, and they are the two who fought beside us at the inn. One is, in truth, a minstrel; the other is son to Duke Dindran."

"So all your suspicions were correct."

Ryl sank into a chair, frowning. "Yes, but I fear it helps us little. The minstrel bears the mark of the Harp already; I think it is in his keeping."

"Then you know where to find it?"

"He must keep it near him, or the fear of the burden would not be so clear on him."

Kensal studied her. "You're worried about something. What?"

"The other—the Duke's son. He has been touched as well, though I think in him the Harp has awakened desire. I wish I dared look more deeply."

"Is that necessary? If we know where it is . . ."

"Lord Flindaran seems impetuous. I fear what the

Harp might do in his hands."

"The minstrel seems a more immediate concern," Kensal said practically. "He has the Harp, after all. I'm glad Flindaran didn't decide to keep it. Taking something from a Duke's son could be a bit awkward."

Ryl smiled and shook her head slowly. "The minstrel is his friend and guest."

"If we can get it quickly enough, Flindaran won't become a problem."

"Do not underestimate—" Ryl stopped. Her head turned, and she went pale.

Automatically, Kensal reached for his sword. "What is it?" Even as he spoke, he knew the answer; the silver harpnotes rang through the room, faint but clear.

"He's playing it," Ryl whispered. "By the Four Lights, he's playing it!"

Kensal darted a sharp look in her direction. Her face was ice-white, and her hands were clenched in her lap. She seemed to be bracing herself against something, like a man holding up a falling wall that threatens to crush him. Kensal's eyes widened. He jumped to his feet and slammed the window shutters closed. The harpnotes continued without change.

Ryl's eyes closed. Her lips pressed together, and she began to shake. Kensal crossed back to her and knelt uncertainly beside her chair. He opened his mouth, then closed it again; distracting her could be dangerous to them both. Finally, he raised his hands and laid them slowly and carefully on top of Ryl's clenched fists.

Strength drained out of him. Ryl's shaking did not lessen, but it did not grow any worse. He wondered how long he could continue to feed her his energy, and what would happen to them both when he had no more to give. He felt himself weakening, but he did not move.

The music drew Emereck through the maze of castle corridors, and he followed it without hesitation. He passed several servants, all frozen in attitudes of listening, and ran up a flight of stairs. A door blocked his way, flanked by a half-ensorcelled guard. Before the man could move to stop him, Emereck burst into the room beyond. He saw Talerith and Gendron turning toward him with expressions of bemused astonishment, and an unfamiliar man bending intently over a still figure in a large, canopied bed. Emereck's eyes swept past them to the source of the music.

Flindaran sat beside the bed, holding the Harp of Imach Thyssel. Some trick of light made it seem polished and undented, as it must have looked when it was new. There was a look of exultation on Flindaran's face as his hands moved surely over the strings. A detached part of Emereck's mind noted that Flindaran had not made a single mistake in his playing, though he could hardly be described as even a passable harpist with an ordinary instrument. Flindaran looked up and saw him, but his hands never paused.

In three strides Emereck was across the room. He jerked the Harp from Flindaran's hands. The music ceased, leaving only a faint echo. He set the Harp carefully on a small table behind him, then turned back to face Flindaran. "You fool!" he said angrily. "Do you realize what you've done?"

As Shalarn began the chant, the four candles lit simultaneously with slender ribbons of fire that were almost as long as the candles themselves. Even as their light flared through the chamber, she felt the faraway tugging cease. Grimly, she continued the spell, forcing herself to ignore the cold certainty of failure that was growing in her mind.

She finished the spell without hope; the silver chain had never even trembled in her hand. As she ended the chant, the candles winked out. She lifted the chain and sphere away from the map, then crossed to a chair and sank into it. She sat motionless for several moments, recovering from the exhaustion of performing sorcery hastily and without proper preparation.

And for what? She could try again later to trace the touch of magic that had awakened her, but it would be a long and tedious process. Even if she succeeded, she would be only one of those seeking for its source; she could not be the only wizard awakened by that pull. She had lost whatever advantage she might have gained by quick action. She slapped a hand against the arm of the chair in frustration.

Well, it was past mending now. She rose and went back to the chest. More by touch than sight, she found a small lamp and lit it. She replaced the gold sphere carefully in its velvet bag, then turned back to the table to put away the map and the candles. She froze, and then gave a low cry of triumph.

The crushed herbs no longer made a small pile above the mark that indicated the castle in which she stood. They had spread into a thin line that led southeast and ended in a second, smaller pile. Shalarn moved forward to study it more closely, and her lips parted in a smile. She had not realized that it was so close. Tomorrow she would make her excuses to Lanyk and be on her way to Minathlan.

The figure in the forest stood listening for a long time. Finally, he relaxed and shook his head. Drops of water flew, striking nearby leaves and branches and knocking still more droplets free. He threw a long, considering look northward. Absently, he fingered a small gold ring that bore the image of a tree with three moons tangled in its branches. At last he turned and started back the way he had come, moving swiftly now as well as silently.

Kensal knew he was weakening rapidly, but he clung stubbornly to his post. Finally, the music stopped. He stayed where he was. At last Ryl's shaking stopped too. He let his hands fall to his side as she opened her eyes. "Thank you," she whispered.

"You're welcome," Kensal said. His voice sounded harsh and rusty, as though he had not used it for a long time. He tried again. "Next time, you'd better find someone younger for that. I almost feel my age."

A ghost of a smile crossed Ryl's face. "I will . . . try to remember. Old man."

He licked his lips. "What happened?"

"Someone played the Harp. I was not prepared for

such a happening."

"Prepared?"

"I will explain later. Now I must rest."

"You're all right?"

"Mostly." Ryl's voice began to fade. "I need rest now, that is all. Do not worry. I only need to . . . rest."

With the last word, Ryl closed her eyes. Kensal looked at her for a long time. Finally, he tried to rise. He almost fell; he had not realized how weakened he was. He tried again, pulling himself up on the arms of the chair, and made it. Carefully, he made his way back to his chair and collapsed into it.

A long time later he raised his head. Ryl lay sprawled awkwardly in the chair where he had left her. Except for the barely perceptible rise and fall of her chest, she looked dead. He sighed and stood up. This time his legs held him. He crossed the room and placed his arms under her, testing his strength constantly to be certain it would last. He decided it would. He picked her up and staggered to the bed. When Ryl was arranged in a more comfortable-looking position, he pulled a chair over to the bedside and settled down to wait.

A tall shadow, cloaked and hooded, stood frowning in Lanyk's tower. So that was what they wanted! No wonder the Dark Ones had been reluctant to explain fully. And no wonder they had been so free with information and . . . other things. They needed hands to bring it to them. Well, if they wanted the thing that had made that music, they would have to find someone else to run their errand. Someone foolish enough to give away such power.

The shadow's eyes narrowed. Time enough for such things later, when the music-maker was safe in Syaskor. First it must be located, and men sent after it. Warding spells must be cast to confuse any other wizards and magicians who might have noticed. And there was Shalarn—she might well have heard the music too, and felt its power. She must be delayed. That Captain of hers would be useful there. The hooded shadow smiled very, very slightly and slid away to plan.

Eleven

*F*lindaran jumped to his feet facing Emereck. His face was hard. "Move aside, Emereck."

"No. You have no right—"

"My brother's dying! Move aside, or I'll throw you."

"No!"

Flindaran's lips tightened, and he reached for Emereck. Then, behind him, a raspy voice said, "What's all the shouting?"

"Oraven!" Flindaran whirled and knelt beside the bed.

"I might have known it would be you," Oraven said with tired good humor. "Can't you do anything without making noise?"

"Oraven, you—" Flindaran stopped and looked anxiously across at the healer.

"Quite remarkable," the little man said placidly in answer to the unspoken question. "He'll need rest, of course, but I believe the crisis is over." He looked speculatively in Emereck's direction. "Interesting instrument you have there."

"Not at all," Emereck said coldly.

"I see. Pity." The healer shrugged.

"Oraven's really all right?" Talerith said breathlessly.

"Yes, of course I am," Oraven said. "Except . . ."

"Except what?" Flindaran demanded instantly.

Oraven grinned broadly. "Except that I feel like sleeping for a week. Stop fussing over me, Flindaran!"

"Flindaran, you did it!" Talerith cried. "Oh, you're wonderful!"

Behind her, Gendron was eyeing his brother with an expression of surprised respect. Under other circumstances, Emereck would have found it amusing. Flindaran flushed very slightly and glanced at Emereck, but he did not speak.

"Quite so. But Lord Oraven should sleep now," the healer said firmly.

"Not yet," Oraven objected. He smothered a yawn. "I've got to talk to Father first."

"Then by all means do so," said the Duke from the doorway.

Like dolls on strings each head turned toward the door. "Father!" Talerith exclaimed.

The Duke surveyed the room. "There appear to be a remarkable number of people present," he commented. "Since Oraven is apparently both out of danger and greatly in need of rest—"

"Oh, Father, it was wonderful!" Talerith said with a gushing enthusiasm that set Emereck's teeth on edge. "Flindaran did it all; he found that Harp on his way home, and—"

Sweet demons, Emereck thought as Talerith chattered on, Flindaran must have told her everything! His anger surged, but he knew he could not confront Flindaran now in the presence of the Duke and so many others. He fought it down.

"I am quite aware of what Flindaran has done, my dear," Lord Dindran said. His eyes flickered to his son. "More so, perhaps, than he appears to be."

"Sir?" said Flindaran.

"I doubt that there is anyone in the city who did not hear your . . . er . . . performance."

"*The whole city?*" Flindaran repeated numbly.

"The instrument would appear to carry well."

"I'm sorry. But I had to do it! Oraven—"

The Duke held up a hand. "Spare me your justifications, I beg you. I have neither time nor inclination to listen."

"Father, you're not being fair!" Talerith objected angrily. "Flindaran saved Oraven's life!"

Lord Dindran looked at her. Talerith flushed. "I think it is time for all of you to go," the Duke said, and waited.

Gendron bowed immediately and went to the door. Talerith moved slowly after him. Emereck turned and picked up the Harp; when he turned back Talerith was glaring at him from the open doorway.

"That's Flindaran's harp!" she said angrily.

"Talerith—" Flindaran said rising hastily.

"Well, it is! He's just a common minstrel. He can't take it. You can't let him!"

Flindaran shifted uncomfortably. "I don't think you understand, Talerith. Emereck and I found the Harp together."

"You saved Oraven with it," Talerith said stubbornly. "It's yours. *He* wouldn't have done anything for Oraven if he'd had it."

"No doubt the two of you find this conversation extremely edifying," the Duke said. "I, however, do not. You will oblige me by continuing it elsewhere."

"But, Father, you can't—"

"Did I ask for your opinion, my dear?" the Duke said sweetly. "I do not recall it."

Talerith turned bright red. "I beg your pardon, Father."

"Very good. No doubt you will also beg your brother's pardon, since it is his rest you are delaying."

"I'm sorry, Oraven," Talerith said. She threw her father a look of mingled fear and rebelliousness, and swept out of the room.

Flindaran started to follow, then hesitated. "Sir, if I may explain—"

"In the morning. And I shall be less interested in your explanations than in what you propose to do now that the Harp is no longer a secret."

"Of course, sir." Flindaran bowed and left. Emereck followed his example. The Duke did not comment; he did not appear to notice Emereck at all. As the door closed behind him, Emereck heard the Duke say, "Now, Oraven, I am entirely at your service."

Flindaran was waiting in the corridor. Emereck walked past him without speaking, but Flindaran turned and fell into step beside him. Emereck glanced at him and shifted the Harp of Imach Thyssel to his opposite arm.

Flindaran flushed. "Emereck . . . I'm sorry."

"Sorry!" Emereck did not try to keep the bitterness from his voice. "It's a little late for that, isn't it?"

"Oh, don't be ridiculous! No real harm's been done."

"No *harm!* Everyone in the city knows about the Harp now."

"You're overdramatizing."

Emereck stopped and glared. "I heard the music myself, and I was all the way out in the courtyard. And I'm not the only one; everyone in the castle heard it as well."

"People heard music, so what? If you'd quit shouting about it, no one will know where it came from."

"How do you expect to keep it secret? Do you plan to lock up the guard and the healer and your sister?"

"Oh demons, Emereck, what's so important about keeping it secret anyway?"

"How am I going to get it back to Ciaron quietly if everyone knows what and where it is? I had a chance when you and the Duke were the only ones who knew about it, but now . . ."

"You're exaggerating!"

"I suppose you think no one else would want it?" Emereck said with biting sarcasm.

"Leave it here, then."

"After what you've done? You had no right to take the Harp!"

"I had to! I don't expect you to understand—"

"Of course you wouldn't," Emereck said bitterly. "I'm just a 'common minstrel.'"

"I didn't mean that, and you know it! You don't have any brothers. How could you understand?"

"Why don't *you* try understanding? Or didn't it occur to you to ask what I thought?"

"Oraven was dying! You weren't there, and I didn't have time to find you."

"You didn't even try."

"I tell you, there was no time! What was I supposed to do, apologize to Oraven's corpse because I went looking for you instead of helping him? I thought you'd be willing to listen."

"You didn't think," Emereck shouted. "You never think! You just go rushing into things without considering anything but what you want. Flindaran, the great hero!"

Flindaran's face was white with anger. "At least I *do* things instead of just thinking about them! Oraven would be dead now if I'd stopped to listen to you."

"And what about the price? Did you think of that when you used the Harp?"

"I don't believe there's any 'price' for playing it!"

"And if you're wrong?"

Flindaran glanced back down the corridor in the direction of Oraven's room. He hesitated, and his eyes turned to the harp Emereck held. His face took on a faraway expression. "It was worth it."

"Worth it!" Emereck spat the words.

"Yes, worth it! You'll never know that, because you'll never dare to play it yourself. You're afraid of the Harp because you're afraid of yourself. I may have made mistakes, but at least I had the courage to try!"

"You'd have done better to have the courage *not* to try!"

"Don't lecture me! That harp's as much mine as it is yours. We both found it."

"The Harp of Imach Thyssel belongs to the Minstrel's Guild!"

"Take it, then! Take it, and much good may it do you!" Flindaran spun on his heel and left.

Emereck stood looking after him. Slowly his anger

drained away, leaving only a numb resentment and a tingling sensation where his right arm rested on the Harp. Hastily, he shifted the instrument to his other arm and began walking toward his own rooms.

Emereck slept very poorly during the remainder of the night, and again his dreams were nightmares of torture. He awoke determined to leave Minathlan as soon as possible. He spent nearly an hour composing a suitably polite message to the Duke, requesting an interview. To his surprise, it was granted at once, and at mid-morning he found himself standing in the Duke's study once more.

"I give you good morning, my lord," Emereck said.

"And I you," Lord Dindran replied politely, and waited.

"And Lord Oraven? How does he do?"

"Considerably better than might have been expected under . . . other circumstances." The Duke studied Emereck for a moment. "Shall we dispense with this pretense? You asked to see me."

"My lord, I—I wish to leave Minathlan. At once. I came to take my leave of you."

"I see." The Duke leaned back in his chair. "I rather thought it might be that."

"Then you have no objection?"

"I have never had any objection to your leaving whenever you wish. The Harp of Imach Thyssel is another matter entirely."

Emereck stiffened. "The Harp belongs in a Guildhall, and the sooner it gets there, the better for us all!"

"Your faith in your Guild Masters is touching," Lord Dindran commented dryly.

"You disagree?"

"Not at all. The Harp of Imach Thyssel undoubtedly belongs in a Minstrel's Guildhall—if, indeed, it can be said to belong anywhere. Which of the Guildhalls will have the dubious honor of watching over it is for them to decide."

"Then I am afraid I do not understand you."

"I am not averse to your departure, with or without the Harp. My objection is to your timing."

"Surely you see why I must go! Flindaran and I—" Emereck hesitated, uncertain of how to finish the sentence.

"I am afraid your quarrel with Flindaran, unpleasant as it may be, has very little to do with this matter."

"My lord, I cannot agree. The use of the Harp has made my position here far more dangerous than it has been."

"Obviously. But I fail to see how leaving Minathlan would make you any safer."

"But Flindaran—" Emereck paused again.

"I would also like to point out that none of the arguments against your journey have changed since yesterday."

"My lord?"

"The northern roads are impassible at this time of year. King Birn remains determined to keep minstrels out of Kith Alunel, and the Syaski grow more active than ever."

"A single traveler may well be able to skirt Syaskor without attracting attention."

"A single traveler may also be easy prey for bandits."

"Minstrels seldom have such difficulties, my lord. Even bandits welcome news and song."

"I will not chance the Harp of Imach Thyssel falling into Syaski hands," Lord Dindran said flatly. "Nor into the hands of the Lithmern, or of some band of robbers. Until I am certain that the Harp can be moved in complete safety, it will not be moved at all."

"You're as bad as they—" Too late, Emereck realized what he was saying and stopped short.

"I believe I shall forget that remark," the Duke said silkily, and Emereck had difficulty keeping from cringing. "Provided you do not make such a mistake a second time."

"I am sorry, my lord; I am overwrought. I beg your forgiveness."

The Duke studied him through narrowed eyes. "I

have no interest in claiming this Harp. You find that surprising? I do not wish to make Minathlan the target of every wizard, thief, and warlord searching for a quick route to fame and power. Which is precisely what will happen if it becomes known that the Harp of Imach Thyssel is here. I also have no intention of endangering Minathlan by allowing the Harp to fall into the hands of Minathlan's enemies, notably Syaskor. Have I made myself clear?"

"Perfectly, my lord."

"Excellent. In that case, I believe we have nothing further to discuss at present."

"Then forgive me for disturbing you, my lord," Emereck said. He rose and bowed, seething inside.

"One last thing," the Duke said as Emereck turned to leave. "After the events of last night, I fear that the Harp has attracted some undesirable attention. I have, therefore, asked my Captain of the Guard to assign someone to guard your room until it is safe for the Harp to be moved. I am sure you understand my reasoning."

"Of course, my lord," Emereck said in a colorless voice. He bowed again and left the room quickly. He had no doubt of the Duke's purpose; the guard would protect the Harp from thieves, but he would also prevent Emereck from leaving without the Duke's permission. He was still smoldering as he went back to his room, and his temper was not improved when he found the promised guard already standing outside his door. Muttering curses, Emereck went inside and slammed the door, as if by doing so he could shut out Minathlan and all its inhabitants.

Twelve

*E*mereck did not leave his room for the rest of the day. He was torn between a desire to find Flindaran and apologize for his part in their quarrel and a continuing anger that Flindaran had been so careless with the Harp. Anything might have happened! Below the anger and regret, buried so deeply Emereck scarcely admitted it to himself, was a strong undercurrent of fear—fear for himself, and fear for Flindaran.

What price would the Harp claim? For Flindaran's sake, he hoped fervently that the legends were wrong, but he did not truly believe it. And no matter what his friend had done, Emereck did not want to watch what the Harp must do to him. Involuntarily, his eyes turned toward the chest that held the Harp, and he shivered. If only he could leave now!

Unfortunately, Lord Dindran was right. Leaving Minathlan made no more sense now than it had two days ago. But how could he remain immobilized here, while "thieves, wizards and warlords" collected and drew nearer? The longer he stayed, the more difficulties would await him when he left at last. Yet leaving would be nearly impossible without the Duke's support, or at least his permission. And even if Emereck could somehow get the Harp out of the castle, how could he keep it safe? Emereck felt like the shield-bearer in "Verrick's Folly" with "seventeen choices and all of them wrong."

Emereck scowled, wishing for a moment that he could give the Harp to the Duke. Let someone else have the responsibility! But he would never be able to come up with an adequate explanation for his Guild Masters. And who could say what the Duke of Minathlan might do once he had the Harp? No, until he reached Ciaron and the Masters of his Guild, guarding the Harp was Emereck's problem. He sighed, and picked up his own harp.

The chest containing the Harp of Imach Thyssel was securely locked, but Emereck watched it warily as he began to play. No silver echoes accompanied his music, and gradually he progressed from scales to exercises and from exercises to ballads. With a kind of malicious glee, he ran through all of the scales and exercises Flindaran hated most. None provoked any response from the Harp, and by the end of the day Emereck began to relax. He was considering whether to go out and face the Duke's family at dinner, when someone rapped at his door.

"Come in!" Emereck called without thinking.

Flindaran stepped into the room and shut the door quickly behind him. Emereck stiffened. Flindaran leaned back against the door, watching him warily. "I came to see whether you were going down to dinner," Flindaran said finally.

"You are considerate, my lord."

Flindaran winced. "I suppose I deserved that. Look, Emereck . . . I want to apologize for yesterday. Last night, I mean." His eyes drifted toward the chest that held the Harp.

Fleetingly, Emereck remembered the exalted look on Flindaran's face when he played the Harp. He wondered what it had been like. He did not say anything.

There was an awkward silence. "I'm sorry, Emereck," Flindaran said at last.

"I believe you mentioned that at the time."

"I thought I'd better do it again." Flindaran looked at Emereck and managed a halfhearted grin. "Somehow I always have to tell you everything twice."

"Well, if you'd get it right the first time . . ." Emereck started, and stopped. They looked at each other, and Emereck looked away. "How is your brother?" he said carefully.

"Mending. The healer says he should stay in bed for about a week, but he'll be fine eventually."

Emereck frowned, surprised, then nodded in understanding. Oraven's wounds had been serious, and Flindaran's use of the Harp had been interrupted. It was entirely reasonable that the Harp had not healed Oraven as completely as it had Emereck. "I'm glad he's better."

Flindaran nodded, and there was another awkward pause. Finally, Emereck cleared his throat. "Flindaran, I—Well, it was my fault, too. I'm sorry."

Flindaran's grin was full of relief, but there was still a touch of hesitancy in his manner. "Then you're coming to dinner?"

"I suppose if I don't, you'll stand there complaining at me all night."

"Not if you're going to start playing scales again. Don't your fingers get tired?"

"How did you know I'd been practicing all day?"

"I was exercising in the courtyard this afternoon, and I heard you." Flindaran nodded toward the open window.

"I hope you enjoyed it."

"I might have if you'd played something besides dah-dah-dee-di-dah," Flindaran said. "How can you stand doing that over and over?"

"How can you stand swinging a sword at a wooden stand over and over?" Emereck retorted.

"It's not the same thing. Come on, or we'll be late for dinner."

"Practice is practice," Emereck said, as he rose and started toward the door. Flindaran grinned, bowed, and swung the door open. Together they left the room and started toward the castle dining hall, still arguing with outward amicability.

Emereck grew more and more restless as the days passed. The Duke of Minathlan showed no sign of allowing him to leave, and a guard remained outside his door at all times. Though Emereck's movements were not restricted, the guard's presence made him feel like a prisoner. He wanted more than ever to leave Minathlan, but he could not bring himself to leave the Harp of Imach Thyssel behind, and he could think of no way of smuggling it out of the castle. In the end, he sat in his room and brooded.

Flindaran tried to distract him by sitting in Emereck's room for hours, talking. Emereck did not know quite what to make of it, until he noticed Flindaran's eyes drifting toward the locked chest in the corner. All of Emereck's earlier misgivings returned with redoubled force. He began to watch Flindaran more closely, and soon discovered that whenever Flindaran thought he was unobserved he studied the chest that contained the Harp.

Emereck lay awake late that night, trying to decide whether to confront Flindaran with his suspicions. The following morning he cornered Flindaran in the courtyard and explained what he had observed.

"You're imagining things," Flindaran said when he finished.

"I don't think so," Emereck said quietly.

"Living with that thing in the same room is affecting your brain. You ought to get rid of it."

"I will, as soon as I get to Ciaron. The Guild Masters are more than welcome to it!"

Flindaran frowned. "I mean sooner than that. Why don't you have it put in the strongroom?"

"With all the guards your father has around this castle, the Harp is just as safe in my room," Emereck said. He did not add that he preferred to keep the Harp under his own control as much as he could.

"Yes, but in the strongroom you won't have to worry

about it all the time," Flindaran said impatiently. "Come on. We can do it now. It will only take a few minutes."

"No. The Harp is my responsibility. I'll be anxious about it wherever it is, and I'd rather have it somewhere where I can keep an eye on it."

"And I thought minstrels only cared about music!" Flindaran said with a mocking sarcasm that was very unlike him.

Emereck shrugged, trying to keep his temper. "At the moment I'm more worried about you than the Harp."

"Worry about your scales, Minstrel, not about me," Flindaran snapped and stalked off.

Deeply disturbed, Emereck returned to his room and his harp. His fingers ran automatically through the long-familiar exercises, while his mind turned over and over the implications of Flindaran's outburst. Finally he rose and bolted the door, then went to the chest that held the Harp. He unlocked it, and slowly lifted out the linen that covered the Harp. Even more slowly, he raised the Harp and set it on the floor beside the chest.

For a moment he stood staring at the dull ivory. The Harp was destroying Flindaran, and destroying his friendship with Flindaran, and he hated it. It was powerful, and therefore dangerous, and he feared it. Yet, despite his hatred and fear, he could understand Flindaran's secretive obsession with the instrument. It was as though the Harp had been meant to obsess people, and that made Emereck fear it all the more.

He pulled his eyes away from the Harp and climbed to his feet. He crossed to the tall wardrobe on the opposite side of the room, opened it, and studied the small selection of garments inside. He removed a sturdy, dark-brown tunic and returned to the chest. After a moment's hesitation, he picked up the Harp and wrapped it quickly in the tunic.

When he was sure that no gleam of ivory showed through the wrapping, he carried the bundle to the wardrobe. He examined the shadowy interior briefly, then set the Harp in the darkest corner. Finally, he adjusted his traveling cloak so that the folds hid almost all of the dark, oddly-shaped bundle.

At last he was satisfied. It was not the most secure of hiding places, but at least the Harp was well out of sight. Carefully, he closed the wardrobe door, then crossed the room and replaced the linen in the chest. He relocked the chest before returning to his practicing.

For the remainder of the morning, Emereck moved restlessly from one thing to another. At last he was driven out of his room into the castle halls. Almost at once he noticed an unusual level of activity. Servants and guards were moving briskly up and down the corridors. Remembering the last, disastrous feast, Emereck stopped one of the men and asked the reason for the stir.

"Preparations for my lord Duke's journey, sir," the surprised man replied, and hurried on.

More puzzled than ever, Emereck continued walking. He was about to question another of the servants when he heard Flindaran's voice hailing him. He turned and saw Flindaran coming toward him.

"So you finally gave up on your scales!" Flindaran said with a grin. "Where away now?"

Emereck blinked. Nothing in Flindaran's manner so much as hinted at the angry words he had thrown at Emereck that morning. It was as though the encounter had been completely forgotten, or had never taken place.

Flindaran's expression changed. "Uh, did I say something?"

"What? Oh, no. I was just wandering."

"Come down to the courtyard with me, then. I've got some things to do."

"You seem a little more cheerful now than you did this morning," Emereck said cautiously as he fell into step beside his friend.

"It's been a good day," Flindaran said vaguely. He glanced down a side corridor, then stopped and called, "Kay! Father wants to see you before he leaves."

Kiannar nodded in casual recognition, and they

continued on. "What's all this about?" Emereck asked.

"Father's going to be away from the castle for a few days."

"This is an explanation? That's obvious. Half the castle seems to be packing things."

"Well, that's about all anyone knows. He hasn't said where he's going or why."

"Is that wise? What if something happened?"

Flindaran shrugged. "He ought to know what he's doing; this isn't the first time it's happened. Besides— you know him. Would *you* want to ask him what he's up to, if he didn't want to say?"

"No," Emereck admitted. "But you must have some idea."

"I don't know, and I'm not going to worry about it. It's just one of his little mysteries; we'll find out when he wants us to know."

A disquieting thought occurred to Emereck. "Who's going to be in charge while Lord Dindran is away?"

"Gendron and I," Flindaran said, and grinned smugly.

"Both of you? Isn't that a little unusual?"

"There's a lot to do, and the healer says Oraven isn't well enough yet to help. Besides, Father is always . . . a little unusual. Hadn't you noticed?"

Emereck laughed, suppressing a twinge of misgiving. "Congratulations, then!"

"It's only for a few days," Flindaran said with unaccustomed seriousness, "but it's a chance to show Father what I can do."

"Have you and Gendron discussed it yet?"

"Of course. He's the eldest, so he'll take over most of Father's public duties. The steward handles most of the details of running the castle, of course, but there will still be a few things he can't do, and the townspeople will—"

Emereck began to relax as Flindaran talked on. The thought of his new responsibilities appeared to have driven all thought of the Harp from Flindaran's mind. And in a few days the Duke would return. Things would be all right in a few days.

*   *   *

Shalarn knelt beside the broken carriage wheel, picking the splinters apart with her fingers. Over a handspan of the rim had been smashed almost beyond recognition by its collision with the rock. Her lips were pressed tightly together in an attempt to suppress the anger she felt at this latest mishap.

"My lady?"

Shalarn looked up into the handsome face of her Guard Captain. "Yes?"

"How much longer do you expect to spend here? It's a long ride to the next town. We'll be lucky to make it by nightfall."

"We'll stay as long as it takes me to find what I'm looking for." Shalarn looked down again to concentrate on separating the pieces of the wheel.

"You suspect sabotage, my lady?" The man's tone was respectful enough, but the question itself was irritating. He might as well be *trying* to distract her. Shalarn sighed noisily and looked up.

"Yes, Captain, I suspect sabotage. This accident is too convenient. And there was the broken harness yesterday, and the delays in Syaskor before that."

"It may not mean anything, my lady."

"I think it does," Shalarn snapped. "Someone is trying to keep me from reaching Minathlan."

"None of the men would do such a thing," the Captain said stiffly.

Shalarn ignored him. Really, the man was becoming impossible. She would have to watch him, or the next thing she knew he would be trying to take her place.

She pulled an old, discolored nail out of the wreckage and dropped it, then scrabbled in the dust of the road to retrieve it. Her finger had brushed something as it fell, a roughness on one side that should not have been there. She found the nail and turned it over in her hands, then was suddenly still.

"What is it, my lady?" the Captain said.

"Sorcery," Shalarn said grimly. A symbol was scratched on one side of the nail, leaving a thread of bright metal showing plainly against the dark surface. Shalarn's jaw tightened as she studied it: four curved lines like over-lapping half-circles opening away from each other. "The Rune of Separation. No wonder the wheel didn't hold!"

"My lady?" the Captain sounded wary and fascinated at once, as he always did when she was involved with matters of magic.

"The symbol on this nail is one of the seven Change Runes, the rune of breaking. I'm surprised the wheel lasted as long as it did carrying this." Absently, she fingered the nail. Clever to have used an old one. She had almost missed it entirely. Who had done it? Lanyk was involved, of course; this explained why he had insisted so strongly on her taking this clumsy, ornate vehicle. Shadows take him and his whole kingdom! But Lanyk was no sorcerer, and only a powerful magician indeed would have knowledge of the Change Runes. Who was helping the Prince of Syaskor? And how much did they know?

Frowning, Shalarn rose. "I think we've lost enough time, Captain. We'll leave the coach; from here on, I'll ride. See to it."

The Captain turned and snapped a command. Shalarn's men leaped to unharness the carriage horses and repack the essential baggage. Shalarn smiled. Tonight she would cast more specific warding spells about their camp; there would be no more delays. In a few minutes the cavalcade was off again, leaving the coach an abandoned shell behind them.

Kensal pushed open the door of the room and stopped short. Ryl was leaning halfway out the window, looking up into the afternoon sunlight. He kicked the door closed behind him, and she turned. "Is that wise?" he asked mildly. "You're not fully recovered yet, and the wind is cold."

"I have no fear of wind, and I am very nearly as well as ever."

"It's the 'very nearly' that worries me. We're running out of time."

"I know. But there is little I can do as yet, and to

move too soon might do much harm."

Kensal looked at her sharply. "That's another thing. Are you sure it was that harp music that made you ill?"

"What is it you fear?"

"Shadow-born."

"It is their doing, certainly, but not recently. The Change they made is always with us, and the spells that defend me from it are . . . delicately balanced. The music of the Harp carries power, and it upset that balance. That is all."

"What if one of those young idiots tries playing the Harp again?"

"I am better prepared for it now," Ryl replied, but a shadow of worry crossed her face. "The remedies you have brought me are good for more than fevers."

"That reminds me. Here." Kensal tossed a small packet in her direction. Ryl caught it neatly, opened it, and made a face.

"I doubt I know which is worse, the scent of this herb or its taste. Are you sure they have no mara leaves?"

"This is a small village, and I've been buying from the largest herb dealer in town," Kensal replied. "If he doesn't have it, no one else will either."

"I can accept it for another day or two, I suppose, but I will be glad when the need is over." She rose and crossed to the water jug. Kensal watched as she mixed the herbs with water and drank. She set the mug down and turned back to look at him. "There is something more, I think?"

"The Duke is leaving Minathlan."

"What? When?"

"Today. The market was buzzing with it. He's leaving two of his sons in charge—the eldest and Flindaran."

Ryl shook her head. "Where does he go?"

"No one knows. The villagers are all speculating, of course, but they don't know anything, and the castle folk don't talk much. The Duke . . . doesn't encourage it."

"And Flindaran is to share his duties while he is away." Ryl sighed and was quiet for a long time. "I do not like this," she said at last. "I do not like it at all."

Thirteen

*I*n spite of the Duke's absence, Emereck's restlessness continued. He was up at dawn the following morning. He joined a startled guard on the sentry-walk atop the castle wall and paced the perimeter of the grounds twice, then wandered through the stables, chatting with the grooms.

As he was leaving, he saw Flindaran and Liana standing near the center of the courtyard, deep in conversation. He was about to pass by, when Flindaran looked up and saw him. "Emereck!" Flindaran called, waving him over. "Come here a minute."

Emereck walked over. "Good morning, Minstrel," Liana said as he joined them, and she smiled warmly. It occurred to him that she seemed always welcoming, always at peace, and that this was one of the things he liked about her.

"Good morning, lady," Emereck replied. "And to you, Flindaran. But what are you doing up so early?"

Flindaran raised an eyebrow. "I don't always sleep until noon."

"Of course not," Liana said before Emereck could reply. "I've seen you up before the sun cleared the walls at *least* three or four times in my life."

"Are you quite sure you aren't exaggerating?" Emereck asked her.

Liana's eyes danced. "Well, perhaps it was only once or twice, now that I think of it."

"Demons take it, don't encourage her, Emereck!" Flindaran said. "I'm having enough trouble with her as it is!"

"You're taking yourself much too seriously," Liana told him.

"And you're not taking me seriously enough. How am I supposed to explain to Gendron? And what do you expect me to tell Father when he gets back?"

"I don't expect you to explain anything. There's no need for it."

"Lee, have you ever tried not answering one of Father's questions? I'll have to tell him *something!*"

"No, you won't," Liana said with unruffled calm. "If he asks, which he won't, I'll be the one who tells him what happened."

"Far be it from me to interrupt such a promising argument," Emereck put in, "but I think it would be easier to appreciate if one of you would explain."

Liana turned toward him. "I have some errands to run in the village, that's all."

"It sounds like a pleasant way to spend a morning," Emereck said cautiously.

"It's Hesta's job," Flindaran said, frowning.

"Things have changed while you were in Ciaron," Liana said gently. "Hesta is getting old, and it's a long walk. I've been doing it for months now."

"This early in the morning?"

"It won't be early by the time I get there. The market opens at dawn, and the shopkeepers don't wait much past it."

"Well, you can't go alone. I don't believe Father would allow it."

"Father isn't here. And Minathlan is not Ciaron; the village is quite safe."

"I don't care," Flindaran said stubbornly. "You can't

go unescorted. It isn't—it isn't proper."

Liana looked at him mischievously. "Neither am I. Besides, Hesta never took anyone with her."

"Hesta isn't my sister."

"Half sister, Flindaran. There's a difference."

"You're still my sister, and you're still the Duke's daughter. And I know how Talerith—"

"Talerith enjoys having guards and waiting women around. I just feel silly."

"That has nothing to do with it!" Flindaran ran a hand through his hair in exasperation and looked at Emereck. "You see my problem?"

"Yes, you've finally found someone who's as stubborn as you are."

Flindaran gave him a look. "Well, you're a minstrel. You convince her!"

"I'll do better than that. I'll accompany her myself—if she is willing to have me," Emereck added hastily. He wondered suddenly why it had never occurred to him to leave the castle grounds. It would be a relief to get away from Minathlan, even if only for a little while.

Liana studied him. "It would make things easier," she conceded. "I warn you, though, I expect to have a lot to carry on the way back, and it's all uphill."

"Then I must certainly join you," Emereck replied, bowing.

Flindaran stared at him. "Emereck, I didn't mean to make you—"

"You aren't making me. I expect to have a delightful morning."

"Shopping? For supplies for the castle? In a village this size?"

"It will give me a chance to see the town," Emereck said firmly.

"Have it your own way, then," Flindaran said. "I have to get back to Gendron. He's got a list of things for me to do that will take all day. Enjoy yourselves!" He sketched a bow and started off across the courtyard. Emereck looked after him in surprise, then turned back to Liana. Their eyes met, and they both burst out laughing.

"Poor Flindaran," Liana said as they left the castle. "He tries so hard to take care of his little half sister, only I don't really need taking care of. But all he can see is that I'm like Talerith, and—"

"You aren't at all like Talerith!" Emereck said.

"I'm more like her than I am like Kiannar, at least in the kinds of things I enjoy. Walking and talking and music and so on."

"Walking you shall have in abundance," Emereck said, gesturing at the cobbled road that led down toward the village. "And I will try to fulfill my half of the responsibility for talking. I'm glad you included music as well, though; if I run out of things to say I can always sing."

Liana laughed. "Altogether a thoroughly enjoyable morning."

The market occupied roughly a quarter of the main square of the village with shops and workplaces creeping out along its edges. Rough wooden carts piled high with winter wheat, new carrots, and early greens filled most of the open center. The narrow aisles between them were full of people, dogs, and an occasional chicken or pig. Most of the crowd was on foot, though now and then a horseman could be seen over the tops of their heads. The people were mainly tradesmen, peasants, and farmers with a few servants in livery scattered among them. Once Emereck saw a man in silks and velvet who could only be one of the town's nobility.

To Emereck, accustomed to the crowded bustle of Ciaron, the number of people seemed unremarkable, but Liana sighed. "It's busy today. This will take longer than I'd expected. I hope you hadn't planned on getting back to Minathlan before noon."

"It makes no difference to me," Emereck said, not quite truthfully. He was relishing his freedom from the oppressive atmosphere of the castle, and already he was reluctant to return.

Liana nodded and led him across the square. They stopped frequently to exchange greetings with various citizens of Minathlan. Liana was clearly popular among the villagers, and Emereck attracted a number of curious glances. Not all of them were entirely friendly; several of the young men they passed appeared to resent Emereck's position at Liana's side. On consideration, Emereck couldn't blame them.

Their first stop was an apothecary's. "This will be a long wait, I'm afraid," Liana said as they entered. "He takes his time mixing remedies. This way."

The shop was large and smelled of dust and herbs. Tall racks of glass jars and clay herb pots combined with cluttered shelves of other merchandise to divide the room into a series of twisting aisles. The apothecary himself was a tall, thin man who peered nearsightedly down at Liana while she explained what she wanted. He nodded vigorously and disappeared into a room at the rear of the shop.

Liana looked after him for a moment, then came over to Emereck. "Would you mind waiting here without me? I'd like to go watch."

"Not at all," Emereck said, though he was a bit puzzled by her curiosity.

"It's not that I don't trust his abilities," she said apologetically. "But it's for Oraven, and . . . well, I just don't want to take chances."

"I understand," Emereck replied, and Liana smiled and left him. A moment later, the apothecary's assistant came in. He gave Emereck one sullen, sidelong glance, then ignored him and began straightening up the shelves.

Emereck retreated to the far end of the room, where he would be out of the way. The herb jars were fewer there, and the welter of miscellaneous merchandise was greater. There was no apparent order to any of it: three heavy iron kettles were stacked next to a delicate fan made of feathers, and a woolen shawl occupied the same counter as a wicked-looking set of hunting knives.

A shadow on one of the lower shelves caught

Emereck's eye, and he bent to look more closely. It was a small wooden drum, brightly painted in the fashion of Rathane. Emereck squatted down and pulled it out to examine it more closely. As he did, he heard the door of the shop open and close. A moment later he heard voices on the other side of the room. One of them sounded familiar, and he poked his head around the shelves to see who it was.

The apothecary's assistant was handing a small packet to a white-haired man in green leather. Emereck blinked, startled. The customer was the Cilhar, Kensal Narryn. Emereck started to rise to greet him, then paused. What was Kensal doing in Minathlan? He and Flindaran hadn't said where they were going, so Kensal could not have followed them deliberately. Unless Kensal knew of the Harp of Imach Thyssel and was following it . . . Emereck gave himself a mental shake. He was being a fool; *everyone* couldn't be after the Harp. The Cilhar's presence must be mere coincidence.

He looked up just as Kensal dropped a few coins on the counter, turned, and left. Emereck watched the door close behind him, then rose. He felt an uneasy guilt at his suspicions, but he was unable to dismiss them. What, after all, did he know about the Cilhar beyond his name? He walked over to the apothecary's assistant and said as casually as he could, "Interesting customer. I'd not thought to see a Cilhar so far from the Mountains of Morravik."

"I'd 'a been just as happy if he'd stayed there," the assistant growled. "Thinks he's better than everyone else, he does."

"Is he difficult to deal with, then?"

"Oh, aye. Knows exactly what he wants and expects it fresh every day, no matter what. Nearly tore the place apart yesterday when it wasn't waiting for him when he wanted it."

"He comes in every day? And I thought all Cilhar were healthy as dune-cats!"

"Oh, it's not for him, more's the pity. It's for his lady-friend." The assistant spat.

"A lady? With a Cilhar?" Emereck felt a twinge of misgiving. If Ryl had accompanied Kensal to Minathlan, it would be a little too much to ascribe to coincidence.

"A wonder, ain't it? They came to Minathlan about a week ago, and she took sick the night the ghost music played."

With effort, Emereck concealed his reaction. The assistant did not seem to notice. "He's been down here every day since," the man continued, "buying sleeping herbs and fever potions. He don't need 'em any more, neither; my cousin who works at the inn says the woman's nearly well. Does that stop him? No, he comes in with his high and mighty airs . . ."

Emereck stopped listening. If what this man was saying was true, Kensal and his companion must have come to Minathlan barely two days after Emereck's own arrival. They had been here when Flindaran played the Harp, and Emereck was suddenly certain that it was the music that had caused the woman's mysterious illness. But why had she been the only one affected? Or had she been? Emereck slipped a question into the assistant's grumbles, and was answered. No one else had become ill; on the contrary, several healings had been attributed, rightly or wrongly, to the unexplained Harp music.

Puzzled, Emereck allowed the man to return to his mutterings. Ryl was a sorceress. It was possible that she was more sensitive to the influence of the Harp than other people. But Emereck had no real basis for assuming that Ryl was Kensal's companion. He wanted to ask the apothecary's assistant for a description of the sick woman, but he did not quite dare. If the two were after the Harp, he did not want word of his interest to reach them. He had already displayed too much curiosity about the Cilhar and his lady.

He shifted uneasily, thinking of the Harp of Imach Thyssel lying unguarded at the bottom of the wardrobe in his room. Well, not totally unguarded, but what could Lord Dindran's men do against magic? Perhaps Flindaran was right to insist that the Harp belonged in the castle strongroom. Emereck frowned. He should never have come down to the village. . . . No, if he hadn't come, he wouldn't have discovered Kensal's presence in Minathlan. The thing to do now was to get back to the castle quickly and tell Flindaran what he had learned. Perhaps they could think of a way to protect the Harp; at the very least, the guards could be warned. Emereck glanced toward the inner door of the shop. How much longer could it take to mix the potion Liana wanted?

Liana and the apothecary emerged at last. Emereck contained his impatience long enough to take his leave politely, but as soon as they were out of the shop he turned to Liana. "Is there anything else you have to do right away?"

"I have a few more errands, but they shouldn't take as long as this one. I'm sorry you had to wait for me this time."

"No, it's nothing to do with you. I . . . saw an old friend, that's all, and I need to talk to Flindaran about it as soon as I can."

"And you want to go back to the castle now."

Emereck hesitated, then nodded. Liana studied him. "This is more important than you're saying," she said at last. "Let's go, then."

"I'm sorry. I hadn't realized I was being so obvious."

As they started away from the square, Liana smiled. "You're nearly as tense as one of your own harpstrings. Is it a secret?"

Emereck hesitated. "Not exactly, but . . . well, it's a long story."

"Tell me."

Somewhat to his own surprise, Emereck did. He was not really giving the secret of the Harp away, he told himself. Liana must know something about it already, if only from Flindaran's healing of Oraven. Besides, it was a relief to share the secret with someone other than Flindaran.

Liana listened quietly, then shook her head. "What are you going to do now?"

"Tell Flindaran, I suppose, and then try to decide what to do about Kensal."

"You don't *know* that he's looking for the Harp."

"I don't know that he isn't," Emereck said defensively. "And I have to be ready if he is. The Harp is too important not to be careful with it."

Liana looked at him. "I wish there was some way you could get rid of that thing right now."

"You mean destroy it?" Emereck was appalled. "I couldn't do that. The Harp of Imach Thyssel is one of the greatest treasures of Lyra!"

"Nobody's missed it for the last thousand years or so, have they? But that's not what I meant. I just wish you could give it to someone else and stop worrying about it. It's making you suspicious of everyone."

"Not everyone," Emereck said, looking at her.

"Well, nearly everyone, then," Liana said, smiling. The smile faded, and she said seriously, "Be careful, Emereck."

"I'll do the best I can. But if someone like Kensal or Ryl tries to take it, I'll have to try to stop him."

Liana gave him a sidelong look. "That wasn't quite what I meant," she murmured. Emereck looked at her in puzzlement, but she did not enlarge on her statement. They walked the rest of the way to the castle in silence.

Fourteen

*E*mereck set a quick pace for the walk back to Castle Minathlan. Liana did not object, and the return trip took very little longer than the outgoing walk had taken. By the time they reached the castle, they were both panting from the exertion. Inside the gate, they paused to catch their breath. "I think that's the quickest trip I've ever made," Liana said. "They won't be expecting us yet."

"Where would Flindaran be at this time of day?" Emereck asked as soon as he could speak easily again.

"It depends on what Gendron has him doing," Liana replied. She frowned, thinking. Emereck glanced around and saw Kiannar crossing the courtyard. He waved, and she turned and came to join them. "Good day, Sword-Wielder," Emereck said as soon as she was within hearing.

"And good day to you as well, Minstrel," Kiannar replied. She nodded a greeting to Liana and went on, "And what service may I do for you and my sister?"

"I'm looking for Flindaran," Emereck said. "Have you seen him?"

"Yes I believe he was looking for you."

"Looking for me?" Emereck said, puzzled.

124

"I saw him heading toward your rooms a few minutes ago," Kiannar said. She gave him one of her unfathomable looks. "Talerith was with him."

"But Flindaran knew I was—" Emereck broke off.

"I may have been wrong. Perhaps they were going somewhere else."

"Perhaps we should go see," Liana said quietly.

"Yes," Emereck said. He found Kiannar's news deeply disturbing. "Yes, let's go."

Together they hurried toward Emereck's room. As they rounded the last corner, Emereck saw with a jolt of foreboding that the guard, ordered by the Duke four days before and a fixture outside his door since then, was gone. He broke into a run. He flung open the door of his room and stood paralyzed.

Flindaran was crouched on one knee in front of the locked chest in the corner, prying at the lock with his dagger. Beside him, Talerith bent over his shoulder. Their heads turned as the door opened, and Talerith's expression changed from eagerness to chagrin. Flindaran froze, his face a mask of sick dismay. Emereck felt Kiannar and Liana come up behind him, and heard Liana's soft intake of breath as she realized the implications of the scene, but he could not stir.

Slowly, Flindaran rose. "Emereck, I . . . I . . ."

"I appear to be back earlier than you had expected," Emereck said around the tightness in his chest. Behind him, he heard Liana slip away from the door, and then the sound of her running footsteps. He wished fervently that he could join her. He saw Talerith tug urgently at Flindaran's arm, and wondered savagely how much of this was her doing.

"I—I thought I heard someone in here," Flindaran said.

"Yes, and we knew you weren't here," Talerith put in. "So we decided we'd better check."

"That's why your father put a guard outside my door," Emereck said pointedly. "I don't suppose you know where he is?"

"How should I? He wasn't there when we came by."

Talerith looked at Flindaran for support, but Flindaran did not appear to notice. His eyes never left Emereck.

"How interesting," Kiannar's voice said from behind Emereck. She pushed past him into the room. Her eyes swept past Talerith and settled on Flindaran. Flindaran stiffened. "And when did guards in this castle start leaving their posts without orders?" Kiannar asked him gently.

"Oh, he probably had some reason or other," Talerith said, tossing her head. "Does it matter? He wasn't here."

Kiannar raised her eyebrows. "And you just happened to be passing by. And just happened to hear something. And since you just happened to know that Emereck had left the castle, you decided to come in and see what it was."

Talerith looked at Kiannar haughtily. "That's right."

Flindaran's lips twitched, and Emereck looked away from the expression on Flindaran's face. His mind screamed at Kiannar, finish this! Finish it and go away.

Kiannar stepped forward and touched the scarred wood around the lock of the chest. "And I suppose you thought whoever you heard had hidden in the chest, and locked it behind him?" Her tone was very dry.

Flindaran's mouth twisted and he lunged at Kiannar with the dagger he still held. Kiannar sidestepped and backed away, without reaching for her own weapons. Talerith screamed. Emereck leaped forward and grabbed Flindaran's free arm. "Flindaran, are you mad? She's your sister!"

With a snarl, Flindaran swung around and aimed a stroke at Emereck. His face was contorted with anger, humiliation, and something that might have been shame. Emereck felt a stab of fear; he was no match for Flindaran in a fight. Light glinted off the blade of the dagger, and he threw himself down and sideways to avoid the blow. His weight swung Flindaran around; then he lost his grip on Flindaran's arm and fell heavily.

The sudden release threw Flindaran out of balance. He staggered, attempting to regain it, and tripped over

Emereck's legs. Emereck saw the dagger's blade flash again as Flindaran threw his hands out in an unsuccessful attempt to catch himself. With a grunt of surprise or pain, Flindaran fell forward into a chair. The chair went over with a loud crash, and then there was silence.

Emereck pulled himself to his feet and started forward. He had no clear idea of what he intended to do; he felt only a sudden fear that was even greater than his grief over Flindaran's second betrayal. Kiannar was before him; Emereck reached Flindaran's side just as the warrior-woman lifted his shoulders and gently turned him over. "Flindaran," Emereck began, and stopped as he saw the spreading red stain around the dagger hilt protruding from Flindaran's chest. "No," he said in a stunned whisper. "Please, no!"

Talerith screamed again. Kiannar ignored her and lowered Flindaran carefully to the floor. She looked up at someone behind Emereck and said grimly, "Get a healer, and hurry."

The room seemed suddenly full of people. A guard stooped to exchange words with Kiannar, then hurried away. Talerith was weeping noisily somewhere in the background, and Emereck could hear Gendron's voice giving orders. Part of his mind wondered how Flindaran's brother had arrived so quickly. Then Flindaran's eyes opened, and Emereck forgot about everything else.

"Kay?" Flindaran said fretfully.

"Don't move," Kiannar told him. "You've got a dagger stuck in your chest."

"Not yours."

"Your own. You fell."

"Yes. I remember." Flindaran grimaced, half in pain, half in disgust. "What a stupid thing to—" A racking cough cut his sentence short, and his face seemed to grow more ashen as Emereck watched. Kiannar held his shoulders still until the spasm passed, then wiped a thin froth of blood from his lips. Flindaran's eyes followed her hand with a dispassionate gaze, then looked at Emereck. "The Harp," he said in a fading whisper.

For a long, shocked moment, Emereck could only

imagine that Flindaran, even now, wanted to possess the Harp. He stared in disbelief, then comprehension came. The Harp of Imach Thyssel could heal! Why hadn't he thought of that himself? He started up, then froze as another realization hit him. To heal Flindaran, Emereck would have to play the Harp, and pay whatever price it required. He couldn't do it! But Flindaran . . . He looked down, and the gray pain on Flindaran's face decided him. Whatever price the Harp demanded, it could not be half as great as the one he would pay for not using it. Emereck rose and started forward.

A second coughing spasm shook Flindaran, and Emereck looked back. Flindaran caught his eyes and tried to smile. "I'm sorry, Emereck," he whispered, and died.

Numbly, Emereck stared down at Flindaran's face. He was distantly aware of Talerith's hysterical sobbing, of Kiannar's hand gently removing the dagger from Flindaran's chest, of Gendron's voice giving orders. They did not reach him. He was alone in his mind with Flindaran's corpse and the knowledge that he, Emereck, was to blame for this. If he had thought of the Harp's healing abilities sooner, if he had not hesitated when Flindaran suggested it . . . But the Harp had never been an instrument of healing to Emereck; he had seen it only as a powerful, dangerous weapon to be safeguarded and kept from the wrong hands, never used. Now it was too late. Even magic could not bring back the dead. Emereck bowed his head, and tears spilled unheeded down his face.

The sound of a low-voiced conversation behind him brought him back to a consciousness of his surroundings. It had been going on for some time, but now a snatch of it penetrated. Emereck rose hastily to his feet and turned. Gendron, Kiannar and Talerith were grouped just inside the doorway; in the hall behind them stood Liana along with several guards and castle servants.

"It wasn't Kiannar's fault, Lord Gendron," Emereck said when they stopped talking and looked at him. It took all his training to keep his voice calm and steady, but he succeeded. "Flindaran attacked her; she never pulled out her own weapons at all."

"I know," Gendron said.

"You know?"

"Liana brought me; unfortunately I didn't quite get here in time. I saw the end of it, though."

Emereck heard the grief in Gendron's voice, and he looked down to keep himself from crying again. He heard Gendron turn away and say, "He's right, Kiannar. It's not your fault."

"No," Talerith said venomously. "It's his fault!"

Startled, Emereck looked up. Talerith was pointing at him. Her face was blotched from crying, and damp straggles of hair hung limply about her neck. "It's his fault!" she said again, and Emereck could hear the edge of hysteria in her voice.

"Be quiet! You've done enough for one day," Kiannar said.

"I will not be quiet! That Harp was Flindaran's! If this Minstrel hadn't taken it, none of this would have happened!"

"Talerith—" Gendron started, but she ignored him.

"He tripped Flindaran because he was afraid to fight! You were here, you can't deny it."

"It was an accident, Talerith."

"It was not! He wanted Flindaran to die so he could keep the Harp! That's why he wouldn't use it to heal him. You saw, you all saw! Flindaran begged him, and he wouldn't! It's his fault."

"Liana, get her out of here," Gendron said over his shoulder.

"I won't go! Not until you take the Harp away from him. It's not his, it's Flindaran's!" Talerith burst into racking sobs. Liana slipped around beside her and began murmuring soothingly, though her own cheeks still glistened with tears. Gendron made a summoning gesture at the guards; two of them stepped forward and began easing Talerith toward the door. "No!" Talerith cried again. "I won't go!"

"I am afraid you will," Gendron said.

"You can't let him keep that Harp!"

"What happens to the Harp is my decision, not yours. In the meantime, you will leave." Gendron's tone was very like Lord Dindran's. Talerith turned and stared. Their eyes locked, a moment later hers dropped and she grudgingly allowed herself to be led away. Gendron's shoulders sagged very slightly as she went out of sight. Then he straightened and turned back to Emereck. His face was stiff as he studied the minstrel. "She has a point, you know," Gendron said at last.

"Duke Dindran has recognized my claim to the Harp," Emereck said as calmly as he could.

"It's not your claim I question. But leaving that thing in your hands is asking for trouble, I think." Gendron glanced briefly in the direction Talerith had taken.

"You can't seriously believe—"

"Hear me out. I propose putting that chest, Harp and all, under triple guard in the armory until my father returns. That should prevent any further . . . mishaps, and it may stop Talerith from spreading too many rumors. You can keep the keys, if you like. Father will be back in a day or two, and then this can all be settled."

"But the Harp isn't—" Emereck stopped short. "I don't appear to have much choice in the matter," he said at last.

Gendron seemed relieved as he nodded to the remaining guards. Emereck watched as they tested the lock to make sure it was still secure, then hoisted the chest and left the room. The servants followed to remove Flindaran's body, and soon the only sign of the recent tragedy was a damp, scrubbed area on the floor.

When the last of the servants was gone, Gendron turned to leave. In the doorway he stopped and looked at Emereck. "If you'd like a different room . . ."

"Later, perhaps. Now I'd just . . . like to be alone."

Gendron nodded and left. The door closed behind him with grim finality. Emereck stood staring at it for a long time, wondering what to do now. He had allowed Gendron to confiscate a locked chest full of linen; the

Harp itself was still resting safely in the bottom of Emereck's wardrobe, where he had moved it the day before. He would have to do something before the deception was discovered, and there was no one he could turn to for help. His only friend in Minathlan was dead, and he himself was to blame. Emereck had never felt so alone in his life.

Fifteen

*F*or a long time, Emereck stared out the window with unseeing eyes. There was no room in his mind for anything but memories and grief. At last he began to pace. Unconsciously, he avoided the scrubbed place on the floor where Flindaran's body had lain, though doing so gave his pacing a crooked track.

On his twenty-ninth trip past the doorway, Emereck's mind began working again. He stopped and stood motionless for several seconds, then turned. With a jerk, he opened the wardrobe and began emptying its contents on the bed.

He had to leave. He did not know how he was going to get out of Minathlan; he only knew he must go and at once. He hated this castle, had hated it even before Flindaran's death, and now . . . He pulled the last of his belongings from the wardrobe and lifted out the Harp of Imach Thyssel. The sooner he got away from this place, the better.

He stared at the Harp, wondering how he was going to smuggle it out of the castle. He could put it in the harp case, but that would mean abandoning his own, ordinary instrument. Emereck thought of making the long journey to Ciaron without a harp he dared to practice on, and pressed his lips together. No. The Harp of Imach Thyssel had destroyed his friendship and killed his friend; he would not let it steal his music as well. He would have to find another way.

If he could disguise the shape somehow . . . Emereck studied the clothes strewn across the bed for a moment, then set to work. By using every bit of clothing and bedding he owned, he eventually achieved a large, shapeless bundle that gave no hint of the Harp inside. He was nearly finished when he heard a soft knock on the door.

"A moment!" he called, and hurriedly knotted the last wrappings in place. He rose and dusted off his knees, then went to the door.

It was Liana, looking pale but composed. "I'm sorry to disturb you," she said before he could collect his wits, "but I'm afraid it's important. May I come in?"

"Of course," Emereck replied automatically, and stepped aside. Too late, he remembered the bundle sitting in the middle of the floor, where Liana could not miss seeing it. So much for any chance of slipping out of the castle unnoticed, he thought, and turned.

Liana was staring at the bundle with a blank expression. As Emereck turned, she looked up and said, "You're leaving. Someone was here before me, then?"

"No one has been here since—" Emereck paused. "—since Gendron left earlier."

"Then why?" Liana gestured at the bundle.

"I can't stay. Surely you see that."

"I understand, but—" Liana stopped. "I'm sorry. I'm doing this all wrong."

"I beg your pardon?"

Liana sighed. "I came because . . . because I don't think it's safe for you to stay here, even if you don't have the Harp any more."

"Why not?"

"Because of Talerith. She—" Liana hesitated.

"She continues her accusations, then."

"I'm afraid so. I've never seen her like this before!

She's demanding that Gendron have you locked up. She hates you, Emereck."

"Do you think she will succeed in persuading Gendron?" Emereck asked, trying to conceal his concern. If he were arrested now, his deception with the Harp was sure to be discovered and he might never get away from Minathlan.

Liana shook her head. "It's not that. Gendron knows what Talerith is like. But Flindaran was popular, and it's no secret that there's been trouble between the two of you these last few days. Talerith sounds reasonable enough, and she's the Duke's daughter. And there are one or two of the guards who would be glad of the chance to demonstrate their loyalty to her, even if it meant doing . . . something rash."

Emereck stared. He could not believe what he was hearing. Yet . . . he could think of half a dozen songs of soldiers and men-at-arms who had dispensed their own justice in a king's absence, or disposed of someone who was an embarrassment to their lord. "Black Dawn in Tarrabeth," for instance, and "Captain Var ri Astar"— he'd sung that one at Talerith's feast. It was, just barely, possible.

And if he were killed? Unlike Ciaron and Alkyra, the lands around Kith Alunel held a minstrel no higher than any other craftsman. His death would be an unfortunate incident for Duke Dindran to explain to the guild, no more. Under the circumstances, no one would ask many questions. A minstrel involved in the death of a nobleman would be an embarrassment to everyone. Emereck felt suddenly cold. "Lord Gendron can do nothing?"

"He's trying, but things are . . . rather tense. It would be easier for him if you took a room at the inn for a while, and safer for you."

"I see." Emereck saw indeed. Liana might be concerned for his safety, but he had no illusions about Gendron. The Duke's heir had seen how the Harp of Imach Thyssel could obsess people; he was taking no chance that Emereck might follow Flindaran's example and try to steal it back.

"It's just until the Duke returns," Liana went on. "And that Harp of yours really will be safe in the armory. Gendron's already spoken to the guards. They won't let anyone in until Duke Dindran comes home."

"Lord Gendron thinks of everything," Emereck said dryly. "It's as well that I'd already decided to leave."

Liana bit her lip and did not answer. Emereck turned and picked up his harp case, then hefted the bundle that hid the Harp of Imach Thyssel, and followed Liana out of the room.

Emereck's horse was waiting in the courtyard. Gendron had clearly been thorough in his preparations for the minstrel's departure; equally clearly, he had no intention of giving Emereck any chance to stay at the castle. Emereck smiled sourly as he took the reins from a sullen guard. Gendron could have no idea how anxious Emereck was to cooperate in this particular plan.

He turned and bowed to Liana. "I thank you and your family for your hospitality, lady," he said formally. "Convey my thanks to your brother."

"I'll come with you," Liana said quickly. Emereck looked at her, and she blushed slightly. "To see you settled at the inn. Gendron will want me to make sure the arrangements are satisfactory."

"Lord Gendron is kind," Emereck said with a touch of irony, "but it is unnecessary."

"I think he feels he owes you something after all this."

Emereck shook his head. "That's not what I meant. I won't be going to the inn."

"But there isn't anywhere else."

"Not in Minathlan. But there's no reason for me to stay here, not now."

"What about the Harp?"

"As you said, it's safe enough where it is," Emereck said without meeting her eyes. "And sooner or later someone will have to report all this to the Guild. I'd rather do it sooner and take whatever penalty they give me."

"Penalty?"

"This whole affair has been a mess from the beginning, and it's my own fault. I should never have brought the Harp to Minathlan. And I doubt the Guild Masters will approve of many of the things I've done here."

"Flindaran's death wasn't your fault," Liana said softly.

"It was, but it's not only that." He paused, searching for the right words to explain the long list of his mistakes and failures. He did not find them. "There are other things," he said lamely.

Liana looked at him. "Couldn't you wait until the Duke gets back? He won't blame you for what happened."

"I doubt that," Emereck said, thinking of his encounters with Duke Dindran. "But that doesn't really matter. I'm not leaving because of your father." Belatedly, it occurred to him that Liana might have accepted that excuse. The Duke was certainly formidable enough to intimidate most people.

"Then why *do* you want to leave?"

"Because I can't stay! There's nothing to keep me here." Even as he said the words, Emereck knew they were not entirely true. Leaving Minathlan would be a relief and a pleasure, but leaving Liana . . .

"I see." Liana studied him gravely. Finally she sighed. "Then I'll come with you."

"*What*?" Emereck's jaw dropped.

"I'm coming with you," Liana repeated composedly.

"But you can't just leave your family and go wandering around the country with no one but a minstrel for company!"

"Why not?" Liana sounded mildly curious.

"You're the Duke's daughter!"

"One of them. I'm afraid I don't see what that has to do with my coming with you, though."

"Lord Gendron won't allow it."

"Gendron has no choice in the matter. He can't tell me what to do and what not to do, and he knows it." Liana looked at him with a glimmer of amusement in her eyes. "Which is more than I can say for you."

Emereck swallowed and tried again. "Why do you want to come with me?"

"You don't know?" Liana looked at him. "Then let's just say it's my duty."

"That's ridiculous! How can it be?"

"You are—You were Flindaran's friend. And someone has to tell your Guild Masters what really happened here."

"I'll do that myself."

"You'll take all the blame," Liana pointed out. "That's not right, and it's not true. So I'll come with you, and explain."

"Your father—"

"Duke Dindran would expect it of me."

Emereck stared, then shook himself. The thought of the Harp of Imach Thyssel burned in his mind; if he let Liana accompany him, it would be almost impossible for him to keep her from discovering it. "It's a long, dangerous trip. You can't go so far with only me for an escort."

"I can, and I will," Liana said calmly.

"I don't want your company!" Emereck almost shouted the lie, trying to make up in volume what he lacked in sincerity.

Liana's face went very still, then she shook her head. "I'm sorry, but you're going to have it anyway," she said firmly. She turned to one of the guards, who had been observing the argument with interest, and began giving him instructions.

Emereck stared at her for a long moment, trying to memorize every detail of her appearance. Then he swung himself into the saddle. "Not if I can help it," he said, and kicked his horse into motion. He caught a glimpse of Liana's hurt, startled expression, and the surprised and angry faces of the guards, and then he was through the gate and riding down the hill toward the town. The horse went faster than was truly safe on such a slope, but Emereck did not draw in his reins until he was well away from both castle and village.

He rode south until he was out of sight of Minathlan,

hoping that Gendron, or anyone else who might be watching, would think he was heading for Kith Alunel. When Minathlan was safely below the horizon, he turned off the road and headed west. Soon he was hidden among the grassy, rolling hills, and he relaxed slightly.

He did not make camp until it was too dark to continue riding. It could hardly even be called making camp, he reflected; he had no provisions for himself or his horse, and he did not even dare to light a fire. If Gendron had sent anyone after him, it would certainly attract their attention. All Emereck could do was gather a few armloads of the long grass, one for his own bed and the rest for his horse.

When he finished caring for his horse, he rolled himself in his cloak and sat staring into the moonless darkness. The wind whispered through the dead stalks of last year's grasses, and the stars were bright and cold. The night had Flindaran's face; even when he closed his eyes, Emereck could not escape it.

Finally Emereck rose and opened his harp case. The polished wood felt warm and familiar to his touch. Harp in hand, he climbed a small hill nearby. He seated himself, facing north and east toward Minathlan, and lifted the instrument. His hands moved surely in the darkness, playing a soft, mournful accompaniment to the wind.

At last he hushed the harpstrings and paused. Elewyth was rising, nearly full now, and the night was quiet, as though it waited for something. Emereck bowed his head and began to play once more. After a time, he realized that the tears were streaming down his face. He turned his head aside to keep from wetting his strings, and let them fall as the music of the "Varnan Lament for the Dead" hung in the air around him.

Shalarn stood in the gathering twilight, arms outstretched, weaving the warding spells around her camp. At last she lowered her hands, and nodded to herself. The spell would hold against all but the most powerful of magics, and she was sure to notice if something that strong were used against it.

She turned and walked wearily toward the fire her guards had made. "You seem tired, my lady," her Captain said as she seated herself.

"Magic can be wearing," Shalarn said dryly.

"Is it really necessary for you to drain yourself this way?"

"Of course it is necessary! Whoever has been causing these delays has not given up."

"How can you be sure?"

"Three times last night I felt someone lurking around the edges of my spell, testing it. It is not the sort of thing I could be mistaken about."

"Yes, my lady," the Captain said stiffly.

Shalarn looked at him and sighed. He was her equal by blood, if not quite in birth, and he was her only real confidant. She did not want to alienate him. "Your pardon, Captain. It is difficult to be polite when I am so exhausted."

"It is nothing. But whom do you suspect?"

"It has to be someone from Lanyk's court, but beyond that, I do not know."

"Could it be Prince Lanyk?"

"I have no doubt that he is behind it, but there must be someone else. He is no sorcerer."

"His wife, perhaps?" The Captain seemed dubious even as he made the suggestion, and Shalarn laughed.

"Tammis? No. Even if she had the courage to try something, it wouldn't be magic. She's some sort of Cilhar, and they're warriors, not sorcerers."

"One of the courtiers, then."

Shalarn nodded. "But which? Think of it, Captain, and if you come to any conclusion tell me later. Right now I wish to rest."

The Captain nodded and fell silent, but the conversation would not leave Shalarn's mind so easily. Who was tracking her? She had seen no sign of magic during her stay with Lanyk, not even a simple warding spell. This sorcerer was either very good or very, very subtle indeed.

Frowning, Shalarn stared into the fire, but that last, unwelcomed thought would not go away. She turned over in her mind the things this sorcerer had done: the small but effective mishaps that had delayed her, the careful probing of her wards, the rusted nail inscribed with the Rune of Separation. Very good, and very subtle. Shalarn shivered and drew her cloak closer around her shoulders, though the night was warm and windless.

The interior of the tent was dark and curiously silent. The noise of men and horses moving outside was muffled, as if the sound were coming from a great distance. In the center of the tent stood a small table of polished mahogany. A tall figure in a hooded cloak sat beside it, bending in concentration over a black mirror.

Light flared suddenly, hard and cold, throwing sharp-edged shadows against the canvas walls. The mirror lit up with a harsh blue-white light that moved like a living thing across its surface. For an instant, a dim, wavering picture formed: a dark-haired woman seated before a fire, pulling a cloak more closely about her. Then it was gone.

The hooded figure sat back and let the unnatural light die away from the surface of the black mirror. No use to try it again. The Lithmern sorceress had set her wards thoroughly. It was a pity she had found the nail. She was suspicious now, and more careful; it would be difficult to slow her any further.

Still, the delays had served their purpose. Lanyk should be at least a day ahead of Shalarn by now, perhaps more. As long as he didn't bungle things, the Prince of Syaskor would have the focus of this power very soon. And once he brought it back, he could be disposed of.

A slender hand put back the hood of the cloak, revealing the brown hair and dark eyes of Tammis, Princess of Syaskor. Her lips were curved slightly in anticipation. Lanyk was in for a very unpleasant surprise.

* * *

The Duke of Minathlan frowned into the night. Behind him, his two guards were putting wood on the fire and feeding the horses. At last he turned to join them, but he had taken only one step when a voice came out of the sprinkling of trees behind him. "Good hunting to you, my lord Duke."

"Ah, Welram," the Duke said, without a trace of surprise. "I had begun to fear you were not coming."

"Your news was irresistible," the other said. He came forward, and the firelight gleamed on pointed teeth in a face that was vaguely catlike and entirely unhuman. Dark brown fur covered his face and arms, and his ears were the shape of a fox's amid a dark mane of hair. The top of his head did not quite reach the Duke's shoulder.

"I thought the Wyrds of Vallafana's Forest would find it interesting. Will you be returning to Minathlan with me?"

"You would find it difficult to keep me away."

The Duke smiled. "Very good. I will give you more details over dinner, if you will join me."

"I would be pleased." The two turned and went together toward the Duke's men. As they seated themselves by the fire, a gold ring flashed on Welram's hand. The design on it was of a tree, with three moons tangled in its branches.

Ryl let out a long, slow breath and opened her eyes. Kensal relaxed fractionally and handed her a cup of water. He waited in silence until she set it aside. "Well?" he asked at last.

Ryl shook her head. "It is as you guessed, or nearly so. Flindaran tried to steal the Harp at his sister's urging, and was discovered. In the quarrel that followed, he fell on his own knife, and died."

"You're sure about that? It sounds a little too . . . convenient."

"I am sure. Did I not tell you that the Harp does not move easily away from one unwilling to give it freely?"

"So the minstrel still has it."

Ryl nodded. "He has it. And he has taken it out of Minathlan."

Kensal raised an eyebrow. "That's hard to believe. Gendron would be a fool to let it happen, especially now."

"Nevertheless the Harp is gone." Ryl's voice was calm and certain. "It moves west toward the Mountains of Morravik and your home."

"All right, then. When do we leave?"

"We do not. The Duke returns tomorrow eve; I would be here when he arrives. There are matters I wish to speak of with him."

"You make having a little chat with a Duke sound easy," Kensal said. "And I thought that getting that Harp was important."

"It is. But the Harp of Imach Thyssel is secret no longer. I sensed a presence as I . . . followed it. Perhaps more than one, I am not sure. If there are to be magicians involved in this, I may need an aid you cannot give me."

Kensal studied her. "The Shadow-born *are* part of this," he said flatly.

"I suspect it."

"And you think the Duke of Minathlan can help against them? What does he know of magic?"

"More than you may think," Ryl replied. "There are traces in this town, recent ones. Though I doubt that the Duke himself is the source of what I have seen." She smiled, as though she considered the idea humorous for some private reason.

"As you will. But I grow tired of this waiting."

"Then it's as well I have another task for you; I would not have you grow bored in my service."

"Boring is very nearly the last word I would use to describe it," Kensal said with an exaggerated sigh. "What do you have in mind?"

"Follow the minstrel. He does not realize how near to danger he is. I think you can overtake him. He has but half a day's start of you."

Kensal grinned fiercely. "I can catch him. But what

do I tell him when I do? He's no fool; I doubt that he'll trust me."

"Tell him the truth, as much of it as he will hear."

"Ryl, are you sure?"

"The time for secrecy is passing. And I think nothing less will convince him of our need in time."

"If he can still be convinced."

Ryl nodded soberly. "Yes. If he can be convinced."

Sixteen

*E*mereck lay still, trying to recapture the dream he had been having. It had been important, he was sure, though he could not have said why. There had been music in it, and tall, gentle people with golden skin, and strange moonlight . . . He sighed as the memory slipped away, and became aware of a crackling sound nearby, and a smell of something cooking that made his mouth water. His eyes flew open, and he blinked in disbelief.

A circular area a few yards away had been cleared of grass and weeds, and a small fire burned cheerfully in its center. Two birds, pigeons perhaps, were suspended over the flames on a small but sturdy wooden spit. Liana sat on the opposite side of the fire, watching the birds cook. Beyond, a dapple-gray mare grazed beside Emereck's horse.

"Good morning, minstrel," Liana said calmly as Emereck sat up, staring.

"Liana, what are you doing here?" Emereck demanded.

"Cooking breakfast," Liana replied. "I hope you like plains-duck; there isn't much else to be found around here."

"That's not what I meant! How did you find me?"

Liana smiled. "I wasn't more than an hour or two behind you. And I'm afraid you're no plainsman; your trail was rather obvious."

Emereck looked at the almost featureless expanse of grass and weeds that surrounded them. "It was?"

"For someone who has grown up around Minathlan, it was. I caught up with you last night, but I . . . didn't think you would want to be disturbed then."

She must have heard his harping. Emereck looked at her and became suddenly aware that he had fallen asleep in his traveling clothes, still covered with the grime of yesterday's journey, and that he was in need of a shave as well as breakfast. He pushed the thought to the back of his mind and said, "You shouldn't be here."

"You made your opinion rather obvious yesterday," Liana said, studying the two birds intently. She leaned forward and adjusted their position, then went on, "But I happen to disagree with you. Besides, you left without taking any provisions, and I thought you might need a few."

"You brought those from Minathlan?" Emereck asked, nodding at the plains-ducks.

"No, I shot them early this morning." She glanced down, and for the first time Emereck noticed a bow and a quiver of arrows on the ground beside her.

"Oh." Emereck had a hard time envisioning Liana shooting anything, but the evidence was unmistakable.

"The Duke insists that all of his family learn to use a bow," Liana said. "It's a tradition of some sort. I'm not as good as Kiannar or Oraven, but I'm better than Gendron. Talerith is just hopeless, but the Duke makes her try anyway."

"I can imagine."

"So I went hunting this morning," Liana continued. "I thought we should save what's in my packs, in case we can't find any game later."

Emereck shook his head. "There isn't going to be a later."

"I beg your pardon?"

"I'm taking you back to Minathlan."

"How?"

"What?"

"How are you going to take me back?" Liana repeated patiently. "You can't very well tie me to my horse, you know, and I can't think of any other way you could manage it."

"I don't believe you'll stay out here alone if I head back," Emereck said, trying to sound more confident than he felt.

Liana tilted her head, considering. "No, I don't suppose I would." Emereck let out a breath of relief. Liana smiled and said, "I'd go on to Kith Alunel, alone. Though I'm afraid it would make things a bit awkward for you when you got back to Minathlan; Gendron would certainly want some sort of explanation."

"What *will* Gendron say about this?"

"Very little, I should think. I talked to him before I left, and he said most of it then." Liana bent forward to examine the cooking birds. "He was almost as difficult as you're being, but he gave in eventually."

"I can't take you with me!" Emereck had to exert all his willpower to keep from glancing at the bundle beside his horse that contained the Harp of Imach Thyssel. It was a good thing he had not taken time to make a proper camp the previous night after all. If he had loosened any of the careful wrappings around the Harp, Liana would surely have noticed it at once.

"You aren't taking me anywhere. I'm coming with you on my own," Liana said. "Now, if you've quite finished your objections, why don't we eat? I'm starving!"

They rode west all morning. At first Emereck was silent, brooding over Flindaran's death, and the Harp, and especially over his failure to dissuade Liana from accompanying him. He had protested throughout breakfast and breaking camp, using every argument he could think of. Liana countered them all with an air of sweet reason that came near to making him wonder whether *he* was the one being irrational.

Liana glanced at him several times as they rode, but did not intrude on his thoughts except to point out very gently whenever he began to drift from the direction he had chosen. After her second correction, Emereck abandoned the vague notion he had entertained of leading her in a circle and so getting her back to Minathlan. Liana was coming with him, and there was nothing he could do about it.

Actually, he reflected, Liana could easily be an asset on the journey. She clearly knew the plains well, at least this close to Minathlan, and judging by breakfast, she was a good enough archer to supply occasional small game to supplement their dried provisions. Most of all, her presence was a welcome distraction from thoughts of the Harp, and of Flindaran. He wondered how long he could keep her from realizing that he was going to Ciaron and not to Kith Alunel, and what she would say when she found out.

It occurred to him that telling her his true destination might be all that was needed to make her return to Minathlan. Surely, she would not insist on accompanying him so far! He took a quick, speculative glance in Liana's direction. On the other hand, she was wonderfully stubborn. And she was sure to ask any number of awkward questions once she learned the truth. Better to postpone that confrontation as long as possible, and simply accept her company in the meantime.

He sneaked another glance, and found her watching him. Their eyes met, and suddenly Liana laughed. "I'm sorry," she said almost at once, "but it seems so silly for both of us to be trying to watch each other when we aren't looking!"

Emereck grinned reluctantly. "I apologize for being such a poor companion," he said. "I'll try to do better in the future."

"I don't know whether you should," Liana said thoughtfully. "It never seems to work when people try to be something they aren't."

"I beg your pardon?" Emereck said, considerably startled.

"Oh, I'm sorry! I didn't mean to imply that I think you're always a poor traveling companion. You couldn't be, or—" Liana stopped short.

"Or what?"

"Or Flindaran would have complained. He—he always did, you know, when he didn't like something."

"Yes." Emereck was silent for a moment. "Flindaran never had much patience." Suddenly he was intensely aware of Flindaran's absence. The journey was too similar to the last one he had made with Flindaran. The countryside, the sound of the horses, the very freshness of the air made him think of his friend, and know that Flindaran was not there, would never be there again . . .

"It reminds me of Ciaron," Emereck said at random.

Liana looked from him to the empty grasslands and back. "This is like Ciaron?"

"Well, not really. . . ."

Liana smiled. "Tell me about Ciaron."

"It's large and crowded," Emereck replied, grateful for the distraction. "There are always at least two Trader caravans passing through. There's a kind of permanent camp for them just inside the walls."

"Do the noblemen really put diamonds on their carriage wheels?"

"You're thinking of Rathane," Emereck said solemnly. "Ciaron is much more conservative; they never use anything more expensive than quartz on their carriages."

"You're joking!"

"Not at all," Emereck said, but he was unable to keep his face straight, and Liana laughed again. She had a very nice laugh, Emereck thought.

"All right, I won't ask foolish questions," Liana said. "But you will have to tell me what Ciaron is really like, and no more well-stretched stories!"

Emereck was quite willing to do so, and they spent the rest of the morning and much of the afternoon in conversation. He told her about the marketplace, where goods from all the lands around the Melyranne Sea were available for a price. He described the fish houses that surrounded the harbor, and the harbor itself, where the great ships floated carefully above the sunken ruins of an older city. He told her of the two-copper magicians, who performed by sleight of hand rather than by true magic, and of the Minstrel's Guildhall that was one of the best on Lyra. Flindaran's memory was a muted counterpoint to every part of Emereck's narrative.

They passed no villages during the day, and few houses. At least one of the houses they saw had been abandoned and was in the process of falling to pieces. Several birds flew out of the crumbling chimney as they approached, and the walls seemed to be sagging under the weight of the roof. They did not stop to investigate.

They traveled farther than Emereck had expected. By late afternoon they were passing occasional clumps of trees, harbingers of the forest for which they were heading. Near dusk, they chose a place and set about making camp. As they groomed the horses, Emereck wondered how he could unbundle his meager belongings without revealing the Harp to Liana. She would certainly think it strange if he slept another night in the clothes he was wearing, and it would be far from comfortable.

He was tempted to simply tell her he had the Harp, but the bitter lessons of recent experience held him back. Besides, they were still too close to Minathlan, and all Liana's loyalties must lie there.

He lowered his saddle to the ground next to his harp case and the somewhat bulky bundle that contained the Harp of Imach Thyssel. Perhaps if he asked Liana to hunt something for their dinner, she would be gone long enough for him to take care of his own needs and hide the Harp once more, as well as set up camp. It occurred to him suddenly that there might be some awkwardness about their sleeping arrangements for the night. After all, Liana was a Duke's daughter, however illegitimate, and Flindaran's sister as well. Not that he, Emereck, would presume . . . but would she know that?

Emereck glanced back toward the horses. Liana was standing on the other side of her mare. All Emereck could see were her boots and an occasional flash of her hair as she curried the horse's neck. He cleared his throat, then paused, not knowing how to begin or even what he wanted to say. He coughed, and cleared his throat again.

"Are you all right?" Liana called.

"Uh, yes, of course," Emereck said hastily.

"Well, you sound as if you're catching something." She leaned around her mare and peered at Emereck. "Maybe I should try to find some horehound. There's bound to be some around; it grows practically everywhere."

"Horehound? Why?"

"Horehound tea is good for coughs."

"I don't need—that is, there's no reason for you to put yourself out."

"Maybe you don't think so, but I'd rather not travel all the way to Kith Alunel with someone who's coughing and sneezing." Liana came around to Emereck's side of her mare and continued her currying.

"Oh." Emereck shifted uncomfortably, wondering why he felt so flustered. "I, um," he said, and stopped.

"What?" Liana looked over her shoulder, then turned and studied him for a moment. "You were going to say something?"

"I was wondering," Emereck said carefully, "where you wanted your bed laid out."

"It doesn't matter, as long as it's reasonably free of rocks and thistles. Why?"

Emereck felt his face growing warm. "I just thought you might have a, er, preference."

Liana stared at him, then smiled. "Oh, *now* I see what's bothering you! I'm sorry; I'm not usually so dense."

"Actually, I wasn't worried about myself."

"Well, you needn't fret on my account. I have quite a few brothers, and I've been camping with them before. You don't have to worry about 'offending my modesty,' or whatever the phrase is in Ciaron."

"I'm not your brother," Emereck said without thinking.

Liana gave him a brilliant smile. "I know."

"I didn't mean—"

"That's all right. I did." Liana grinned at his confusion. "I'm going to find something for dinner. Put the beds wherever you want them." She gave him a mischievous look, picked up her bow and arrows, and was out of hearing before Emereck could think of an adequate response.

Emereck stared after her, then realized that this was his chance to unwrap the Harp. Without enthusiasm, he went over to the small pile of his belongings, knelt, and began untying the knots that held his careful camouflage together. His thoughts were full of Liana; he hardly even noticed what his hands were doing.

Had she known what she was offering when she told him to put the beds wherever he wanted them? She must have; Liana was no fool. His breath caught at the thought, then, regretfully, he laid it aside. He had been the cause of trouble and division in her family since his arrival in Minathlan; he was responsible for her brother's death; he had taken the Harp of Imach Thyssel against her father's expressed commands. He had lied to her about where he was going and why, and because of those lies she was determined to come with him on this long and dangerous journey. He could not add to the list of wrongs between them by taking advantage of her offer now, however much he might want to. His fingers moved on the harpstrings to pluck the first sad chords of "The Swordsmith and the Lady," when he realized just what he was about to do.

He dropped the Harp and was on his feet in an instant. He stood two paces from the Harp, staring down at it, and waited for his shaking to stop. How could it have happened? He had been about to play the Harp of Imach Thyssel as if it were an ordinary instrument with no purpose but to make music, and he had not even noticed. He might have brought every wizard and thief between Kith Alunel and the Kathkari Mountains down on their heads. He might have told Duke Dindran what he had done and where he was. He might . . .

He might have played the Harp of Imach Thyssel.

Somehow, the thought did not terrify him as much as it had barely a few days before. His own carelessness frightened him far more than the Harp. He stepped forward and picked up the instrument. The ivory was cool and smooth against his palms, but he felt no urge to play it. That obsession had died with Flindaran.

He set the Harp down and covered it, then set about making camp. By the time Liana returned carrying a brace of rabbits, the Harp was safely rewrapped and Emereck was seated before a small fire, staring into the flames. She did not refer to their earlier conversation, though she must have noticed the two piles of grass on opposite sides of the fire. Emereck, watching her skin the rabbits she had brought, could not decide whether he was glad or sorry that she did not mention it.

Seventeen

*E*mereck was shaking—no, someone was shaking him. His eyes flew open and he saw Liana's face above him, washed in moonlight. But the nightmare still clung to him; she seemed to be melting into darkness as he watched. He sat up with a breath that was half sob, and realized that it was only a cloud crossing one of the moons. He waited until he was sure his voice would be steady, then said, "Thank you."

"You're welcome," Liana said. She hesitated, then went on, "I wasn't really sure whether I ought to wake you, but . . ."

"I'm glad you did. I managed to miss the worst part this way."

Liana hesitated. "This has happened before?"

"Yes, nearly every—" He stopped, staring into the night, going backward in his mind. "Nearly every night since we found that cursed Harp," he said slowly.

"How can it be the Harp?"

"I don't know. But it's the same dream, every night, and it started when we found the Harp."

"What do you dream?" Liana asked softly.

"I see a city, and tall people with golden skin and eyes. It is night, and Kaldarin is rising. Elewyth is just ahead of it, but most of the light comes from a silver moon that's bigger than either of them. Then something reaches out and touches the silver moon, and it . . . hurts. The air goes dark, and everything starts twisting. I see the golden people melting and . . . changing, and I know they are screaming but I can't hear them. It goes on, and on, and the silver moon cracks and falls and everything is dark, and it still won't stop—"

Liana laid a hand on his arm. For a long time they sat in silence. At last Liana shook herself. "It doesn't sound to me as if it has anything to do with the Harp. But I think it's just as well you had to leave it in Minathlan."

"Yes," Emereck said after a pause during which he carefully did not look at the place where the Harp lay hidden among his belongings. "I suppose it is."

They broke camp as soon as it was light and went on. The land was dry and dusty; here and there, great outcroppings of stone reared starkly above the plain. They reminded Emereck of bones, the bones of the world poking through a dry, dead skin. He decided that his nightmares were making him morbid, and tried to stop thinking about it.

Near mid-morning they stopped to rest the horses. Emereck paced restlessly while the animals grazed, unsure why he was so nervous but unable to keep still. Finally he left Liana sitting in the meager shade of one of the stones and climbed a small hill. He stood looking out over the plain, thinking of the Guildhall in Ciaron, of the songs he needed to practice, of anything except the Harp and Flindaran and the last few days at Castle Minathlan. At last he turned to rejoin Liana. Halfway down the hill, he halted abruptly. There was a small cloud of dust on the northern horizon.

Emereck ran the rest of the way. Liana looked at him in surprise until he pointed out what he had seen. She studied it briefly, then nodded. "Horses," she said. "Probably five or six of them, coming this way."

"One of your border patrols?" Emereck asked without much conviction.

"No, we're well past the borders of Minathlan by now."

"Then Gendron must have—"

"I don't think so. They're coming from the wrong direction to have ridden straight from the castle."

"Well, who do *you* think they are?" Emereck said crossly.

Liana frowned. "I suppose they could be from a Trader caravan, but I can't imagine what would bring one out here. Or they could be travelers."

"Or bandits," Emereck said. Or wizards, he added silently, or thieves, looking for the Harp. "And I don't want to stay here and find out which of us is right. Maybe we can outrun them."

"Running will just attract their attention," Liana objected.

"All right, we'll ride slowly," Emereck said over his shoulder as he walked toward the horses. "But let's go!"

They rode southwest, angling away from the approaching riders. For a time it seemed they had succeeded in keeping clear, but soon it became apparent that the riders had changed direction to intercept them. "I don't like this," Emereck said. "Come on."

He kicked his horse into a trot, then a canter. Liana followed. A few minutes later, Emereck heard her call, "They're gaining on us," and then, "Syaski soldiers!"

Emereck glanced back. He saw with shock how close the riders had gotten, and only then did he note their uniforms. He gestured at Liana to hurry and leaned forward to urge his own horse to greater speed. Together they crashed on through the tall grass. Emereck's world narrowed down into the heat of the sun on his back, the smell of dust and horses, the sea of waving grass ahead, and the sound of hooves like funeral drums, growing louder as the Syaski gained on them.

Emereck's horse began to falter. Desperately, he dug his heels into the animal's sides, but even as he did one of his pursuers passed him. Emereck twisted his reins, hoping to put a little distance between himself and the

Syask. His tired and thoroughly frightened mount did not respond in time. The Syaski horseman swerved in front of Emereck.

Emereck's horse shied, then plunged sideways. For the next several minutes, Emereck was completely occupied with trying to stay in the saddle; he had no attention to spare for what was happening, or even for thoughts of escape. When he finally succeeded in bringing the terrified horse under control, he and Liana were surrounded.

There were seven Syaski, all wearing similar uniforms of leather dyed a dark blue. Their horses formed a circle around Emereck and Liana, and a smallish, brown-haired man rode forward. Emereck saw Liana's eyes widen. "What is it?" he whispered.

"That's Prince Lanyk!" she hissed back, then fell silent as one of the soldiers fingered his sword hilt suggestively.

Lanyk studied them for a moment with the narrow-eyed gaze of a cat studying a mousehole. "Who are you?" he said at last. His voice reminded Emereck of a poorly-made melar—all surface polish and no depth of tone.

"Minstrel Emereck Sterren of the Ciaron Guildhall, my lord," Emereck said, half-bowing.

"And the lady?"

"Liana Dinfar, milord," Liana replied.

"And what are you doing out here that makes you so eager to avoid our company?" the Prince asked.

"Is it surprising that two travelers prefer not to encounter a larger group they know nothing of?" Emereck countered. "There are bandits—"

"Very few on these plains," Lanyk said, cutting him short. "Which you know, or you would not be traveling as two alone. Try again."

"Oh, tell him, Emereck," Liana said.

Emereck turned, surprised by the petulance in her voice, and intercepted a sharp look of warning. "But, Liana—" he began uncertainly.

"Then I will!" Liana turned to the Prince, and smiled.

"We thought you were from Minathlan, you see."

"From Minathlan?" Lanyk stared at her, nonplussed.

"Yes, from Minathlan. I was one of the waiting ladies for the Duke's daughter, Lady Talerith, and Minstrel Emereck has been playing there this past month, and we, well, we became friends." Liana looked down modestly, and one of the soldiers smothered a snicker.

Emereck held his face in a mildly anxious expression he hoped would be suitable for whatever tale Liana was spinning. Inwardly, he marveled at Liana's performance. She sounded flighty, thoughtless, entirely empty-headed, completely incapable of deceiving anyone. He wondered how many other unexpected talents she possessed, and whether she would be able to persuade Prince Lanyk to let them go.

"I don't see what Minathlan has to do with your running away from us," Lanyk said.

"But the Duke didn't like it!" Liana said as if it were the most obvious thing in the world.

"Like what?"

"Emereck and me! So we ran away. And of course when we saw you, I thought he, the Duke, I mean, had sent you to bring us back. You can't imagine how glad I was to be wrong." Liana gave the Prince of Syaskor another dazzling smile.

"And where are you running to?" Lanyk asked smoothly. "Not Kith Alunel, certainly, the way you were heading."

"Oh, that was Emereck's idea," Liana said blithely. "If we don't go straight there, the Duke won't be able to find us so easily."

"I see." Lanyk's smile held the faintest suspicion of a sneer. He turned and studied Emereck. Emereck tried to look innocuous. Lanyk's sneer grew more pronounced. "Forgive me for not offering to escort you on your way, but I have other business to attend to."

One of the soldiers, a small man wearing a somewhat more elaborate uniform than the others, cleared his throat. "My lord, shouldn't we go on? These don't seem to be the ones we're looking for, and you did say there wasn't much time."

"In a moment," Lanyk said without turning his head. "I wish to make certain." He reached inside his cloak and brought out a small box. He flipped it open, glanced down at it, and stiffened in his saddle. When he looked up, his eyes were hard and cold. "They have it. Get them off those horses and search their bags."

Emereck felt the words like blows in the stomach. To have been so close to escaping and then to lose everything . . . The Syaski were certain to find the Harp; what else could they be looking for? He hardly felt the hands pulling him from his horse. He had failed again, and in some ways this was the worst failure of all.

One of the Syaski held the horses while the others tramped down a circle of grass and began spreading out the contents of the saddlebags. They unwrapped the Harp of Imach Thyssel almost at once, but to Emereck's amazement, they continued their work as though it was of no importance. Liana gave Emereck a single, sidelong look when she saw it, then returned to contemplating her bow and arrows, lying just out of reach.

Lanyk grew visibly impatient as the work progressed. Finally he dismounted and walked among the clutter, watching the box in his hand. He hesitated briefly before a small bag that belonged to Liana, then went on. When he reached the Harp, he stopped and his lips parted in a humorless smile. "A harp," he said. "How appropriate."

"I don't understand. That's just—"

"Stop your games, minstrel!" Lanyk snapped. "It was clever of Dindran to hide it among a minstrel's belongings, I'll admit. Pity he wasn't clever enough to guess I'd have magic of my own to find it with." He waved the box in Emereck's direction, then flipped it closed and bent forward to pick up the Harp.

The air sang a hard, high note. Lanyk straightened, clutching at his throat. Emereck caught a glimpse of something black and sharp and spiky, and then Lanyk made a gurgling noise and toppled slowly sideways. Emereck stared, uncomprehending, while the soldiers around him drew their swords. He came out of his shock only when the man holding him jerked, choked, and fell to his knees, another of the black weapons embedded in his throat.

The man guarding Liana was down as well. "Run!" Emereck shouted. He dove toward the Harp of Imach Thyssel, hoping that whoever was throwing things would be too busy with the Syaski to worry about a mere minstrel.

One of the soldiers shouted as Emereck snatched up the Harp. Another swung at him. Emereck ducked and kept on running. From the corner of his eye he saw Liana running toward him, closely followed by one of the Syaski. He turned to shout a warning, and something swept his feet from under him.

As he went down, he twisted frantically to keep from falling on the Harp. He heard a loud clang above him, the sound of two swords meeting, and then he landed heavily on his side. He lay half-stunned, only distantly aware of the fighting going on immediately in front of him. His head began to clear a little, and he tried to push himself away from the conflict.

Something swished through the air above him. A Syask Emereck hadn't noticed before pitched forward across his legs, pinning them. The black tip of one of Liana's hunting arrows protruded from the Syask's back. Emereck shoved at the body, but the fighting was still going on in front of him, and he did not dare raise his head and arms enough to get good leverage.

He glanced quickly upward just as the Syask swordsman fell, run through, giving Emereck his first clear look at the other fighter. Emereck froze. It was Kensal Narryn.

There were only two Syaski left. One was directly in front of Kensal; the other was hovering indecisively halfway between Kensal and Liana. Kensal pulled a dagger from his belt with his left hand and faced them. "You know what I am," he said. "You had better lay down your weapons."

One of the men wavered visibly, but the other looked at Kensal with hatred fueled by fear. "Surrender to a

Cilhar? We are Syaski! We'll die first."

"As you will have it, then," Kensal replied, and stepped forward. His sword seemed to blur in his hand; Emereck did not even see the stroke that ended the Syask's life. An instant later there was a dull thud, followed by a cry, and the last Syask fell, Kensal's dagger buried in his chest.

Kensal bent to wipe his sword, and Emereck saw him shake his head. Then Liana's voice, slightly shaky but still clear, called, "Don't move, Cilhar. Not at all."

"Certainly," Kensal said. "Anything to be obliging."

"Emereck? Emereck, are you—"

"I'm all right," Emereck called, wriggling out from under the dead Syask. "A little battered, that's all." He braced his legs to keep from trembling with reaction, and stood up.

Liana, white-faced but determined, stood ten paces away, aiming an arrow at Kensal. "Emereck . . ."

"I would appreciate it if you would aim elsewhere, lady," Kensal said in a conversational tone. "Failing that, I would at least like to straighten up. This position is somewhat uncomfortable."

"Drop your sword, then," Emereck said.

Kensal opened his hand and the sword fell. "And now?"

"You can stand up." Emereck picked up the Harp and made a wide circle around Kensal to Liana's side. Kensal watched with an expression suspiciously like amusement. Emereck wondered what to do with the Cilhar. They couldn't stand there watching him all day.

"What are you doing out here?" Emereck demanded at last.

"Following you," Kensal replied promptly. "And it seems to be a good thing I was. You'd be dead and Lanyk would be riding north with that Harp by now, if I hadn't."

"You're after the Harp, too, then," Emereck said wearily.

Kensal hesitated. "In a manner of speaking. But I'm not fool enough to try to steal it from you or take it by force. I'll swear to that, if you like."

Liana's arms were beginning to tremble from the strain of keeping the bow drawn. Emereck sighed. "Swear."

"I swear before the Mother of Mountains that I will not take the Harp of Imach Thyssel from you unless you give it to me freely and in full knowledge. Is that sufficient?"

Emereck nodded, and Liana lowered her bow with a sigh of relief. Kensal smiled, then bent and picked up his sword. He wiped it carefully before sheathing it. Then he looked up. "I suggest we clean up a bit and then find a place to sit down and be comfortable. I think we have a lot to discuss."

Eighteen

*K*ensal began his "cleaning up" by retrieving his dagger, wiping it carefully, and returning it to its sheath. Then he crossed to the nearest body and removed the spiked throwing weapon.

"What *are* those things?" Emereck said.

"They're called raven's-feet." Kensal plucked another of the black spiky-looking things from the next Syask's throat and held it out for Emereck's inspection.

Emereck swallowed and took it. It was deceptively simple. A small steel ball formed the center from which four slender spikes protruded, each as long as Emereck's middle finger. The spikes were arranged so that no matter how the thing was dropped, it would rest on three of them with the fourth pointing straight up. One of the spikes was wet with blood. Hastily, Emereck handed it back, and Kensal went on with his task.

"Do you want your arrow?" Kensal asked Liana when he had collected his arsenal.

"No," Liana said. "I never want to see it again."

Kensal turned and studied her. "It's not the fault of the arrow that the man is dead."

"I know." Liana still looked rather white. "But I—I've never killed a person before. I'd rather not be reminded."

"These," Kensal pointed out, "are Syaski."

Liana turned away. Emereck glared at Kensal. "You could at least try to understand, Cilhar."

Kensal shrugged. "I understand that they would have killed you if I hadn't been here. Don't ask a Cilhar to grieve for Syaski; we have seven centuries of reasons not to."

"It's all right, Emereck," Liana said hastily. "I mean, it's too late to change now, so there's no point in my fretting about it."

"You're sure?" Emereck said.

"Yes." Liana straightened her shoulders and looked at Kensal. "And I'll take my arrow back."

Kensal smiled and handed it to her. "And perhaps you would be kind enough to retrieve your horses." He waved at the Syaski mounts, which had scattered during the fight. Liana looked at him without moving. Kensal sighed. "Someone must do it, and I don't know which horses are yours. We'll be on our way more quickly if you collect them while your friend and I take care of the bodies."

Liana bit her lip. "All right, then."

"What's your hurry?" Emereck asked Kensal as Liana started off toward the horses.

Kensal gave him a look. "If you think Prince Lanyk was wandering around this far from home with only six guards and no luggage to speak of, you don't know much about rulers."

"You mean there are likely to be more of them?" Emereck said.

"It's not likely, it's certain. Come help me with these." Kensal bent over the nearest body and began dragging it toward one side of the trampled circle.

Reluctantly, Emereck moved to help with the unpleasant task. They piled up the bodies and covered them with the cloaks the Syaski had been wearing. It was all they could do; there was no time to dig a grave or build a cairn, and no wood for a pyre. By the time they finished, Emereck was feeling queasy. He also had a vivid understanding of why most heroic ballads stopped with the hero victorious on the field of battle, without detailing the aftermath.

"Whew," Kensal said when they finished. "I'm getting too old for this sort of thing." He sat down and began cleaning the raven's-feet. Emereck turned to gathering up the belongings the Syaski had scattered over the ground. He was nearly finished when he ran across the small box Lanyk had used to identify the Harp. He picked it up, wondering whether he should keep it or destroy it. As he hesitated, Kensal looked up. "Found something?"

"In a way," Emereck said, and held up the box. "Lanyk seemed to be using this to track us."

"Interesting," Kensal said. "May I see it?"

Emereck hesitated, then handed it over. Kensal held the lid shut and turned the box over in his hands. "The style of carving is Lithran," he said, frowning. "I don't like this."

"Lithmern are no worse than Syaski," Emereck said.

"If you'd said 'no better' I'd have agreed. Or don't you believe what your Guild Masters tell you?"

"What are you talking about?"

Kensal did not seem to hear. "Well, no sense waiting," he muttered, and flipped open the lid of the box. He glanced inside, and his expression hardened. "Shadow-scum!" he snarled. In one fluid movement, he dropped the box and rose to his feet. Before Emereck could protest, he crushed box and contents together beneath the heel of his boot.

"What—"

"Look there," Kensal said, indicating the shattered remains on the ground. Emereck leaned forward. Amid the splinters of the box were several shards of smoky black crystal. He reached out to pick one up, and Kensal knocked his hand away. "Don't touch it!"

"Why not? Why are you so—" Emereck saw Liana approaching, and broke off. She was leading the horses she and Emereck had been riding, along with one of the Syaski mounts.

"Here they are," she said as she joined Emereck and

Kensal. "We can leave any time."

"Good," Kensal replied. His tone was grim.

"Something's wrong?"

"Yes."

"No."

Liana looked from Kensal to Emereck. "I see. What did I miss?"

"This," Kensal said, nudging the crystal shards with the toe of his boot. "Have you seen anything like it before?"

"No," Liana said positively. "Why?"

Kensal sighed. "Good. I think. It will make it harder to explain, though."

"What is it?" Emereck demanded.

"I'll tell you as we ride." Kensal was already tying Emereck's saddlebag to one of the horses.

"Ride? But—"

"Unless I am much mistaken, we need to get away from here, and quickly. I don't know just how much time we have."

Emereck opened his mouth to object, then closed it. Kensal had saved their lives, and it was clear from his manner that he felt this was urgent. But could he be trusted? He knew too much about the Harp for Emereck's comfort. And how *had* Kensal managed to be out in the middle of the plains at precisely the right time and place to save Emereck and Liana from the Syaski? He had promised not to take the Harp himself, but he could still lead them into a trap.

Liana settled the matter. She studied Kensal briefly, then handed Emereck the end of the leading rope and began packing her own things. She wasted very little time; she simply scooped most of them into a pile and jammed the pile into a saddlebag. "I didn't find your horse," she told Kensal as she worked. "I brought you one of the Syaski ones instead."

"Let it go," Kensal said. He grinned, and gave a shrill, carrying whistle. A few moments later, Emereck saw a sturdy brown mare round one of the stone outcroppings and head toward them. Liana looked up, nodded, and began untying the Syaski horse. Kensal turned to Emereck. "Get your harp, and let's be off."

Feeling frustrated, angry, and a little afraid of what might happen next, Emereck did as he was told. Kensal watched in silence as Emereck wrapped the Harp of Imach Thyssel, tied it to his saddle, and carefully checked the knots. Emereck was irritated that Kensal did not give him an opportunity to refuse an offer of help. He finished the knots and swung into the saddle. Beside him, Liana plucked a handful of long, stiff grasses and switched the extra horse to make him move.

"Pick a direction," Kensal said, "and let's go."

Emereck looked at the Cilhar in surprise, then understood. If he, Emereck, chose their path, there could be no question of Kensal's leading them into a trap. The knowledge only irritated Emereck more. He scowled and pointed. "West. We can make the forest in another day if we push, and it'll be easier to hide if there's trouble." He looked challengingly at Kensal.

The Cilhar nodded gravely. "It is always easier to avoid trouble. If possible." He made a clucking noise to his horse, and started off. Liana threw the switch after the Syaski horse and followed. Feeling vaguely dissatisfied and thoroughly unhappy, Emereck kicked his horse into motion and went after them.

Wind rustled the branches of the trees outside the tent, casting shivering shadows across the walls and roof. Inside, Tammis, Princess of Syaskor and sometime sorceress, paced angrily up and down between a cot and a small mahogany table. On the table lay a black mirror that reflected none of the tent's interior, only a clotted crimson stain.

Lanyk had failed. Worse, the secondary link had been destroyed. And they had been so close to success! Mother of Mountains, how *could* he have bungled it? He had been within reach of the power they sought, might have been actually holding it. So close—and now this. Her small mouth was set in a thin line.

The situation was intolerable. Lanyk was dead, the

patronizing little fraud, and she had not even had the satisfaction of killing him herself. As soon as the Syaski found out, what little direct influence she had would end, unless she was prepared to use raw power to enforce her claim to the throne.

The corners of her mouth relaxed slightly as she pictured the consternation of the courtiers. Most of them had believed in her carefully planned mousiness. Did they really think a Cilhar would be so helpless? The smile faded and she shook her head. It was too soon. She could not ensorcell an entire country, not without help. And to get the help she needed, she had to have the . . . whatever it was. She ground her teeth in frustration. Lanyk could have at least used the link to let her know what he had found before he got himself killed!

Firmly, she brought her mind back to the immediate problem. Once the Syaski heard of her husband's death, it would be only a matter of time before some ambitious general or courtier decided that assassinating an unpopular Cilhar princess was the quickest way to the throne.

Very well, then; they must not hear of Lanyk's death. She could manage that, at least. But how long would it be before the soldiers grew restless anyway, waiting for their precious Prince to return? That was easy; they were restless already. She could handle them, but . . .

Tammis's frown deepened. She could hold the Mother-lost soldiers, but to do so she would have to stay here, watching her chances of reclaiming her birthright fade as the real prize slipped out of reach. And sooner or later her hold would slip, too, and the Syaski hatred of Cilhar would take over. No, it made no sense to stay. Better to risk everything on the chance of seizing the thing for herself. With careful preparation, it could be done. She was no bungler.

She turned to the table and passed her hand over the surface of the black mirror. The red stain faded and was replaced by a murky reflection of the tent's interior. Satisfied, Tammis wrapped it carefully in a piece of silver-colored silk, then placed it in a flat oak box. She seated herself beside the table and frowned in concentration. There was that boringly single-minded Shalarn and her soldiers to deal with, as well as the group she was seeking. And someone else had brushed her mind recently; that one would need special handling. Tammis smiled and began the list of the things she would need to take with her.

In the study of Castle Minathlan Duke Dindran sat behind the polished desk. His face was an expressionless mask, but the lines around his mouth seemed deeper than they had been. Beside him sat the Wyrd, Welram, on the shortest chair the servants could find. Gendron was across from them, watching his father. When the silence became unbearable, he cleared his throat. "Sir, I—"

The Duke cut him off with a wave. "I do not blame you for what has happened, Gendron."

"I should have watched Flindaran and Talerith more closely. And I should have guessed that the minstrel would never leave without that Harp."

"You could not have predicted Flindaran's actions."

"The responsibility is still mine."

"I left you and Flindaran in charge. It is as much my fault as yours. More," the Duke added, half to himself. "Practice at raising children appears to have made me worse at it, not better."

Gendron looked at him in concern. "Father, I . . ."

"Dindran!" Welram was staring toward the door, his ears pricked forward like a fox hearing a rabbit in the underbrush. "Someone comes."

"No one will get past the guards," Gendron said, torn between irritation and respect. "The orders—"

"Guards and orders cannot stop magic," the Wyrd said. "And there is a very powerful and subtle magician coming this way."

Gendron looked at the door as though he had just been told it was made of human bones, then looked back at Welram. "You're sure? How can you tell?"

"One magician knows another."

"Enough," the Duke said. "Welram, how long—" He broke off as someone knocked at the door. A moment later, the door swung open and a lanky blonde woman wearing servant's garb stepped inside. She glanced at the Wyrd without surprise, closed the door behind her, and stood waiting with a serene confidence that was out of keeping with her appearance.

"It seems that you were correct, Welram," the Duke said.

"It is no fault of your guards and servants that I am here," the woman said. "I arranged matters myself."

"Did you. You make yourself quite free of my home."

"It was necessary. I apologize for disturbing you, but I have need of a few words with you and your guest."

"Indeed." The Duke leaned back. "And would it be presumptuous to inquire who you are?"

The woman smiled. "I am one of the Five who have been Watchers and Guardians of the world since before Varna sank, since before the Shadow-born were bound, since before Tyrillian fell. I am one of the last of the Eleann, and my name is Rylorien." The words rang through the chamber like a bell tolling.

There was a moment's silence; even the Duke looked slightly shaken. "Guardians?" Gendron said at last. "What Guardians?"

Welram answered him without taking his eyes from the woman before them. "When the third moon fell and the Eleann died, they left five Guardians behind them. Their names were Elasien, Amaranth, Iraman, Valerin, and Rylorien."

"Anyone may claim a hero's name," Gendron said uncertainly.

Rylorien looked at the Duke. "Your library proclaims you a scholar, lord Duke. Have you studied the small green book that opens only to the touch of the Dukes of Minathlan and their kin?"

"How do you know of that?"

Rylorien smiled. "I was there when it was written. Have you studied it?"

"I have."

"Then watch." Rylorien raised a hand. Her form shimmered, grew, changed. Her skin was a pale golden color, her slanted eyes a golden brown, her hair the color of clear honey. She stood a head taller than the Duke. Dindran stared for a long moment; then he bowed. Rylorien smiled and began to change again. The golden shape shimmered and ran, and then a small, dark-haired woman stood composedly before them. Gendron closed his mouth and swallowed hard.

The Duke studied the dark-haired woman for a moment, then raised an eyebrow. "Your first demonstration was quite convincing. There was no need to display your, er, adaptability further."

"This is the form in which the minstrel Emereck knows me. If we are to seek him, I think it wisest to make recognition easy for him."

Gendron looked at his father. "You're going after that Harp?"

"Welram and I had intended it," the Duke replied. "You will remain in charge here."

"You'd trust me after what happened last time?"

"If I did not, I would not have made that decision." The Duke looked at Rylorien. "Have you an objection to such an expedition?"

"None at all. I wish to come with you. There is magic gathering against the Harp, and I think we may help each other."

The Duke inclined his head. "An excellent idea."

Shalarn rode at the center of the small column of men. Behind the silk scarf that kept the dust out of her face, she was frowning. In another three or four days they would reach Minathlan. Everything had gone smoothly since she had begun her warding spells, yet she was uneasy. The feeling had been growing since the previous day, and she knew better than to ignore such hunches.

She turned in the saddle and beckoned to her Captain. "We will stop here for a few minutes," she said when he pulled his horse up beside hers. "There is something I wish to investigate."

"Yes, my lady."

As he turned and began giving orders, Shalarn pulled her horse to a halt and slid to the ground. While her men and horses rested, she took a map, a box of herbs, and a black velvet bag from their special places in her saddlebags. She went a little way off the road and set up the spell, slowly and with great care. She did not want to waste even a fraction of her power.

When the preparations were complete, she took a small gold sphere on a silver chain from the velvet bag. She dangled it carefully over the map, and spoke the words that set the spell in motion. There was a flash of heat and the pile of herbs under the sphere crumbled into ashes.

Shalarn finished the spell and lowered her hand. Her eyes widened, though she had half expected the result. The source of the power for which she searched had moved. The line of ashes pointed west of Minathlan now. She studied the map until she was certain she had memorized the pattern, then cleared away the traces of the spell.

She rose to her feet, dusted the last traces of ash from her hands, and walked back to her men. "Captain!"

"My lady?"

"My plans have changed. We will go southwest from here, instead of continuing to Minathlan."

The Captain looked at her with wary curiosity, then nodded. Shalarn smiled as she remounted. She and her men could overtake these others in a day or two. Provided the ones she sought had no magic to hurry them along, she reminded herself. She would work the tracing spell every night when they camped to make sure she had not lost them. When she caught up to them— well, she would choose that road when she reached the crossing.

Nineteen

As soon as they were well underway, Emereck rode up beside Kensal. "I believe you promised us an explanation, Cilhar," he said.

Kensal sighed. "So I did. You saw the pieces of crystal?"

"I saw them."

"That was a shadow-stone. It's a kind of link to the nastiest bunch of sorcerers I know of."

"A link?" Liana said.

Kensal nodded. "Under the right conditions, the sorcerers can use their power through the stones, cast spells through them, perhaps even travel through them somehow. And they and their servants can find one of those stones anywhere on Lyra."

"That's why you smashed it," Emereck said numbly. "To keep them from finding us."

"Yes. Soldiers and fighting men I can handle, if there aren't too many of them, but wizards are another matter. Magic isn't my specialty."

"Then why are you helping us?"

"I owe you a life for your help at Ryl's inn," Kensal said after a moment. "And even if I did not, I am a Cilhar; I would do far more than this to keep the Harp you carry out of Syaski hands."

Kensal's explanation sounded reasonable, but Emereck was sure the man had not told him all his motives. He frowned, searching for the right way to ask the question, and Liana said suddenly, "Who are these sorcerers you spoke of?"

"They are called Shadow-born. They're the ones responsible for the Lithmern invasion of Alkyra a few years back."

"The Lithmern were defeated," Emereck pointed out.

"Defeated doesn't mean wiped out. The Lithmern are still there, and so are the Shadow-born."

"But if the Alkyrans killed some of them—"

"They didn't," Kensal interrupted, shaking his head. "Apparently the Shadow-born can't be killed, only bound."

"Can't be killed?" Emereck said incredulously. "That's ridiculous!"

"Ridiculous it may be, but it is true nonetheless." Kensal looked at Emereck curiously. "You're a minstrel. You must know the songs."

"What so—" Emereck stopped. "The Pallersi Cycle? The Wars of Binding?"

"Exactly." Kensal looked pleased, like a Master Minstrel whose apprentice has just correctly answered a difficult question.

"But those wars were three thousand years ago!"

"What is time to things without bodies?"

"No bodies?" Liana said. "I thought you said they were wizards!"

"They are," Kensal replied cheerfully. "They just aren't human wizards. Or Shee ones, or Neira, or Wyrd for that matter. It's a pity in a way; Shee or Wyrds would be easier to deal with."

"No one's seen a Shee or Neira or Wyrd for centuries!" Emereck said, feeling more confused by the minute.

Liana looked as if she were about to say something, then changed her mind. Kensal shrugged. "Shee and Wyrds and Neira are just as real as Shadow-born. And it's not true that no one has seen them for centuries;

they've been all over Alkyra for the last four years."

"I—" Emereck shook his head. He knew there were Guildhalls that considered the songs of the Pallersi Cycle to be literally true, but he himself had always thought that the songs and stories of the Wars of Binding were half poetry and half myth. Oh, there had certainly been some great magical conflict, but most of the Master Minstrels of Ciaron felt that it must have been an interracial war. Hadn't the three nonhuman races—the Shee, the Wyrds, and the Neira—withdrawn from humans after the war? The "Shadow-born," according to this interpretation, referred to those members of the Four Races whose hatred had begun the war. Some of the Masters even regarded the three nonhuman races as myths, though there were Alkyran records barely two hundred years old that mentioned Shee and Wyrds. "I would have heard of it in Ciaron if what you say is true!"

Kensal shrugged. "Talk to the Alkyrans. Talk to the minstrels who were there during the invasion. Your Grand Master himself crowned the new queen of Alkyra. Talk to him!"

"I know, but . . ." Emereck's objection trailed off. If Shadow-born were real beings, not metaphor . . .

"But what are they, really?" Liana asked. "These Shadow-born?"

"Powerful, ambitious, and dangerous," Kensal replied promptly. "I don't know much more than that, and I don't want to."

"And you think they're following us?" Liana persisted.

"The Shadow-born? No. One of their servants, perhaps. But that could be almost as bad."

"How do you know all this?" Emereck asked suspiciously. "You said yourself you're a fighter, not a wizard."

"Ryl told me when she asked me to help her get the Harp of Imach Thyssel."

Emereck's head snapped in Kensal's direction. For a moment he simply stared, trying to absorb the implications of Kensal's statement. He and Ryl were working

together, and they were after the Harp. But why had
Kensal admitted it? He must know how Emereck would
react. He might be trying to demonstrate his good faith.
Or was he only trying to fool Emereck into thinking he
was being open? "Please explain," Emereck said at last.

"Ryl is one of the Five Eleann Guardians," Kensal
began. "I don't know much about them, but one of their
main jobs seems to be keeping an eye on the Shadow-
born. Other than that, they don't meddle much in the
affairs of the Four Races.

"The Harp of Imach Thyssel was one of the exceptions
to that rule. Somehow when Imach Thyssel was
destroyed, the Guardians got hold of the Harp. They
couldn't or wouldn't destroy it, so they hid it in Castle
Windsong."

Emereck made a choking noise. "How do you know
about—"

"I'm telling you. Now, I think I mentioned earlier that
the Shadow-born were behind the most recent Lithmern
invasion of Alkyra. The Lithmern were looking for a
quick way of working sorcery and they released about
fifteen of them. They must have thought they had a
chance of keeping fifteen under control. The rest—"

"The rest? How many of these things are there
supposed to be? And what does this have to do with the
Harp?" Emereck said, bewildered.

"I'll get to that. There are several hundred Shadow-
born, I think. Most of them were bound under Lithra;
there are a few others scattered across Lyra in other
places. May I go on?"

Emereck nodded, not trusting himself to speak.

"The released Shadow-born got out of control rather
quickly. For some reason they didn't unbind the others
right away, just weakened their bonds or something.
Maybe they didn't want to share their freedom; maybe
that's just how Shadow-born think. Anyway, they
loosened the spells holding the other Shadow-born, then
went off to war with Alkyra and got beaten."

"How could the Alkyrans defeat those things, if
they're as bad as you say?" Emereck demanded.

"That's what the Four Gifts of Alkyra are for," Kensal said impatiently. "Surely you knew they'd been found again?"

"Yes." The tale had been a sixteen-days wonder at the Ciaron Guildhall. "But—"

"Who's telling this story? The Alkyrans used the Gifts to bind the fifteen Shadow-born who'd come with the Lithmern army, but they didn't do anything about all the others under Lithra. I don't think they guessed there were more. And, after a few years, the Shadow-born in Lithra started working loose, and the Guardians had to go down and stop them."

"I still don't see what this has to do with the Harp."

"Patience. The Guardians got to Lithra before the Shadow-born had gotten completely free, but they still had a hard time getting the Shadow-born thoroughly bound again."

"I don't see why," Emereck said sarcastically. "There were five of them and only a hundred or so Shadow-born."

Kensal looked at him. "The Guardians are very powerful. Unfortunately, they have to use most of their power to maintain the spells that keep them alive and whole. If they're distracted too much, or if they're forced to use a spell that's too powerful, they . . . Change. It's something the Shadow-born did to them a long time ago. They twist and melt and . . . it's not pleasant. I think that's why there are only five of them left, and why they hate Shadow-born."

"I can understand it," Liana said, shivering.

"You believe this . . . this fairy tale?" Emereck demanded. His voice was harsher than he had intended; Kensal's description reminded him of his nightmares, and he did not want to be reminded.

Liana looked at him oddly. "I am of the blood of the Dukes of Minathlan. I've seen some of their private histories. I'm willing to listen, and I'm surprised that a minstrel isn't."

Emereck felt as if he had been slapped. He wanted to say that it was not his training that made him skeptical,

it was the Harp. Kensal's tale sounded unreal, like
fragments of ancient ballads and songs strung together,
a story meant to beguile a minstrel. He could not speak,
and after a moment he realized it was just as well.
Anything he said would sound defensive or self-
justifying, and neither would do him any good in
Liana's eyes. He turned to Kensal. "Go on."

"The Shadow-born fought back when the Guardians
sought to keep them bound. Even though they weren't
wholly free, they were very powerful. And there are
quite a few of them. Before the Guardians bound them,
the Shadow-born managed to distract one of them a
little too much."

"That spell you mentioned?" Liana said.

"The Change. Yes. To save his life the other
Guardians cast a spell that threw him into a . . . place
where time itself is frozen. He must remain there, like a
moth trapped in resin, until the other Guardians find a
way to bring him back without letting the Change finish
him." Kensal paused. "His name is Valerin. He is—or
was—a good friend to me."

"I'm sorry," Liana said softly.

"The Harp of Imach Thyssel is the only way the
Guardians have of freeing Valerin safely. Ryl asked me
to help her retrieve it. If it hadn't been for those
Lithmern at the inn, we'd have been at Castle Windsong
before you, and none of this would have happened."

"I wish you had," Emereck said bitterly, thinking of
Flindaran.

"Then you'll give us the Harp?"

"No!"

"I'm going too fast for you, I see. My apologies."

"Emereck . . ." Liana said.

"I won't do it," Emereck said flatly. Liana looked
hurt, but he did not try to explain. He was not really
certain he could. He had been almost forced to accept
responsibility for the Harp. Having done so, he could
not simply relinquish it to a person he barely knew on
the basis of a story he only half believed. The real
problem was that he was beginning to like Kensal. He

wanted to trust the Cilhar, but he did not dare. He had
trusted Flindaran . . . "If it's Ryl who wants the Harp,
why isn't she here?"

"Ryl stayed behind to talk to the Duke; I assume
she'll be following us later. She sent me after you
because she feared you were in danger. I think circumstances have shown that she was right." Kensal paused,
frowning. "I wish there were some way of warning her."

"Warning her?" Liana asked.

"About that shadow-crystal. She could be terribly
vulnerable, if one of the Shadow-born's servants finds
out who and what she is."

Emereck was silent for a moment, then he said, "Why
didn't you come to me in Minathlan and tell me all
this?"

"What did we know of you? You arrived at the inn
just before the Lithmern attacked. You lied about who
you were, or at least one of you did. And you went
straight to Castle Windsong and took the Harp. Would
you have trusted us, if that were all you knew?"

"No," Emereck admitted. "But in that case, why are
you here now?"

"There was no other choice," Kensal said simply.

"You could have stolen it."

"Ryl knows more of the Harp of Imach Thyssel than
anyone. And she claims force and trickery are difficult
and . . . unwise ways to try to take it. After what I've
seen, I believe her."

Emereck looked at him sharply, then realized he was
referring to the dead Syaski, not to Flindaran. "In that
case, why did she send you after us?"

"I said it was difficult to take the Harp by force, not
that it was impossible."

"Oh." Emereck frowned, digesting that.

"I don't suppose you'd consider—"

"No," Emereck said sharply. He saw Liana looking at
him and said, more to her than to Kensal, "I need time
to think."

Liana smiled, and Kensal nodded. For a time the
conversation lagged. Emereck's horse drifted a little

away from the others, and he made no move to stop it. Kensal's talk of Shadow-born and Guardians had confused and frightened him. These were matters for the Guildmasters, even the Grand Master himself, not for a mere wandering minstrel barely out of his journeyman's rank. Emereck could hardly believe it was true. Yet if the legendary Harp of Imach Thyssel were real, why not other things from the ancient songs as well?

The thought shattered the last remnant of Emereck's composure. His thoughts ran in endless circles and reached no conclusion. What conclusion could there be? Against the power of the Shadow-born wizards, he would be helpless. No, not helpless, for he had the Harp of Imach Thyssel. But could he bring himself to use the Harp, even in a time of need? Would he dare not to use it? And what of the price the Harp would demand? He shook his head, and Flindaran's voice sounded suddenly in his memory: "It might be worth it."

Emereck swallowed a lump in his throat and glanced over his shoulder toward the Harp. It made such an ordinary lump hanging from his saddle. Yet it had cost so much already. He scowled at it, wondering how much of what had happened was the Harp's doing. He was beginning to think of it almost as a person, he realized. He snorted and turned back to his horse and his brooding.

Liana glanced over at him several times, but Emereck deliberately showed no response. Finally, she started a conversation with Kensal about life in the Mountains of Morravik, and soon she was laughing at some comment the Cilhar had made. Kensal certainly seemed to be popular with one of them, Emereck thought sourly. He turned away. Liana could afford to trust Kensal. The Harp wasn't her responsibility. She—

"Emereck," Liana's voice said beside him.

He turned, startled, and saw that Liana had pulled her horse over to his. "Yes?"

"I said, isn't it a lovely day." There were lines of suppressed laughter around her mouth.

Emereck blinked. "We're out in the middle of the

plains with nowhere to hide and we're being looked for by Syaski, Lithmern, and possibly Shadow-born, all of whom probably want to kill us. You think that's lovely?"

"Well, no, it isn't. But it has nothing to do with how lovely the day is, either." She grinned at him. "And since we can't do anything about any of it anyway, we may as well enjoy the weather. So—isn't it a lovely day?"

Reluctantly, Emereck smiled back. "Yes, I suppose it is."

"Then stop sulking and come tell Kensal the name of that song you sang at Talerith's party. The one about the dragon and the blacksmith. He says it sounds like something he heard once in Col Sador, but I didn't think it could be." She smiled again, and Emereck put aside his worrying for the moment, and joined her.

Twenty

*T*hey rode until late in the evening, pushing the horses as hard as they dared. Emereck felt exposed on the plains, and he was anxious to reach the cover the forest would provide. He also had a feeble hope that Kensal would leave them once they gained the woods. He appreciated the Cilhar's protection, but he could not rid himself of a certain uneasiness about the man.

When they stopped at last, it was Kensal who chose their campsite. It was a small hollow formed at the base of three hills, out of the wind and partially hidden from view. It was a good spot, but Emereck was irked by Kensal's casual assumption of command. He did not say so; the journey was uncomfortable enough without adding to the friction between himself and the Cilhar.

They took turns watching that night. Liana took the first watch and Emereck, the last. His dreams were chaotic and unpleasant, but the recurring nightmare of the melting city had not begun when Kensal woke him. Emereck breathed a quiet sigh of relief and rose to take his watch. The thought of explaining the dream to the imperturbable Cilhar had not appealed to him at all.

He climbed the nearest of the hills and settled down to his vigil. The stars were bright above him; the waning half-circle of Elewyth was low on the western horizon, with Kaldarin's dull red crescent lagging reluctantly behind. A warm breeze rippled the grass, tossing it like the waves of the Melyranne Sea in the moonlight. Emereck felt small and insignificant surrounded by so much space, yet curiously peaceful as well. Whatever happened to himself and his friends, whatever happened to the Harp of Imach Thyssel, the stars and the night and the whispering wind would still be there, unchanged.

Emereck leaned back and stared out across the waving grass. Flindaran had loved these plains. The unbidden thought brought with it a sudden, vivid impression of Flindaran's presence. Emereck found himself looking over his shoulder, half expecting to see his friend climbing up the hill toward him, calling some remark about dreamers with their heads in a fog. There was only the wind and the darkness, and again Emereck felt a dull ache of loss.

He rose to his feet and scanned the plains, half hoping to see something that would distract him from his thoughts. There was nothing, but the action itself helped. Slowly, he turned and climbed down his hill and up the next, watching the moonlit grass. The light was fading now as Elewyth set, and the night seemed colder as well as darker.

At the top of the hill Emereck stopped and turned in a full circle, peering uneasily out across the plain. Still he saw nothing. His discomfort grew as the silver-green moon sank lower, and he remained standing. As the last sliver of Elewyth vanished below the horizon, leaving Kaldarin alone in the sky, Emereck saw the city.

It stood, impossibly, where there had been nothing but grass a moment before. The elegant spires seemed made of crystal mist; even in the dim light, he could see the grass waving through the walls. With a shock of fear, he recognized it. It was the city of his nightmares. He stood paralyzed, wondering if he were going mad, as the sequence of the dream began to play itself out before him. The graceful people of the city appeared: tall, transparent images in starlight. Then the explosion, and the images began to writhe and melt, their mouths open wide in silent screams. With a moan, Emereck closed his eyes to shut out the sight. When he opened them the city had vanished.

Shaken, Emereck stared at the empty plain. Had it been a vision, or a kind of waking dream, or was he going mad? And what could he do about it in any case? Demons take the Harp of Imach Thyssel and all its works! Why was it doing this to him?

He discovered that he was trembling and sat down abruptly. He closed his eyes and forced himself to breathe in long, slow breaths until the shaking stopped. Then he opened his eyes and sat scowling at the night.

The city he had seen wasn't Imach Thyssel, he was sure. The bits of description in "King Loren's Lay" did not fit the dream-city at all. The people, too, were unfamiliar in appearance. Their height and slightly slanted eyes fit descriptions of the Shee, but their coloring did not. Neira, then? But that was no underwater city he had seen. And *three* moons in the sky . . . Emereck wished fervently that he had listened more closely when the occasional adept of the Temple of the Third Moon had stopped at the Guildhall.

He wracked his brain for hours, but he could find no clue to the meaning of the dreams. The only things that seemed to fit at all were the scraps of information Kensal had dropped about the Guardians and the "Change." Emereck grimaced. He was beginning to think he would have to tell Kensal about the dreams after all. Perhaps the Cilhar could give him a clue as to what was happening to him and why. Emereck resolved to try, come morning.

When morning came, however, Kensal was very little help. He listened to Emereck's tale with no comment and an increasingly worried expression. "Ryl said nothing of this to me," he said when Emereck finished. "And I am afraid I have already told you as much as I know of the Guardians and the Change. I am sorry."

"Perhaps we should wait here for Ryl, then," Liana suggested.

"No," Emereck and Kensal said together.

Emereck looked at Kensal in surprise, and the Cilhar smiled slightly. "Ryl will catch up with us when she chooses," he explained. "Right now it is far more important for us to avoid the rest of Lanyk's men."

Emereck nodded. His own reasons for wanting to postpone an encounter with the innkeeper-sorceress-Guardian were less practical and more emotional. He had expected to meet people who would try to take the Harp of Imach Thyssel from him by force or trickery before he reached the Guildhall, and he had been prepared to guard the Harp from them as well as he was able. He had not expected to be asked calmly and politely to give the Harp away. That decision was for the Guild Masters to make. Yet if Kensal's tale were even partly true, Ryl was the rightful guardian of the Harp, and Emereck had no right to keep it from her. And that was a problem Emereck did not want to face just yet.

The memory of his waking nightmare stayed with Emereck through the day's ride, making him tense and irritable. His training enabled him to maintain a civil manner, but as soon as they finished making camp that night he picked up his harp and left, muttering something about needing practice.

The familiar routine of tuning the harp relaxed him. He set his hands to the strings and let his fingers wander. He was halfway through the second verse when he realized that he had unconsciously begun with one of the ballads Flindaran had hated most, as he always did when his friend was not present to be irritated by them. His hands faltered, and then the rhythm firmed and the notes flowed on. But as soon as he finished the verse, he stopped and began a different tune.

Some time later in the middle of a complicated sequence from "The Song of Gasinal," he heard a rustling behind him. He muted the harpstrings and turned. Liana stood behind him, holding a battered tin bowl. "I thought you might want something to eat," she said.

"Thank you," Emereck replied. He set his harp aside and took the bowl from her. She stood watching him as he began to eat, then dropped to sit in the grass beside him.

"Emereck . . ." she started, then hesitated. He looked at her inquiringly, and she said, "Why are you so unfriendly with Kensal?"

"I'm sorry. I didn't think it was that obvious."

"It is to me. You aren't still worried that he'll try to steal the Harp from you, are you?"

"Not exactly. But he still wants it, and he expects to get it. He's too sure of himself."

"Emereck, no Cilhar would break an oath on the Mother of Mountains! Can't you trust him a little?"

"I trusted your brother—" The words were out before Emereck thought. He cut himself off in mid-sentence, appalled by what he had just said.

Liana stared at him. "No," she said slowly, "you didn't trust Flindaran. That was part of the problem."

"What do you mean?"

"If you trusted him, why didn't you ever talk to him about the Harp? Why didn't you discuss your plans with him?"

"What makes you think—"

"I heard some of his talks with Talerith. He was worried about you, Emereck."

Emereck stared. "Worried about *me*? But he was the one—"

"How do you know?"

"The way he was acting . . ."

"Was it so different from the way you were acting?"

"He never said anything."

"Neither did you. That's what I mean." Liana shook her head. "You don't trust anyone when it comes to that Demon-cursed Harp."

Emereck blinked, surprised and hurt by the bitterness in her voice. "I—I trust you, Liana."

"Do you?" Liana said evenly.

"You're the only person I *know* doesn't want the Harp."

"Do you?" she said again. "You haven't been acting like it."

"I don't under—" Emereck stopped, then went on in an altered tone, "I *couldn't* tell you I had it with me. Surely you see that! It was too dangerous."

"Was it any less dangerous for me to come with you not knowing about it?"

"I tried to make you stay in Minathlan!" Emereck responded, stung. "But would you listen? No, you insisted on following me whether I wanted you to or not! You're stubborner than Flindaran ever was."

"Probably," Liana said calmly. "But I wasn't complaining about the risk. I was simply asking whether this trip would have been any more dangerous for me if you'd told me about the Harp that first morning, when I caught up with you."

"I suppose not," Emereck said after a moment's hesitation. "But the Harp isn't . . ."

Liana made a small, exasperated noise. "If the Harp of Imach Thyssel is too powerful to even *talk* about with anyone else, then it's too powerful for you to handle alone."

"Do you think I don't know that? All I want is to get back to the Guildhall in Ciaron and let the Masters have it!"

"And in the meantime you're going to curl up in a shell like a garden snail?"

"The Harp of Imach Thyssel is too important to take chances with."

"So you trust me as long as it isn't too important." Liana stopped and her expression changed. She shook her head in apology. "I'm sorry, Emereck. I didn't mean that the way it sounded."

"I deserve it," Emereck said. "I wanted to tell you about the Harp, but we were still so close to Minathlan. . . . I should have trusted you, but I wouldn't let myself. I couldn't take the chance."

"The way you want to trust Kensal now, and won't let yourself?" Liana said softly.

"I—" Emereck paused. "I don't know." He looked at

Liana through the growing gloom. "Do you think I should give the Harp to Kensal, then?"

"No. But I think you ought to *think* about it a little more, instead of just rejecting it out of hand."

Silence fell. Slowly Emereck finished his meal. Liana made no move to leave; she sat gazing into the deepening twilight with a look of abstraction. Emereck sighed. How could one small woman, hardly more than a girl, make him feel so confused and uncertain? He wanted to shake her; he wanted to shout at her; he wanted to tell her . . . tell her . . . he didn't know what he wanted to tell her.

His eye fell on his harp. Almost without thinking he picked it up and began to play an old country song from somewhere in the north:

> "Oh, where are you going this warm summer day?
> How long will you travel alone on your way?
> What wish set you walking on what private quest
> That keeps you from dancing at home with the rest?
> What goal do you look for, that drives you so fast?
> And what will you do when you find it at last?
>
> "I go where my love goes, I follow her song.
> I'll walk 'til I find her, no matter how long.
> I wish for her laughter, the smile she can't hide;
> I lost it because of my anger and pride.
> My love is my goal, and that we'll never part
> I'll ask her forgiveness, and offer my heart."

The last notes of the plaintive melody seemed to linger in the air. Emereck looked up to find Liana watching him with a slight smile. He set the harp carefully aside, as though it was the harp and not the mood that he feared would break. There was a long silence. Finally he took a deep breath. "Liana, I—Well, I'm sorry about everything—the Harp, and Flindaran, and . . ."

There was a rustle in the darkness as Liana leaned forward. "Hush," she said, and kissed him.

For a long moment Emereck forgot about Flindaran,

the Harp of Imach Thyssel, the Syaski, and everything else. Then, reluctantly, he pulled away. "Liana, I . . . If it weren't for that blasted Harp . . ."

Liana looked at him. "I don't see what the Harp has to do with it."

"It has everything to do with it." Emereck swallowed hard. "I can't make any promises until this business with the Harp is settled, one way or another."

"Why not?"

"Because I might have to break them, or worse. I'm already responsible for Flindaran's death—"

"That's the silliest statement I've ever heard. In the first place it was an accident, and in the second place he was trying to steal your precious Harp. If anyone was responsible for his death it was Flindaran himself! And I don't see what it has to do with kissing me."

"Will you listen? I'm stuck with the Harp. With all the wizards and Syaski and who knows what else looking for it, there's a good chance I'll be killed before we get to Ciaron. And even if I make it . . ."

"Yes?"

Emereck sighed. "I'm a minstrel; music and stories are all I know. After the way I've bungled this whole business, I'll be surprised if the Guild Masters don't throw me out."

"You've done the best you could. They'll know that."

"Maybe. And maybe not. But either way, I can't make promises or ask for them until . . . I know whether I have anything to offer."

Liana looked at him until he was forced to meet her eyes. "I don't need promises, Emereck," she said softly.

"I do," Emereck whispered.

Liana was silent. Then she said slowly, "I think I under-
stand. I don't know whether you're right or not, but I think I understand." She lifted her head and smiled at him, then leaned forward and kissed him again. "I'll wait."

Before Emereck could think of an adequate reply, she rose to her feet, picked up the bowl, and went down the hill toward the camp. Emereck sat looking after her for a long time.

Twenty-one

*N*ext morning, Emereck found that he had more difficulty in facing Liana than Kensal. The need to keep her at a distance angered and frustrated him. He took refuge in irritability, but Liana did not seem to notice. Eventually, her casual conversation coaxed him out of his dark mood, and by the time they reached the outskirts of the forest he had pushed the problem to the back of his mind.

Once they were past the bushy growth at the forest's edge, Emereck relaxed at last. He had not realized how nervous the wide openness of the plains had made him until he left it behind. His troubles were far from over, he knew, but at least there would not be a repeat of the hopeless flight from Lanyk, with nowhere to run or hide.

Kensal took the lead for the afternoon's ride, and for once Emereck was pleased to let him. His own skills as a woodsman were adequate to the needs of a wandering minstrel, but no more. The Cilhar's expertise was obvious, and the small group of almost-fugitives might need every advantage they could get.

Next morning, they continued west. The trees were large, and their heavy canopy of leaves hid the sun almost completely. At first Emereck enjoyed the shade, but after a while he became uneasy. He felt eyes on his back, watching him, waiting for him to make a mistake. He tried to dismiss the feeling, but it would not go away.

"Is something wrong?" Liana asked, after he had looked over his shoulder for the fourth time in as many minutes.

"I don't think so," Emereck said apologetically. "These woods just make me nervous."

She raised an eyebrow. "I thought it was the plains that bothered you."

"This is different. There, I was worried about being found by Syaski. Right now I feel as if the trees themselves are watching me."

Liana looked thoughtfully at the woods. "Maybe they are, but I don't think it's anything to worry about."

"You feel it, too?"

"In a way. I thought at first it was just because there aren't many trees around Minathlan, but it's more than that. This place is . . . alive somehow."

"Most forests are," Kensal put in.

"I don't mean just growing! I mean—well, awake and aware."

"I don't like it," Emereck said.

"It isn't threatening or evil or anything," Liana said, surprised. "It's just *there*."

"I still don't like it. Maybe we should head farther south and try to go around it."

"I don't think we can," Liana said.

"And I don't think we should try," Kensal added. "We don't know anything about this whatever-it-is you're feeling. Turn south and we could be heading farther into it, instead of out."

"I suppose so," Emereck said reluctantly. "But it makes me—"

"Shhh!" Liana said suddenly. She pulled her horse to a stop and motioned Emereck and Kensal to do likewise.

"What—"

"Quiet, please! I thought I heard something."

All three of them sat motionless, listening. Emereck heard nothing but the small noises of a forest: leaves whispering quietly in the breeze, birds twittering at each other, the rustle of some small animals passing. "I don't hear anything," he said at last.

"Nor I," Kensal said.

Liana frowned. "It's that way," she said with certainty, pointing slightly north of their westward path.

"Um." Kensal looked at her. "What was it you heard?"

"I'm not sure. Pipes, I think, or—"

"Pipes?" Emereck's stomach felt suddenly hollow. "You mean, music?"

"Well, yes, but not like anything I've ever heard before."

Kensal looked at Emereck. "Are you thinking what I think you're thinking?"

"It can't be!" Emereck said with a vehemence that surprised him. "We aren't anywhere near that castle!"

Liana's eyes widened. "You mean the place where you found the Harp? *That's* what I heard?"

"That's what he means," Kensal said. "Castle Windsong."

"But how can I be hearing it? And why couldn't you?"

"You are of the blood of the Dukes of Minathlan," Kensal said with a shrug. "According to Ryl, that's all it takes."

"I don't believe it," Emereck protested. "That castle was at least four days' ride from the edge of the forest, maybe more. We haven't come anywhere near that far."

Kensal smiled wryly. "Castle Windsong has a mind of its own, indeed."

"It isn't possible! Castles don't jump around from place to place like frogs!"

"Perhaps this one does. There's only one way to find out." Kensal turned his horse in the direction Liana had indicated.

"No!" Emereck said firmly.

"Emereck, what's the difference?" Liana asked. "It's

not far out of our way."

"This isn't a pleasure outing! There are Syaski hunting us, remember?"

"We don't know that for certain," Liana replied mildly.

"And if there are, Castle Windsong may well be the safest place for us," Kensal said. "Only the family of the Dukes of Minathlan can find it."

"And if it isn't Windsong? It could be a trap," Emereck said.

"I doubt it. I don't think even the Shadow-born could imitate Windsong well enough to fool one of the Duke's kin."

"It doesn't feel dangerous," Liana put in. "And if it *is* Windsong, I'm curious about it."

"Then go by yourself. I'm not going back there." With a jerk that made his horse toss its head in protest, Emereck pulled the animal around and started off, heading almost due south. After a few moments, he heard the sounds of the other horses behind him, but he did not turn. He was ashamed of himself, and appalled by his loss of temper.

But how could he explain? He had found the Harp at Castle Windsong. The chain of events that ended with Flindaran's death had begun at Castle Windsong. He was afraid of the place: afraid of falling victim to its magic and its music; afraid of finding Ryl there to demand the return of the Harp; afraid of losing Liana as he had Flindaran.

The thought froze him. He hunched his shoulders, trying to relax muscles that had gone taught as harpstrings stretched to breaking. He told himself firmly that it couldn't be the same castle. The place they had found the Harp was miles away, farther north and much further west. Liana was safe from— He jerked in the saddle as the wind brought him an echo of unmistakable music.

"There it is again!" Liana said.

"It's definitely Windsong," Kensal commented. "And we seem to be getting closer."

"I heard it," Emereck said grimly, and pulled his horse to a stop. At the same moment he realized that the sound had come from directly in front of him. He looked angrily at Liana. "I thought you said it was coming from back there!"

"It was, then."

"I suppose you're going to tell me it moved."

Liana looked at him. "No. I'm not going to tell you anything at all."

Savagely, Emereck turned his horse west. "Keep this up much longer and we'll be going in circles," Kensal commented. Emereck ignored him. The breeze died, taking the music with it, but only for a brief time. When the wind and music resumed, both were coming from the west. And the music was louder. Emereck reined in once more.

"I think you might as well give up," Kensal said.

"Are you doing this?" Emereck demanded.

"Of course not. I'm a soldier, not a magician."

"Then how—"

"None of us can answer that unless we stop trying to avoid it," Liana said.

Emereck looked at her. "I suppose I really don't have much choice," he said at last.

"Then let's go," Kensal said, and lifted his reins. His mare started forward. Liana followed; Emereck, still fuming inwardly, brought up the rear. He still did not understand how they could be heading for the place where he and Flindaran had found the Harp, but he did not doubt that it was so. He feared the castle and mistrusted it, the same way he feared and mistrusted the Harp. Yet there seemed no way to avoid it now.

He heard Liana gasp and urged his horse forward. The others had stopped at the top of a low rise. He pulled his horse to a halt beside them and looked down. Below was the field of halaiba flowers and the high, white wall surrounding the castle and its gardens. He noted absently that this time the gate was facing them. They would have only a short ride through the flowers to reach it. Emereck frowned suddenly. How long had it been since he and Flindaran were here? Nearly three weeks, and the halaiba were still blooming. He gave a mental shrug and added it to the list of strange things in and around the castle.

"It's beautiful," Liana said softly.

Emereck glanced at her uneasily, wondering what she saw that he did not. A white wall rising from a sloping sea of blue flowers certainly made a striking picture, but beautiful? He remembered Flindaran's reactions to the forest and the castle, and his uneasiness grew. "Liana, maybe we shouldn't go on."

"I don't think we *can* stop now," Liana replied, giving him an odd look. "Besides, we haven't found out anything yet." She urged her horse forward without waiting for Emereck to answer, and the sweet scent of crushed halaiba rose strong and heavy in her wake. Kensal glanced at Emereck and followed her, leaving Emereck little choice but to join them. All the way down the hill Emereck felt the eyes of the forest on his back.

The gates opened at Liana's touch. They rode inside and dismounted. The garden was as green and cool as Emereck remembered, but he did not find its sameness comforting. Liana, however, was delighted. "I've never seen such lush plants!" she said. "And are those the sculptures you told me about? Will it hurt anything if I look at them?"

"I doubt it," Emereck said. "I did it last time." He watched her for a while as she went from one of the statues to another. Then he turned to Kensal. "Well, what do we do now?"

"I suggest we make camp. This is the safest place I can think of, and I suspect Ryl will be here soon. We may as well wait."

"Ryl. Of course."

"You'll have to face her some time, you know."

Emereck looked away. The Cilhar seemed to have read his thoughts, and it was not a pleasant feeling. Furthermore, the man was right, and admitting that, even to himself, was not pleasant either. What *was* he going to do with the Harp of Imach Thyssel when Ryl asked for it? Would he have any choice? He scowled. "Go ahead and make camp," he said.

While Kensal unloaded his mare, Emereck went over to his own horse. He unstrapped the Harp and stood looking at it for a long time, as if by doing so he could somehow determine what he ought to do. Finally, he shook himself. He started to set the Harp down beside the rest of his belongings, then paused. The habit of concealment was still strong; he did not feel comfortable leaving the Harp in plain view, even if Kensal and Liana were the only ones around to see it.

With a sigh, he picked up the Harp and carried it to one side of the low stairs leading into the castle. He opened his saddlebag and piled clothes and bedding over the Harp until it was thoroughly hidden. Feeling a little foolish, he went to get his own instrument. Perhaps a few hours of practicing would help him think.

As soon as they were well within the forest, the Duke pulled his horse up next to Ryl's. "Have you some idea how far ahead of us they are?"

"A day's ride, at least, though we have gained some time thanks to your horses."

"And thanks to Welram's work with them," the Duke replied, nodding to the Wyrd. "I wish my grooms had your talents."

Welram grinned, showing white, pointed teeth. "Some skills come naturally to certain people."

"Quite so," the Duke said dryly. "If one happens to be a Wyrd. But how much more time can we gain, and how quickly?"

"That depends."

"On what?"

"On how much you value your horses. There are limits even to the magic of the Wyrds."

"I see." The Duke glanced at Ryl. "I don't suppose you might be able to do something about the problem."

"I fear not, but it is unimportant."

"Unimportant?" The Duke raised an eyebrow.

"Now that we are within the forest, you can bring us

to our goal. Or rather, bring our goal to us."

Duke Dindran stared at her, for once nonplussed. "I?"

"We have passed the border of the lands that once were ruled from Castle Windsong. You are of that line of rulers; within these lands you can call it to you, if you will. And the ones we seek are there."

"I . . . see."

"Can-you not feel it?"

"I believe there is something."

"Perhaps we are still too close to the border," Welram suggested.

"That is possible," Ryl said, frowning. "The castle should grow easier to call as we come nearer to it. Wait, then, and try again in a little while."

"As you request," said the Duke.

Shalarn's Captain rode toward her through the trees and pulled his horse to a halt. "We have found them, my lady," he said, bowing.

"Good! How many of them are there?"

"Only three. One is a minstrel, one a young woman." He paused. "The third is the Cilhar warrior we caught at the inn."

"Kensal Narryn! You are sure?"

"I cannot swear to his name, my lady, but I am certain it is the same man."

"And the woman—was she his companion at the inn?"

"No. I have never seen her before."

Shalarn frowned, wondering what this might mean. "How far away are they?"

"Just ahead, about ten minutes ride. We took care that they did not see us, as you commanded."

"Then we will follow them. And we will continue to avoid being seen."

"My lady, there are ten of us. Even a Cilhar cannot—"

"That is what you thought last time," Shalarn said sharply. "Your mistake has made my task more difficult. I am sure the Cilhar will remember you. I cannot force him to help me, and after the way you treated him at the inn he is not likely to trust me."

"But—"

"Enough! We will follow them without being seen, while I test their abilities. Then *I* will decide the time and place to meet them."

"Yes, my lady!" The Captain turned and gave the orders. Shalarn smiled inwardly. He was a trifle over-eager at times, and he had a regrettable tendency to think he knew more than she did. Still, he had a deep respect for her more unusual abilities; she would have no further trouble with him today.

For the rest of the morning, they followed the Cilhar, the minstrel, and the woman. Shalarn rode in a kind of half-trance, letting her body's reflexes keep her in the saddle while her mind cast tiny, questing spells at the group ahead. The Cilhar and the woman noticed nothing, but the minstrel felt something; she could tell by his growing nervousness. She had almost decided to stop her efforts, when she felt the first glimmerings of a new spell. She called her men to a halt at once.

"We ride into magic," she told them. "It is a spell of confusion to make us lose our way, and it is very old and very powerful. Stay with me and follow my lead, no matter how strange it seems, or you will be lost."

The men nodded. Shalarn turned and began the slow task of picking her way through the forest. She quickly realized that her only hope was to follow the Cilhar and his companions. She had no time to cast a proper spell; she would have to do the best she could without the benefit of her tools. She cast a tenuous linking spell to hold her mind to their path. Twice the fragile thread failed. When it caught hold at last, she clung tenaciously to it, tracing it slowly and carefully to avoid losing or breaking it.

The work seemed to go on for hours. Then, suddenly, it was over. Shalarn opened her eyes. Her horse stood at the top of a small rise looking down over a wide clearing filled with shrubby blue flowers. Strange music rose from a large, walled area in the center. The whole place reeked of magic.

Shalarn smiled in satisfaction and turned to her men. The smile vanished. Only three had managed to stay with her during the long, twisting ride while she sought the path through the forest. Only three.

"What are your orders *now*, my lady?" the Captain said.

Shalarn's eyes narrowed at his tone. "Why, the same as before. Though now I am certain you will agree with them. Three men are not good odds against a Cilhar."

"Yes, my lady."

"All three of you will come with me. You will not provoke them, and you will make no threatening move unless I myself am actually attacked. Have I made myself clear?"

"Yes, my lady."

"Then come." Trying to look more confident than she felt, Shalarn rode down the hill to the gate. The massive iron door was not latched; she waited until her men caught up with her, then pushed it open. "Dismount," she commanded. Leading their horses, they walked inside.

They stood in a garden surrounded by music and greenery. Shalarn glanced quickly around, and her eyes found the Cilhar almost at once. He had risen at their approach, and stood watching them through narrowed eyes. Behind him an unfamiliar girl slipped away through the trees. Of the minstrel there was no sign.

Shalarn motioned to her men to stay where they were. She stepped forward two paces and stopped, careful to keep her hands in sight. She waited, but he said nothing. Finally, she nodded. "I am the Lady Shalarn sa'Rithven, lately of Lithra. If you are Kensal Narryn, I would like to talk to you."

Twenty-two

*E*mereck was just finishing his third pass through the bridge of "Darneel and the Firebird" when the music of the singing statues changed dramatically. He stopped his own playing and listened carefully, wondering what had caused the change. The music still sounded like the work of a master improviser, but the key had risen a full step, and the style of playing was completely altered. Emereck frowned. The wind did not seem to have changed, and the statues were fixed in place. How could the music change so suddenly?

He looked up and saw Liana hurrying toward him around the ruined wing of the castle. He rose hastily. "What is it?" he said as she approached.

"Four people just came in—at least I think there are only four. Three soldiers and a noblewoman. They're talking to Kensal now."

"Ryl! And you left her with Kensal and the Harp?"

"I thought you would want to know. Besides, I don't think it's Ryl. Kensal didn't seem to recognize her."

Emereck stifled a curse. So much for Kensal's assurances that no one but Ryl could find Windsong! He snatched up his harp and ran through the garden toward the gate, Liana at his heels. When he rounded the end of the ruined wing, he went more cautiously, keeping out of sight behind statues and clumps of bushes and motioning Liana to do the same. He stopped when they had worked their way close enough to hear. Panting slightly, he peered around the edge of a bush.

A striking, dark-haired woman stood several paces in front of Kensal. She was dressed in an elaborate riding costume of red silk and brown velvet, trimmed in gold, and her hair was coiled on top of her head in the fashion of Lithmern noblewomen. Behind her, just inside the iron gate, stood three men in uniforms, holding horses and watching Kensal through narrowed eyes. Two of the men were completely unfamiliar. The third Emereck recognized at once, and a chill ran down his spine. He was the leader of the Lithmern who had attacked Ryl's inn.

"You can hardly expect me to believe that," Kensal was saying. "This is not the sort of place one comes to by accident."

The woman smiled, like a cat discovering the cream untended. "Just so. And you and your companions had as much purpose in coming here as I."

"We will leave my companions out of the conversation for the moment," Kensal replied. "At the risk of sounding inhospitable, I must point out that you are the ones who must explain your presence. And before you spin me any more fairy tales, I will tell you that I have recognized your Captain."

"I regret the inconvenience he caused you at your last meeting," the woman said. The look she gave the unfortunate Captain would have cracked stone. "He overstepped his authority."

"Really." Kensal's voice was politely noncommittal.

"I wished only for the opportunity to speak with you."

"You have it now."

"I have heard that you know something of interest to me."

"Anything's possible. But I'm still waiting for an explanation of your presence here."

The woman sighed. "I am seeking something."

"Which is?"

"A way to destroy the Shadow-born."

Emereck stiffened, and his hand tightened involuntarily on the branch he was holding. The woman's head turned toward the faint rustling, and she said, "Your companions seem to be returning at last, Cilhar."

Emereck went forward at once, feeling a little foolish at being discovered so easily. Liana followed at a little distance. The Lithmern woman's eyes widened slightly when she saw him, as if in recognition. Emereck studied her unobtrusively, but he was certain he had never seen her before. He wondered who she thought he was.

Kensal nodded as Emereck joined him, and said, "Emereck, meet Shalarn sa'Rithven of Lithra—noblewoman, sorceress, and the person behind that attack at Ryl's inn."

"Not the best recommendation I've ever heard," Emereck said, trying to match Kensal's tone. Inwardly, he felt numb. This was the woman Gendron had mentioned, who had been staying with Prince Lanyk. Had they been working together? Was she aware of the Prince's death?

"I have already apologized for the overzealousness of my men," Shalarn said.

"Quite so," Kensal said blandly. "You were about to explain who or what these Shadow-born are that you wish to destroy."

"If you seek to test me, Cilhar, I shall pass," Shalarn replied with a touch of impatience. "The Shadow-born are things without bodies, powerful and intelligent beings that live below the surface of the earth. To walk in sunlight they must use others' bodies. They are old beyond imagining, and wise in magic."

"And your reasons for wishing to destroy these wise, powerful, and ancient beings?"

"They are responsible for the loss of my home and the current unfortunate position of my country." Her voice was even, but Emereck could hear the undercurrents of anger and hatred.

"Um." Kensal studied her. "I suppose it's possible."

"It is more than possible! You are familiar with the details of our war with Alkyra a few years ago?"

"We have heard of it," Kensal said, glancing sideways at Emereck.

"Our king knew the war was coming, and he knew that the Alkyrans are sorcerers. So he prepared sorcery of his own to counter their magic, and encouraged others to assist him. He called on the Shadow-born for help, but they betrayed him. They destroyed our sorcerers and took command of the army, then led it into a trap."

"And how is it that you managed to escape?" Kensal asked mildly.

"I was lucky," Shalarn replied simply. "I had friends who helped me, and I was careful not to use magic until I was out of Lithra. Since then I have sought for a way of punishing the Shadow-born for what they have done."

"I see. And just how do you expect a Cilhar soldier to help you?"

"You have a . . . thing of great power. You cannot deny it. I have felt its presence, and I have tracked it since you or one of your friends made use of it a week ago in Minathlan."

"And you want it."

"I want it. I am being open with you, you see."

Emereck tensed. Kensal shot him a warning glance, and he forced himself to relax. Shalarn seemed to think Kensal had the Harp; he must do nothing to correct that impression. Kensal turned back to Shalarn and said, "What makes you think I would give it to you? Assuming, of course, that I have such a thing to give."

Shalarn smiled and lowered her eyelids. "I have learned a great deal in four years of searching. You are an enemy of the Shadow-born. I think you will help me because our aims are the same."

"Perhaps," Kensal said. "And perhaps not. You will allow me time to consider?"

"Of course."

"In the meantime, let me show you and your men around the gardens. They are quite fascinating."

"I would be pleased." Shalarn turned and motioned to her men.

"Show her the gardens? Kensal, are you mad?" Emereck whispered as soon as her back was turned.

"I want to see how her men move. The Captain looks as if he might be good; if it comes to a fight, I want to be prepared."

"We can't just let them stay here!"

"How would you suggest we get rid of them?"

"I don't know, but there must be some way. They're after the Harp."

"Of course they are!" Kensal sounded exasperated. "But as long as we know that, it's safer to have them here where we can watch— Are you ready, lady? This way, then." Kensal started around the castle, Shalarn and her men trailing in his wake.

Emereck scowled after them, wondering what he could do about them. After a moment, Liana joined him. "Do you believe her?" she asked.

"I believe she wants the Harp. I don't know about the rest of it."

"She makes the Shadow-born sound very different from what Kensal described."

"She's Lithmern. But frankly, right now I'm not sure who to believe. Or trust." Emereck stared after the little group disappearing among the trees.

Tammis rode slowly through the forest, half-hidden from accidental discovery by the leaves and the spells she had wrapped around herself. She could feel magic ahead, the strong fire of the thing she sought and another, more nebulous presence that pushed her, trying to turn her from her path. It required all of the skill she had learned during the long years in the north to keep herself on the right heading. If she had not been warned of something like this, or if she had not had the beacon of the power she was looking for, she knew she would

*   * ˙ *

have lost her direction, possibly without ever realizing she had gone astray.

The thought made her concentrate all the more. Her progress slowed, but even at a snail's pace it grew harder and harder to keep her horse on the correct path. Finally she realized that she must abandon the horse or lose her way. She hesitated only briefly. If she succeeded in her task, she would have no problem in obtaining a new mount; if she failed, it would not matter.

She dismounted and stood motionless until the horse was out of sight. Then she renewed her concentration. Carefully, she felt out the path through the invisible maze that hemmed her in. Her progress was slow; her eyes told her that she was walking in a drunken circle, while her magic said she was drawing closer to her goal. She forced herself to ignore the evidence of her senses, and went on.

Finally she reached the top of a low rise, and knew her journey was at its end. Below, treetops showed above a long, white wall, and she could hear music from the other side. What interested her most, however, was the bright flame of the power she had followed so far. It was there on the other side of the wall; she could feel it. She smiled a small, cold smile, and started down the slope toward the gate.

She paused when she reached it and listened. She heard nothing but music. Cautiously, she pushed at the gate. It swung open; the fools were depending on the magic to guard them. She slipped inside and glanced quickly around. She counted seven horses, four of them still saddled, but no people.

Her eyes narrowed suddenly. That gray was Shalarn's horse, she was sure of it. So the Lithmern sorceress had managed to get here first! And the brown mare was a Cilhar's mount; she hadn't seen one of the small, sturdy animals since she'd left the mountains.

Her eyes swept the garden once more and fastened on an untidy pile of clothes beside the stairs. She almost laughed aloud. *That* was a hiding place? She started forward, but she had taken only two steps when she heard the sound of voices approaching through the trees. She hesitated; it was so close! But she had no time. Cursing beneath her breath, she slid away into the bushes.

"How far do you want to go before you try again?" Welram asked.

"I'm afraid you will have to ask Rylorien," the Duke replied. "I've never done this before."

"Not far, I think," Ryl said. "In fact—" She stopped. The Duke was not listening. He was looking intently into the forest ahead of them, his eyes narrowed and his lips pressed tightly together.

Welram dropped his reins and reached for his bow. "What is it?"

"I don't know," the Duke said slowly. "But something seems to be wrong."

Ryl frowned, concentrating, When she looked up, her eyes were full of concern. "Something is wrong indeed. Time grows short. Call Windsong now, if you can, or we may be too late."

The Duke nodded. He sat motionless for a long moment, staring at nothing. Then he shook his head and his eyes focused. "This way," he said, turning his horse. "It's only a few minutes more."

Welram cocked an ear at the Duke. "You're quite sure? I thought you hadn't done this before."

"Some skills come naturally to certain people," the Duke said blandly.

"Quite so," Welram replied with a fierce grin. He looked at Ryl and picked up his reins. "Well, if there's trouble ahead, we don't want to keep it waiting. Let's go."

Twenty-three

*W*hen Emereck caught up with the others, Shalarn was chatting easily with Kensal. Her men seemed no more pleased by this than Emereck, particularly the Captain. Emereck found himself trying to split his attention three ways so that he could watch Kensal, Shalarn and the Captain with equal care. He was not particularly successful. By the time they came in sight of the gate once more, he had learned nothing whatever and he was beginning to get a headache.

"Emereck."

Liana's voice roused him from his musings and he turned. "What is it?"

"Did you see something just now by the gate?"

"No, but I wasn't really paying attention." He glanced at the gate and frowned, puzzled. "It does seem different, somehow."

"No, no, I didn't mean that it looked any different. I thought I saw something move."

"There's nothing there now. Maybe . . ." Emereck's voice trailed off as he realized what it was that made him think the scene had altered. "The music's changed again!"

"Has it?" Liana was still staring toward the gate.

"Not much, the key's the same. But the style is—"

"Something's wrong."

"What?" Emereck looked around. Shalarn and Kensal were standing beside one of the wind-music statues, still talking. The rich silks and velvets of her riding costume made a sharp contrast to the faded green leather of the Cilhar's uniform, and the curving shape of the bone-white statue beside them added a touch of strangeness to the picture. Shalarn's men were scattered through the nearby garden, looking uncomfortable and extremely out of place against the rich greens and browns of the lush plants. The two guards were watching Kensal with obvious unease; the Captain was edging toward the horses just inside the gate. Emereck looked back at Liana. "I don't see anything."

"I don't know what's wrong. And I don't know how I can tell, either, so please don't ask."

Emereck glanced back toward Kensal and Shalarn. "Can you at least—" He stopped and blinked. All of the shadows in the garden had just shifted. He spun and looked up at the sun. It was a good three finger-widths to one side of where it should have been.

"What was *that*?" Liana said breathlessly.

Emereck's head jerked down to look at her again. "You felt something?"

"Didn't you?" They looked at each other. "If you didn't feel anything, why did you jump like that?" Liana said at last.

"I saw the shadows change. I think the castle may have moved again."

Liana looked over her shoulder at the sun. "I think you're right. I wonder where we are now?"

"I'm more concerned with why it happened. Look, will you make sure Kensal knows? And try and find out if that woman noticed anything. I'm going to check the Harp."

Liana nodded and started toward Kensal and Shalarn. Emereck turned and walked swiftly toward the front of the castle. The pile of garments that hid the Harp looked untouched; with Shalarn's men watching he did not dare check more closely. He breathed a quiet sigh of relief and walked on, trying to look as if he had been heading for his horse all along.

The Captain scowled, but stepped back to let Emereck pass. At the edge of his vision, Emereck saw Shalarn approaching from what was now the south side of the gate. Liana and Kensal had fallen a little behind her, and Shalarn's two guards had moved in to flank them. Emereck frowned, wondering what they were planning. Then his attention was jerked away by a ripple of movement ahead of him. The castle gates were swinging open.

Emereck stepped back a pace. Behind him, he heard the soft ringing of a sword being drawn from its sheath, and then the gates were open far enough to reveal the riders on the other side. Emereck recognized the Duke of Minathlan and Ryl at once, but the sight of the third rider drove all other thoughts from his head.

His face and arms were covered with a fine, dark brown fur. From a mane of the same color emerged two ears shaped like a fox's but with short tufts of hair at their ends. He wore a loose tunic of dark green, belted at the waist. He carried a bow and a quiver of arrows at his back, and he rode bareback on a shaggy pony.

Emereck closed his mouth and swallowed hard as the three rode inside. A Wyrd! And riding with the Duke of Minathlan and Ryl. He tried to force his stunned mind to think, to consider the implications, but he could not do it. He could only remember the legends: the Wyrd attack on Basaraan during the Wars of Binding, their cities made of living trees, their magic and their songs.

The riders dismounted, and Emereck shook himself and glanced around. Shalarn and her men were staring in wonder at the Wyrd. Liana seemed less astonished, though she watched the Wyrd with curiosity. Only Kensal showed no surprise; his lips quirked in a wry smile as he bowed to Ryl, but that was all.

The Duke's eyes swept the company, and he gave a small, stiff nod of recognition in Emereck's direction. Emereck bowed in return. The Duke's lips tightened;

then Liana stepped forward, and the lines around his mouth softened fractionally. "I am glad to find you well, my dear," he said.

"Thank you, sir," Liana replied, and curtsied. "Allow me to present my companions: the Lady Shalarn sa'Rithven of Lithra and her guard, and Kensal Narryn of the Cilhar."

Shalarn darted a sharp look in Emereck's direction when it became apparent that Liana was not going to continue. The Duke's head turned to look at her. "Lithra. I see." He looked at Ryl. "I believe we have found the source of that wrongness we were discussing earlier."

"I think not," Ryl replied. "She bears no taint of shadow."

"You are sure?"

"I am. Open yourself to the castle and you will be sure as well."

"She claims she is looking for a way to destroy the Shadow-born," Kensal put in.

"And so I am," Shalarn said, controlling her anger with obvious effort. "You cannot deny it."

"True," Kensal said. "But I also can't confirm it. We have only your word, either way."

"The Wyrd Glens of Alkyra sent word long ago of Lithra's dealings with the Shadow-born," the Wyrd said. His voice was deeper than Emereck had expected from so small a person.

"Do you think everyone in Lithra believed their promises?" Shalarn said. "And do you think we all believe them still, after they destroyed our sorcerers and forced our army into the trap at Coldwell?"

"'Who can be fooled once, can be fooled again,'" the Wyrd quoted.

"Peace, Welram," Ryl said. "Have I not said she is no knowing servant of the Shadow-born?"

"Knowingly or unknowingly, I serve no one but myself!" Shalarn said. "I seek to destroy the Shadow-born. They will pay for what they have done to me and to Lithra."

"Revenge is overrated," the Duke said. "As well as being rather difficult in this case. The Shadow-born are not lightly disturbed."

"Nevertheless, I will do it! That is why—" Shalarn stopped and glanced at Kensal.

"That is why she has been following me," Kensal said. He looked at Ryl. "She wants what we came for."

"Ah." Ryl looked at Shalarn, and there was something like pity in her eyes. "If what you say is true, I am afraid it would do you no good. If the Harp of Imach Thyssel could destroy the Shadow-born, we would have used it long ago to do so."

"The Harp of Imach Thyssel!" Shalarn's eyes flew from Kensal to Emereck. "So it is the minstrel I want!"

"No," Ryl said gently. "Did you not hear me? The Harp can undo certain of the works of the Shadow-born, for it is older even than they, but it cannot harm the Shadow-born themselves."

Shalarn turned back to Ryl. "How do you know?"

As Ryl started to answer, Emereck took one step backward, then another, until he was standing outside the little knot of conversation. He saw Kensal's eyes flicker, then the Cilhar stepped casually between Shalarn and Emereck. Emereck let out a slow breath and turned slightly, so that he could watch the hidden Harp as well as Shalarn and her two guards. He frowned suddenly and looked quickly around. Shalarn's Captain was nowhere in sight.

Uneasily, Emereck took another step backward. Where had the man gone? Shalarn was still arguing with Ryl. She did not seem to have noticed him, but Welram and Liana were both looking at him curiously. He shook his head, hoping fervently that they would look away before Shalarn noticed and turned to see what they were staring at.

Emereck glanced around once more and saw the bushes to the right of the gate quiver. A moment later, the missing Captain appeared from behind them. Emereck's vague fears vanished and he felt foolish; the man must have gone into the bushes to relieve himself, that was all.

The Captain came forward, swinging wide around the little clump of people. Emereck backed up again, so that the Captain would not pass between him and the Harp. The Captain ignored him. Emereck's misgivings returned and he frowned, wondering what the man was up to. The Captain's attention seemed concentrated on Kensal, as though the Cilhar was the only one of the group who really existed.

Emereck's eyes shifted to Kensal. He waited for the Cilhar to turn, to shift, to show by the most imperceptible change in position that he knew the Captain was there and that he was ready for him. Kensal did nothing, and Emereck's frown deepened. The Captain was directly behind Kensal now, and moving forward; he seemed to be heading for a position between Shalarn and the Cilhar. It was an eminently reasonable thing to do, and yet . . . Emereck took a deep breath, intending to add some comment to the conversation and thus call Kensal's attention to what was happening behind him. An instant later, he let it out in a cry of warning.

He was not quite in time, but he was not quite too late, either. Kensal started to turn, and the Captain's dagger struck his left side just below the shoulder, instead of his heart. Kensal staggered. His right hand flickered once, then reached for his sword. The Captain cried out and clutched at his left shoulder. One of the black, spiky raven's-feet protruded from it.

At almost the same instant, Shalarn gave a cry of pain. Emereck turned his head and saw another of the raven's-feet buried in her right arm. His eyes jumped back to Kensal; could even a Cilhar have thrown two of the weapons so quickly?

Shalarn's Captain had no such doubts. "Cilhar treachery!" he shouted. "To me, and defend the lady Shalarn!"

Shalarn's other two guards sprang forward, drawing their swords. "Treachery indeed," the Duke growled as he pulled out his own weapon and stepped forward to meet them.

"Stop this!" Shalarn cried. "Stop it at once!"

Her men ignored her and kept on. Kensal was already engaged with the Captain, their swords moving more rapidly than Emereck would have believed possible. Emereck shook off his momentary paralysis and dove for his belongings. There was a dagger in there somewhere, a gift from Flindaran long ago; he spared a mental curse for his stupidity in not wearing it. Without a weapon there was nothing he could do to help Kensal and the Duke.

It took only a moment to find the dagger. As his hand closed on the hilt, he heard Liana cry out. He whirled and started back before his eyes had time to take in what was happening.

Liana was unharmed. She had evidently been circling the combatants, possibly with the same idea as Emereck; she was standing halfway between the fight and the bushes where the Captain had emerged. Kensal and the Captain were still engaged, though both seemed to be tiring. Of the two, Kensal was in worse condition; the left side of his uniform was soaked with blood. Duke Dindran stood nearby. His sword had been dropped or wrenched away. He stood weaponless, one hand pressed against his side. A trickle of red crossed the back of the hand, and Emereck caught a glimpse of a black spike projecting out from between the fingers. One of Shalarn's guards lay unmoving in front of him. The other had his sword raised for a death stroke at the Duke.

There was no way Emereck could reach them in time. He cried out in frustration. The guard's sword started down—then dropped from his suddenly limp hand. The man stared in dumb surprise at the small wooden dagger hilt sticking out of his chest, then toppled. Beside Ryl, Welram grinned fiercely and lowered his throwing arm. He said something Emereck could not hear, and pointed toward the bushes.

Ryl nodded and raised her arms. *"Ri shera fin niterbarata il fina garhan lasa!"*

The bushes shivered, and Emereck heard an angry cry. With a rustle and a crackle, a woman came through them, walking as though she were being dragged. Her hair and eyes were dark. She was tall, taller than the Duke; a loose cloak hid most of her figure. Her right hand held a raven's-foot poised to throw, but she seemed unable to move it. Her left was clenched in anger. Her face showed no trace of fear, only fury.

"*Tammis?*" Shalarn said incredulously.

The Captain's head turned toward the new arrival, and his eyes widened. "No! You said no one would know, you—" The sentence ended in a gurgle as Kensal's sword ran him through. Kensal pulled the weapon free, breathing hard. The Captain fell, still staring reproachfully at the woman called Tammis.

Ryl's eyes had not left Tammis and the raven's-foot she held. "Drop it," Ryl commanded, then when the woman did not obey, "*Bespyl pori!*"

The raven's-foot fell harmlessly to the ground. Emereck saw a flash of surprise mingle with the fury on Tammis's face, then her eyes narrowed. "Who are you?" she demanded, staring at Ryl.

"We might ask the same of you," the Duke pointed out. He had removed the raven's-foot from his side, but kept his hand pressed to the wound. It did not appear to have any effect on his usual manner.

"That will not be necessary," Kensal said. He had turned to face Tammis, and his voice was colder and harder than any Emereck had ever heard. "I know who she is. Tammis Fenrel, traitor and renegade. The Cilhar banished her ten years ago for deliberately leading her attack team into a trap."

"That's ridiculous!" Shalarn said emphatically. "She's the Princess of Syaskor!"

"Maybe, but she's also a Cilhar outlaw."

Tammis laughed suddenly. It was not a pleasant sound. "Kensal Narryn. I should have guessed; only you would still care about such ancient history." She smiled mockingly.

"I wish you had chosen to do your fighting yourself," Kensal said. "I would have enjoyed beating you."

"Easy enough to say to a woman who can't move."

Kensal turned. He seemed to be holding himself

upright by sheer force of will, but he still managed to lift
his sword and say, "Let go of her, Ryl."

"No. Wounded as you are, you would be no match
for her, and I would not have you die to no purpose.
And she is the source of the evil I have felt here." Ryl's
voice was calm, but her face was tense with concentration.

"*She serves the Shadow-born?*"

Ryl nodded.

Kensal looked at Tammis as though she were a snake
three days dead and crawling with maggots. "You
should have been killed ten years ago. And paralysis or
not, I'm going to do it now."

"I think not," Tammis said. Her smile widened
fractionally. "Not when I know exactly who your
companion is."

"You can't," Kensal said flatly.

"You forget—I, too, know the traditions of the
Cilhar. And you should not have chosen such an
obvious alias for such an exceptionally powerful sorceress." Tammis inclined her head very slightly in Ryl's
direction. "She can only be the Guardian Rylorien."

"There's nothing you can do about it."

Tammis laughed again. "I've learned more than you
think since I left the Mountains of Morravik. I know the
weakness of the Eleann."

The fingers of her left hand began to uncurl, one by
one, and Emereck saw that she held something within it.
Kensal started forward, but before he could reach her,
Tammis cried loudly, "*Arsklathran fin!*" and pointed at
Ryl. At the same moment, Emereck saw exactly what
she held in her hand. It was a slender crystal of smoky
black.

Twenty-four

As Tammis spoke there was a sudden wailing discord from the musical statues. The air darkened and grew colder. A ripple of distortion seemed to move outward from the crystal Tammis held. As it reached him, Emereck felt a twisting stab of pain in every bone and muscle of his body. He wanted to cry out, but he could not move. Then the ripple passed, leaving him gasping. A moment later Ryl screamed.

The sound froze Emereck's blood. He knew it, recognized it, though he had never heard it before. It was the scream of the golden people of his nightmare as they twisted and melted and changed, the scream he had never quite been able to hear in the dream but had always known was there. Slowly, reluctantly, his head turned, and he looked at Ryl.

She was lying on the ground, curled in on herself, her dark hair falling in a tangled veil around her. Her body shimmered and slipped out of focus, then solidified briefly. The outline of her form seemed to blur and run like butter melting slowly on a hot griddle. Her shape firmed again, and for a moment she lay gasping on the ground. Emereck had a momentary hope that she had succeeded in throwing off whatever was happening to her, then the cycle began again.

Kensal, too, had glanced at Ryl. He hesitated, apparently torn between rushing to help her and attacking Tammis. Then Welram threw himself to his knees beside Ryl and took her hand in one of his. His eyes narrowed to thin slits and he bared his teeth; it was a moment before Emereck realized that the Wyrd was concentrating on something.

That was enough for Kensal. He lunged toward Tammis, sword outstretched. Tammis raised the crystal. A shaft of blackness darted from her hand to Kensal, and the Cilhar crashed to the ground in front of her. She looked down. "Old fool," she muttered.

When Kensal lunged, Emereck had begun edging slowly toward the overgrown garden on his right. He still had his dagger. If he could get behind Tammis, perhaps he could stop her. He knew it for a faint hope, at best; he was a poor fighter by any standards while she was both Cilhar and a sorceress. But he had to do something. Ahead of him, he saw Liana moving with the same caution toward her bow and quiver. He would have smiled encouragement, but he did not want to distract her or to draw Tammis's attention in their direction.

As Kensal fell, the Duke started forward. Welram caught at him with his free hand. "Not with swords," the Wyrd gasped, so low Emereck could hardly hear him. "Need magic. Use Windsong."

"You!" Shalarn's voice surprised Emereck; he had almost forgotten her presence. She was staring at Tammis with undisguised loathing. "Servant of the Shadow-born!"

"How clever of you to notice," Tammis said. "Yes, I serve them. As you have."

"No! I hate them!"

"You have served them nonetheless. How do you think I found out about all this in the first place? Your Captain was helpful, but hardly knowledgeable enough to lead me to this."

"My Captain?" Shalarn stared down at the man's body.

"Your Captain," Tammis said, mimicking Shalarn's tone. "Why do you think he started this fight?"

"*You* told him to?"

"Very good. There were a few too many of you for me to handle alone, but you killed each other off quite nicely. Rylorien was a surprise, but she's no threat now."

"I'll kill you!" Shalarn's fingers curled into claws.

"I think not." Tammis smiled with maddening certainty. "I'm afraid I took the precaution of smearing poison on my raven's-feet. Neither you nor the Duke there will last much—"

Tammis broke off, and her head snapped in the Duke's direction. "What are you doing?"

Duke Dindran had not moved, but somehow he seemed to have grown taller and more substantial. His expression did not change, but his eyes met Tammis's and she swayed as though she had been struck. Shalarn glanced quickly from Tammis to the Duke, then reached into a black velvet pouch by her side and withdrew a small gold sphere. She breathed on it, then closed her eyes and muttered something under her breath.

Tammis was concentrating on the Duke. She raised the smoky crystal, and the darkness in the air intensified. The Duke's lips tightened as though he were bracing himself for something. At that instant, Shalarn opened her eyes and threw the gold sphere like a dagger at Tammis.

With a brilliant flash of light, the sphere struck the blackness that surrounded the Cilhar sorceress. Tammis jerked, and the bolt of black energy she had intended for the Duke skimmed over his head and demolished part of a tree. The music of the wind-sculptures grew louder, and the darkness thinned.

Tammis whirled. Shalarn's face was pale and tense with concentration. The golden sphere hung coruscating in the air, slowly eating away at the shadows Tammis had made. With a snarl, Tammis struck at it with her crystal, then spun back to face the Duke once more.

The sphere exploded in a shower of brilliant sparks.

Shalarn turned chalk-white; as Emereck watched, she swayed and slid slowly to the ground. The Duke's eyes narrowed. The wind-music skirled angrily, and the darkness around Tammis thinned still more.

Emereck was almost close enough to strike. He looked quickly around. Liana was barely two paces from her bow. Ryl was still fighting the spell Tammis had thrown at her, but it was clear that both her strength and that of the Wyrd was dwindling.

Emereck's eyes flew to the Duke, but Lord Dindran showed no sign of weakness. The invisible battle continued unabated, with the shadowed air and the swirling changes of the wind-music the only outward indications of its progress. Tammis took a step backward, then another. Emereck held his breath and raised his knife.

A ray of blackness licked out from the crystal Tammis held, but it struck Liana, not the Duke. The arrow Liana had been aiming went wide. "No!" Emereck screamed, and brought his knife down. Tammis dodged in a sinuous sideways motion, and Emereck's blade caught only the edge of her cloak.

"Stop!" Tammis cried. "One more move from either of you and the girl dies."

Emereck froze. Half-unbelieving, he looked at Liana. She had not fallen; relief made his knees weak. Then he saw the dark glow that surrounded her like a bubble of black glass. His skin crawled, and he looked back at Tammis in horror. She was panting slightly, her hand still holding the crystal high. Her eyes were fixed on the Duke, who had turned to look at his daughter.

Duke Dindran turned back, and his face was grim. "No," he said. "I cannot—"

As he turned, Tammis gestured. One of the black rays stabbed at the Duke. He reeled and fell to his knees. Emereck tried to lunge at the sorceress, but found himself unable to move. Tammis struck again. The Duke raised an arm as though to block her, then toppled. The music of the garden slowed, became a dirge. Breathing hard, Tammis looked at her erstwhile opponent.

"You almost won," she said, half to herself. "I can see I will have to learn more about this castle."

She turned to Emereck and gestured. He staggered and almost fell as the spell holding him vanished, then he struck at Tammis. She avoided him easily and raised a warning hand. "Not so fast! Have you forgotten?" She clenched her fingers around the black crystal and squeezed. Liana screamed.

"Stop it!" Emereck shouted.

"Drop your knife."

Emereck did. He felt numb and dazed. "Why don't you just kill me?"

"There's no need. You're no threat to me, and I dislike meaningless waste."

"What do you call all this?" Emereck said bitterly.

"Necessary." Tammis smiled coldly. "Now, bring me the Harp."

"No!"

"Do as I say, or . . ." Tammis closed her hand, and Liana screamed again.

Emereck shut his eyes in pain. "All right! Just stop it."

Tammis nodded in satisfaction, and the screaming stopped. Emereck's shoulders sagged in defeat as he turned and walked toward the Harp's hiding place. He had failed again, and this failure was the worst of all.

He bent and brushed the concealing clothes and bedding away. Underneath, the Harp leaned against the white stone of the terrace. It was shimmering faintly with a cold, white light, and Emereck hesitated. It seemed a desecration to give the Harp to Tammis, but what else could he do? He was neither a warrior nor a wizard, only a minstrel.

"Bring it!" Tammis commanded.

Emereck bent and picked up the Harp. A flash of power shot through him as he touched it, like a joy so intense that it was painful, bringing with it a crowd of memories. Flindaran's voice: "It might be worth the price." The Duke: "I will not chance the Harp of Imach Thyssel's falling into Syaski hands." The exaltation on

Flindaran's face as he played the Harp. Liana: "Be careful, Emereck."

Emereck rose and turned, holding the Harp of Imach Thyssel. For the first time since he had found the Harp, he felt certain of what he must do. He smiled in pure relief, and drew his hands across the harpstrings.

The Harp came alive in his hands. Power crackled through him as he played. He felt it spreading out through the castle and gardens around him, shredding the darkness of Tammis's spells and making the air sing like chiming crystal. For a moment he thought he had won, then he saw Tammis turn with the slow inevitability of a dream and clench her fist around the smoky crystal.

Emereck tensed as a wave of darkness swept toward him, but his fingers did not falter. The shadows closed around him and he could no longer see the garden or Tammis, but it could not muffle the song of the Harp. The music buoyed Emereck up. As the darkness touched him, he felt only a distant twinge, like an old memory of pain or the faint echo of a broken chord. He almost laughed aloud. Tammis could not reach him! He plucked a chord of triumph, then began a run of notes to dispell the cloud around him. And then he heard Liana scream.

Fear stabbed him. The Harp seemed to catch at the emotion and intensify it. The darkness that hid the garden was swept away in an anxious ripple of notes. He saw Tammis's tight smile as Liana crumpled to the ground, and his fear exploded into murderous rage.

He stared at Tammis, and with a sudden, sure knowledge shaped nightmares in music. The Harp sang of loss and power and revenge beneath his hands: deep notes of menace, eerie minor chords of fear, a steadily building rhythm of anger and hatred. He saw Tammis lift her hand once more, and he plucked a single high note on a string that shimmered with a faint silver-green light.

The black crystal shattered in Tammis's hand, showering her with tiny slivers. Her face twisted in terror, and Emereck grinned in savage triumph. With all the power that ran singing through him, he sent her worst fears back to her in music, willing them to destroy her.

The garden began to shimmer and fade around him. Emereck saw only Tammis, drowning in the sea of music he was making. Exultantly, he forced his fingers to move even faster. Tammis screamed, writhed, then faded, leaving Emereck alone with his song of madness and revenge. Emereck laughed, feeling the power of the Harp of Imach Thyssel. His harp. He played on.

Faces began to form in the haze around him: a Guild Master he disliked, a fellow student who had been deliberately offensive, a merchant who had cheated him. Emereck smiled. With the Harp to call on, he could send retribution on them all. He could do anything, he could—

Another face formed in the mist before him. Emereck's heart lurched and his fingers slowed. It was Flindaran. He looked gravely at Emereck, without speaking. The memory of Flindaran's betrayal swept over Emereck, bringing with it a mad desire for revenge.

Emereck drew a sobbing breath. The other images disappeared; Flindaran had done far more to hurt Emereck than any of them. The face hung in the air, waiting, while the strings of the Harp pulsed with a song of revenge and hatred and insanity. Waiting for Emereck to set the magic of the Harp free to do its work.

"No," Emereck whispered, and muted the droning of the lower strings. His mind cleared a little, and he shuddered at the thought of what he had almost done. He was worse than Flindaran; his friend had never sought to use the Harp in anger and hatred. Emereck looked up. "I'm sorry," he said in a low voice. "About everything."

The last shreds of the hunger for revenge left him. Flindaran smiled. As the haze around Emereck began to clear, the smile became Flindaran's old, mischievous grin, and then the apparition vanished.

The Harp of Imach Thyssel still hummed beneath Emereck's fingers. He looked up from his playing, and saw Tammis lying motionless in front of him. Involuntarily, his head turned toward Liana, and the Harp sang sorrow in his hands. Then, as he started to turn away, he saw her fingers twitch.

Almost without his willing it, the music of the Harp swelled once more. His mind seemed to spread out along with it, filling the garden. He could hear the song of the castle, powerful and complicated and constantly changing. Held within it was a soft, fading melody that was Liana's. link to Windsong. He heard another similar melody as well, deeper and stronger but slowly waning; the Duke, too, was not yet dead. Only the magic of Castle Windsong had kept them both alive this long.

Quickly Emereck plucked two high, sweet chords, sending a surge of healing toward Liana and another toward the Duke. The magic did its work almost instantly; he could hear their new strength in the music that was Windsong. Then he remembered Kensal and tried to find him. There was nothing, not even a dying echo. Emereck felt a stab of sorrow, but he had no time to indulge his grief. There were still Ryl and Welram to consider. Emereck turned his attention in their direction.

Instinctively he recoiled from what he heard. Ryl was trapped in a harsh jangle of sound, a twisted parody of music that should never have existed. He heard it below the music of the Harp, behind the music of the garden, as a greedy, strident discord. A delicate web of harmony was all that kept the deformed spell away from her. Welram's magic was a steady accompaniment supporting the fragile defense, but it was clear from the slowing tempo that the Wyrd was almost exhausted.

Cautiously, Emereck plucked a chord, then another. Power vibrated through the Harp, but he dared not add it to Welram's efforts. The balance of harmony in Ryl's defenses was too delicate; one wrong note, or one played a fraction too loudly or too late, and the protective melody would be drowned out by the twisted horror around it. Emereck paused, listening to the inaudible echoes of the spells. Then he began to play, improvising an accompaniment to the distorted music of Tammis's twisted spell.

It took all his skill to follow the changing dissonances, but he made no mistakes. His fingers danced over the strings, resolving phrases the spell left hanging, modulating from one key to another, shaping the disordered cacophony into something like music.

Power poured from the Harp as he played, reshaping the spell as he reshaped the music. As the harshness of the noise began to soften into melody, Emereck added a run of high, sweet notes, sending healing toward Ryl and Welram as he had done for the Duke and Liana. The sounds of their magic grew stronger, surer. And slowly they began to win.

Finally it was finished. Ryl sat up, blinking; beside her, Welram relaxed in relief. Emereck smiled and let go of the magic that flowed into him from the Harp. But the music did not stop. Emereck's smile faded, and he tried to stop playing, to pull his fingers from the strings, to throw the Harp aside. He could not do it.

His hands continued to play without his willing it. He looked up, and the garden was changed. More clearly than ever, he could hear the web of magic woven through it, molding the wind and the music of the statues. Liana and the Duke were part of it, focal points that fit seamlessly into the overall harmony that was the castle. Welram was a warm, deep sound, like a set of bass pipes. And Ryl . . . if there was anything Ryl resembled, it was the music of the Harp itself, clear and pure and powerful.

Again Emereck tried to stop playing, without success. He could not halt the magic that flooded him. He could feel himself drowning in the music, as Tammis had drowned, and he was afraid. He thought of the price the Harp exacted, and of the Prince of the Kulseth who had been crippled by the power of the Harp. Perhaps this was what had happened to him: the Harp out of control and the power of its music building and building, until at last it burned him up from the inside. Emereck swallowed hard, wondering how long it would take.

He could hear nothing now except the music of the Harp, and the ringing power in his ears, and, very faintly, the song of the wind on the sculptures. The song of the wind . . . Emereck's eyes widened in sudden hope. He could not set the Harp down, but he might be able to control what he played. And if he tried to play simply to make music, instead of to use the Harp for revenge or healing, perhaps the power would stop.

Emereck looked down at the Harp, trying to shut out everything except the movement of his fingers and the music of Castle Windsong. He began to improvise more consciously, choosing notes himself rather than allowing the Harp to direct his fingers. He ignored the power that filled him, then forgot it. His whole being was concentrated on the music.

The harpnotes wove in and out of the melody the castle played. After a few moments, Emereck realized that the music of the castle was changing, adapting with the skill of a Master Minstrel to what he played on the Harp. Emereck grinned. This was a game he knew well. At the Guildhall students had often displayed their skills by improvising a duet, each trying to outdo the other. His fingers flew over the strings, and music swirled through the garden.

A small part of his mind was aware that his gamble had succeeded; the power of the Harp was draining away. Emereck no longer cared. He was a minstrel, and the Harp was meant to make music. Nothing else mattered. He called on all the skill he possessed, for no reason but the sheer joy of creation.

At last he stopped, exhausted. His fingers hurt from plucking the harpstrings; his arms were sore from holding the instrument for so long. He sighed in satisfaction and set the Harp on the ground, then lowered himself to sit beside it. Only then did he realize that Ryl, Liana, Welram, and the Duke were standing beside the castle gate, watching him.

Twenty-five

Ryl broke the silence. "Well done, minstrel, and very well done. I did not think it possible for anyone to do what you have just done."

"I didn't do anything," Emereck said, still feeling somewhat bemused. "It was the Harp."

"The Harp of Imach Thyssel has great power, but your mind and will directed it."

Emereck looked at the bodies sprawled behind her and shuddered. Shalarn lay face down where she had fallen. Slightly ahead of her the three crumpled heaps of the Captain and his guards formed a half-circle around Kensal. Just beyond was a body so twisted that it was only by eliminating everyone else that Emereck could identify it as the Cilhar sorceress, Tammis. Emereck thought of the music and the madness and the glee with which he had hurled nightmares at her. He looked away, feeling sick.

Liana's eyes followed his. "You can't blame yourself for all this, Emereck," she said.

"Can't I? None of it would have happened if I hadn't been fool enough to take the Harp."

"Then remember that there has been healing here as well as death," Ryl said sternly, "and do not seek to carry more blame than is your share."

"There has been healing," Emereck said in a low voice, "but not enough." His eyes sought Kensal's body once more.

"Kensal told me that few Cilhar die peacefully," Liana said half to herself. "I don't think he really wanted to be one of them."

"He chose his death," Welram put in unexpectedly. "I saw it in his face."

"Yes." Ryl's voice held a distant sorrow. "He knew more than to expect a sword to be of use against such magic as Tammis wielded."

"Then why did he attack her?" Emereck said.

Ryl looked at him. "Why did you?"

Emereck glanced at Liana and felt his face grow hot. "I had to," he said shortly.

"As did Kensal. I think he hoped to distract Tammis enough to allow one of us to defeat her." Ryl sighed. She looked back at Kensal's body, and her expression became remote. "I will remember him."

There was a moment's silence. Then the Duke of Minathlan said, "My sympathy is yours, lady. But do you have any objection to disposing of the bodies now?"

Ryl did not respond. The Duke seemed about to repeat his question, when there was a brilliant flash of light from where Kensal's body lay. A wave of heat struck Emereck. When the brief dazzle cleared from his eyes, Kensal's body was gone. A dusting of ash hung in the air, to be dispersed almost at once by the singing winds.

"The Cilhar burn their dead," Ryl said. "So much, at least, I owed him. Do as you will with the others."

The Duke nodded. Emereck climbed to his feet, foreseeing an unpleasant interval of hauling bodies. Then he stopped. The Duke had not moved, but there was a line of concentration between his eyebrows. Behind him, the bodies of Shalarn and her men were sinking into the ground, slowly but steadily. Emereck stared until the surface of the grassy courtyard closed over them and smoothed out into firm, hard ground once more. Only Tammis's twisted corpse remained to show that anything had happened.

"Very good for a beginner," Welram said. "But what about the last one?"

Duke Dindran frowned. "I have no desire to allow such as she to remain in my lands, even in death. Yet I confess I am not certain of the best way to remove her."

Welram gave the Duke one of his pointed-tooth grins. "Perhaps Ryl and I can help you. I think it's safe enough now?" He added the last with a questioning look at Ryl.

"It is safe for a little time," Ryl said. "Come, then."

She held out her left hand, and Welram took it in one of his own. With her right, she sketched a figure in the air. "*Avoc arat!*" she said. Emereck felt the words pull at him, and Tammis's body vanished.

"My thanks," the Duke said, bowing.

"It is a small enough thing to do for the prince of Castle Windsong," Ryl replied.

"I don't understand," Liana said. "What did you do?"

"We sent the body away to an empty part of the plains on the other side of Minathlan," Welram said.

"Yes, but why?"

"Tammis was a servant of the Shadow-born," Ryl replied. "All her magic, she learned from them, and much of her power came through the link she carried."

"The black crystal!" Emereck said.

"Yes. She bore the taint of shadow willingly, and even in death it would not leave her. To bury such a one in a place of power would be . . . unwise, at best."

"It could have given the Dark Men a way into Windsong," Welram said.

"Or a way to destroy it," Ryl added. "Windsong has long been a stronghold for the enemies of the Shadow-born."

"Then why was it ever abandoned?" Emereck asked.

Ryl smiled a little sadly. "It was not abandoned, exactly. The princes of Windsong became one with their domains; they *are* the castle and the lands around it. The last of them merged with the land centuries ago."

"I thought they had gone to Minathlan."

"Minathlan was settled by a younger son at a time when the family was numerous. There were other such colonies, but they have all died out over the centuries. The Dukes of Minathlan are the last."

Liana looked at the Duke. "And you mean to live here, my lord?"

"To claim it at least. There appears to be no one else who can do so with any justification."

"But Minathlan—"

"I believe I am sufficiently aware of my responsibilities that you need not remind me of them."

"Then what *will* you do with Windsong?" Liana persisted.

"As I understand it, the only requirement is that one who is 'of the blood' of the Dukes of Minathlan rule here," the Duke said and paused, looking pointedly at Liana.

"It would be a good job for Oraven," Liana said hastily. "He's needed something to distract him for a long time."

The Duke raised an eyebrow. "An excellent suggestion. I do not think he will refuse the offer."

Ryl smiled. "Then one good thing, at least, has come of this confusion. It will be good to have Windsong occupied again."

"That reminds me." The Duke turned and looked at Emereck.

Emereck stiffened. "My lord?"

"I believe you are in some measure responsible for 'this confusion.' Now that things have, er, quieted, perhaps you would be good enough to explain how you happen to be here with my daughter and the Harp of Imach Thyssel."

"Of course, my lord. But the story is a long one. Will you be seated first?"

"When did a minstrel ever tell a story briefly?" But the Duke moved toward the paved terrace at the front of the castle, and the others followed.

Emereck brought the Harp with him, and set it close

beside himself. When everyone had found a place, he began his tale. For Welram's benefit, he began with a summary of the fight at Ryl's inn, the finding of the Harp, and the events leading up to Flindaran's death. He covered his escape from Minathlan and the journey across the plains in greater detail. He was interrupted only once. When he tried to gloss over Liana's presence, she broke in and pointed out with great firmness that coming with him had been her own idea.

At last he finished. The Duke looked at him. "Well, minstrel—"

"My lord," Liana interrupted. "May I speak?"

The Duke raised an eyebrow. "I seem unable to prevent you."

Liana smiled, completely unabashed. "Thank you, my lord. Emereck does not do himself justice in his account."

"I see." Duke Dindran looked at her. "And what interest do you have in the matter?"

"I wish to marry him, Father, with your blessing."

Emereck's head jerked toward her, the Duke forgotten. "Liana!"

Liana raised her chin. "You must have heard me, or you wouldn't look so shocked."

"Liana, this isn't the time for—"

"It is, too. If my father agrees." She looked at the Duke.

"And if I don't, you will be sweet and reasonable until I change my mind," the Duke said. He sighed. "In some ways you are very like your mother, Liana."

Liana rose and curtsied. "Thank you, my lord."

"My lord, you can't let her marry me!" Emereck said.

"Why not?" Liana demanded. "Do stop making objections, Emereck."

"Why not, indeed?" murmured the Duke. "It seems . . . fitting." He smiled blandly at Emereck's shocked expression. "After all, I appear to owe you both my life and my daughter's."

"Thank you, Father," Liana said demurely.

Emereck looked at Liana, and a crescendo of joy

began building within him. "I—I thank you as well, my lord. With all my heart." He leaned forward, and his hand brushed the Harp beside him.

The joy froze within him. He had played the Harp of Imach Thyssel; now he would have to pay the price. And if Liana's life became part of that price, he could not bear it.

"Emereck, what is it?" Liana said.

"The Harp," Emereck said dully. "There is a price for playing it, and until I have paid it I cannot—"

"No." Ryl was shaking her head.

"What?" Emereck turned to look at her.

"There is no price. The Harp is a tool, no more."

"How can you say that?" Emereck demanded. "Everyone who has ever played it has payed! King Loren, and the Prince of the Kulseth . . ." And Flindaran, he added silently.

"And Karth of Rathane, and Veleday of Tyrillian before that. But it is not the nature of the Harp that extracts a price for its use."

"Then what?"

"It is the nature of men."

"How do you know?" Emereck demanded, torn between his desire to believe her and his fear of the consequences if she were wrong.

"I know the Harp." Ryl smiled. "I played it once, long ago, before the first ancestors of those who built Imach Thyssel walked the ways of Lyra. Before the Shadow-born brought the Change down upon us all."

Emereck stared. "Kensal's tale was true, then. You are one of the Eleann."

"Did you doubt it after what you have seen and done?"

"I don't understand," Emereck said, bewildered.

"It was the Change itself that you beat back with the music of the Harp. Tammis called it down upon me when she realized what I am." Ryl shook her head. "It was a foolish and dangerous thing to do. Once it is awakened, the spell is impossible to control; it could easily have struck her as well."

Welram's ears twitched. "I doubt that the ones she served would have told her that," he said dryly. "No matter how well they know it themselves."

"The moon exploding, and people melting," Emereck murmured, and shivered.

Ryl looked at him sharply. "You have seen visions of the Change?"

"I thought they were only dreams," Emereck said. "No, not dreams. Nightmares."

"Neither dreams nor nightmares, I think. I should have guessed that the Harp might have such an effect on you."

"Why?"

"You are the first true minstrel to hold the Harp of Imach Thyssel since Iraman and his friends breached the Valley of Silence. You are suited to it by your profession, and thus more sensitive to its sendings."

"Sendings?" Emereck said uneasily.

"The Harp was made before the Change. Among its powers is that of holding and amplifying the emotions of the one who plays it. The Change was . . . an extremely emotional time. It does not surprise me that the shadow of that event engraved itself on the Harp. As long as the Change spell lingers those emotions will resonate in the Harp, sometimes more strongly, sometimes less so. When they were strong, you had your dreams."

"As long as the Change lingers?" Liana said. "I thought that was over centuries ago!"

"No," Ryl said. "The Change was not so simple a spell. It still endures. Even now the few Eleann who are left must be constantly on guard against it. If we turn too much of our power away from the spells that protect us from it, we . . . change. As you saw." She paused. "Valerin was distracted. We . . . sent him away to save him."

"And the Harp of Imach Thyssel is the only way to bring him back safely," Emereck finished, remembering the story Kensal had told them.

"Yes. And I have little time left. If I do not return with the Harp today, or tomorrow, it will be too late."

"How many Eleann are there?" Liana asked softly.

"There are only five of us left now, of all the Eleann." Ryl looked at Emereck. "Only four, if you will not give me the Harp."

Emereck hesitated. Welram put a hand to his bow. Emereck's lips tightened. "I seem to have little choice."

Ryl shot a glance at the Wyrd. "No. I will not have it taken from you. Speak your will, and we shall abide by it."

Emereck thought fleetingly of the Guild Masters, then set the thought aside. This decision was his alone. He looked down at the Harp. He had lost his fear of it, and he no longer desired its power, but he wanted it now more than ever. Not because of its magic, but because it was an unsurpassable instrument. He remembered the feel of the strings beneath his hands, warm and alive with music.

He looked at Ryl. "Take it."

Ryl smiled and rose to her feet. "Thank you," she said, and the joyous relief in her voice made Emereck forget to worry about what he was going to tell the Guild Masters.

She came forward. Emereck picked up the Harp and rose to meet her. He held out the Harp, and Ryl took it from him. As the weight of the instrument passed to her hands, her form began to shimmer and grow. Emereck cried out, remembering his nightmares and all Ryl's warnings about the Change, but almost before he could begin to worry the shape before him solidified. Emereck looked up in awe.

She was tall, nearly seven feet. Her skin was a transparent gold; her long hair was the color of mead. Her brown eyes slanted slightly upward above a straight nose and small mouth. She wore a loose robe of dark green trimmed in pale silver. Her hands on the Harp of Imach Thyssel were graceful and long-fingered. Good hands for a musician, Emereck thought.

"Rylorien," Welram said, and bowed.

Rylorien smiled at him. "I thank you for your help; without it I could not have held off the Change so long as I did."

"Any of us would have done the same."

"Still, I was grateful for it. And for your help, Lord Dindran, as well. I am glad of your friendship."

"And I of yours," the Duke replied.

"Liana." Rylorien looked at her and smiled. "I wish you well with your minstrel."

Liana curtsied without speaking, and Rylorien turned to Emereck. "Again, I thank you, minstrel. Do not worry about the Masters of your Guild; we have some little influence among them."

Emereck nodded and bowed, hardly realizing what he was doing. He was too dazed by the rapid turn of events.

Rylorien's smile broadened, but it was not unkind. "Fare you well, my friends." She set her hands to the harpstrings and began to play. Emereck was immediately absorbed in the music, though he could never after remember it. A bright haze began to grow around her. Through it Emereck caught a glimpse of a slender bridge of silver-edged crystal arcing across a sea of mist, and a shining silver castle amid the gardens beyond. Then the haze grew too bright to look at. A moment later it was gone, and Rylorien and the Harp of Imach Thyssel with it.

Emereck stood blinking at the empty air. "I wonder whether the Harp will actually do what they want it to," he said at last.

Liana smiled and came over to his side. "I think she'll find a way to let us know," she said.

"I, for one, have no intention of standing here waiting for it," said the Duke. "It seems we shall be spending the night here, and as the castle does not appear to be habitable as yet, I think it would be wise to set up some sort of camp."

"I'll join you," Welram said, with a glance at Emereck and Liana. Wyrd and Duke set off into the gardens. As soon as they were out of sight, Emereck took Liana in his arms and kissed her.

"Much better," Liana said breathlessly a few moments later. "I take it you're willing to marry me after all?"

"Willing!" Emereck provided her with another demonstration of his enthusiasm.

"How soon can we be married?" Liana asked a long time later.

"As soon as we can get a minstrel here from Kith Alunel to perform the ceremony," Emereck said, grinning.

Liana smiled back at him. "And where do we go then?"

"Back to Ciaron, I think. I owe the Master Minstrels some explanations, even if Ryl thinks she can make everything right with them." Emereck's smile faded, and he stared off into the setting sun. "So much has happened."

Liana looked up at him, then snuggled closer and rested her head on his shoulder. "Yes, it has. It will make a wonderful song."

Emereck blinked. It hadn't occurred to him, but Liana was absolutely right. He would make it a memorial for Flindaran and Kensal. How should he start it? *Long was the road to the castle gate, Wherein the Harp did lie . . .*

He felt Liana smile against his chest and realized he had spoken aloud. He tightened his hold on her. "It *will* be a wonderful song," he said. "It certainly will."